SAFETY FROM THE PAST

By
Fredrick A. Stewart

e mail address: fastewart@shproductions.org

First paperback edition June 2023
ISBN 979-8-218-19949-4

www.shproductions.org

A SPECIAL DEDICATION

I dedicate this book to my wife, Anthonetta Stewart, who departed this life December 2, 2021. You would be very proud of the girls, The older two have both accomplished their dream of becoming nurses and are doing well. Your namesake is growing up much faster than I would like, but I am so proud of her, I know you would be too. Your absence has affected us all as we struggle to deal with your loss. You are loved and missed by family, friends, and coworkers. In God's arms I pray you have found peace and rest.

I also dedicate this book to my father in heaven. Thank you for your love, protection, and guidance, I couldn't have made it this far without you. When I feel like I can't go further, or the burden is too heavy to bear it's you that guides my steps and lightens my load. I thank you for the gift of creative mind, and the ability to write entertaining stories. I give you all the praise, honor and glory, for you are worthy. In your son's name, I give thanks.

ACKNOWLEDGMENTS

I acknowledge you,

not because what you have given

but for the support that you've shown.

You've watered me

with your words of encouragement

that has motivated me to grow.

Anthonetta L. Y. Stewart: When you were a little tornado tearing up the house, you provided me with material to write about. From Sockmonster to Precious Pearl, you have been my inspiration. Now that you are a young lady growing into your own, you provide me with motivation to keep pressing on. In a few more years, I'll have to let you go out into this crazy world. Until then, I'll hold onto you like I did when you were born. I am so proud of you for overcoming the adversity you have faced. I love you. You will always be daddy's munter booties.

Isiah McGill: Bro! First, let me say thank you for being my biggest supporter when it comes to my writing career. I appreciate your continued promotion of Ten Miles to Safety, and I hope you will enjoy this book, just as much. Secondly, thank you for being my friend. You've been there for (us) during good and bad times. I appreciate you. I pray God continues to bless you beyond anything you can imagine. Love you bro.

Janine M. Seals: Ms. Seals, you have played a significant role in my life for a very long time, for that I say thank you. I appreciate your willingness to help me reach and achieve my goals. To know I can still call you friend after all these years, means the world to me. Thank you for lending your voice, time, and support to my dreams and aspirations. You are truly one of my most favorite people, and I feel blessed to have you in my life.

To my family, friends, and everyone who has contributed to the journey of award-winning published author, I say thank you. Your support has not been taken lightly. You are all greatly appreciated.

Contents

•••

CHAPTER 1.

First Date

•●•

SAFETY FROM THE PAST

FREDRICK A. STEWART

Tonight, ended like many other nights before it. I lay awake, lost in the internal assessment of my mind. Reflections, memories, and thoughts traveled at hyper speeds in and out of my subconsciousness, seeking to make sense of what I think I know and what I've been taught. I pursued the resolve of who I am and how it intertwines with my purpose. Although my body longed for the essential need for rest, my mind was unwilling to compromise. It's times like these I strive to break down the complexities of life.

While on this planet, I have absorbed significant amounts of data and intel. The complexity of life has shown me its versatility. I've been privileged to witness life as it takes its first breath outside the womb and the jubilation of knowing what love at first sight means. I have also seen the dimming eyes of those struggling to stay amongst the living. My conclusion was clear. 'Life has many faces; it can be as cruel as beautiful.'

What is life without failures, accomplishments, and victories? Nothing sparks this inquiry more than the woman lying next to me. Her beauty used to be her curse, now, it is the exquisiteness that tantalizes my spirit. As beautiful as she is, her former life embarked on a time when she was cold, callous, and relentless.

Her life resembled the raucous vocals of an inner-city rap song, depicting the harsh reality of the urban streets, where violence and survival were much a part of her everyday life, as breathing. As life evolves, so does the desire to change. She is not who she used to be. Now, she is the sexy sway of a saxophone, accompanying a smooth jazz piece. Her body is curvy, tempting, and attractive. The air that is forced through her produces a rich, vibrant sound.

Her keys are pressed and released in perfect unison, producing a melody that eases and invigorates the mind. The seductiveness of her descant is enticing, while her harmonic vibrations seduce me into her rhythmic erotica.

I believe with my whole heart that Shada and I meeting the way we did was no coincidence. She has gone through so much in her short time on this planet. She has lost life, taken life, seen life wither away, and now she has surrendered her life to God. We spent time learning about one another before we arrived at our current relationship. No topic was off-limits. Our shortcomings, as well as our strengths, were discussed. We took a chance and reviled our hearts, allowing vulnerability to be our status quo.

After we returned from Safety, I reported to Drill Instructor School. Although we didn't physically see each other while I was in training, we conversed daily via phone or video call. As much as we thought we knew about each other, we realized we had only scratched the surface of what would be discovered.

Our goal was to acquire as much about each other as possible during our physical separation. We discussed the good, bad, and ugly—our non-negotiables and possibilities. When I finished training as a drill instructor, I began teaching recruits to be highly motivated Marines. With all the training classes, a revolving cycle of recruit trainees, and special assignments, it has been almost eight months since I last seen Shada.

I finished getting my last class of recruits through boot camp and took a leave. That's when Shada and I went on our official first date. The traditional dinner and a movie, song, and dance wouldn't cut it. I sought to provide an encounter she could remember with fondness. I struggled to come up with anything outside the norm of regular. I wanted something spectacular and exciting. Not just a date but an experience. A first for both of us that we could share.

Many of my fellow marines have been married for some time. I figured they might have some good intel to help with my dilemma. I sought the knowledge of the ones who have been married the longest. After hearing their suggestions, I realized motivated Marines are probably not the best to ask about romance. Their ideas were intriguing. Everything from sky diving to bungee jumping, I concluded I was trying to impress her, not have a near-death experience with her.

One night while I was relaxing and catching up on some sports scores, a commercial came across the screen that was exactly what I was looking for. I grabbed my phone and called the number. The customer service representative was eager to assist once I explained to her what I was attempting to accomplish.

She assured me this was the perfect idea. At times, I felt like she was trying to shoot her shot, but we pressed on. Her helpfulness allowed me to secure the ideal setting for a memorable and enjoyable first date.

After I hung up, I felt I needed to beat on my chest a little. I was beaming with pride. Thoughts of, 'you're the man!' boosted my ego. After I basked in my glory for a bit longer, I called Shada to give her the good news.

"Hello, beautiful."

"Hello, handsome," was our standard greeting; we've made it our thing. "So, you know I have leave coming up soon, and I was thinking we could get away for a little bit."

"Mason Barringer, are you asking me out on a date?"

"Well, something like that."

"Ok, well, I'll have to check my schedule and see if I can pencil you in."

"Pencil me in! Woman, you better pencil me in, ink me in, and carve it in stone."

We both laughed hard and loud at our silliness. "Yes, Mr. Barringer, I would love to go on a date with you. What do you have in mind?"

"I may have already booked a little getaway excursion for us."

"So, you have it all planned out!"

"You know, that's how I roll."

"You were sure I was going to say yes."

"Yes! I was. I imagine you kept checking your phone, waiting for it to ring so that you could hear my deep, strong, masculine voice."

"Don't be acting like you know me." Again, laughter filled our airways. "When is this excursion taking place?"

"Our reservation is next Thursday morning; we'll be gone until Sunday."

"Wow, that sounds nice. Am I going to be safe with you all that time, alone together?"

"Nothing's going to happen that you don't want to happen."

"Yeah, therein lies the problem. I don't know if you'll be able to resist all this sweet, tender, juicy, luscious caramel."

"Yeah, that does sound pretty tempting. But the real question is will you be able to resist this tall glass of ripped abs, bulging biceps, massive chest, and big..."

"Ok, ok, ok. You win. You're going to make me have to take a cold shower."

"What? I was going to say, big feet."

"Yeah, I'm sure you were. Anyway, what time do I need to be ready?"

"I'll pick you up at seven."

"Seven, I keep forgetting you're an early riser."

"We have a little drive to make before we get to our initial destination."

"Ok, no problem, I'll be ready and waiting."

"And one more thing, this is a trip for two. Crazy doesn't get to come on this trip."

"I don't know, she won't be happy about that. You might have to tell her yourself."

"I'll send her an email."

"That's ok. I'm pretty sure I'll be safe and in good hands."

"Oorah!"

We finished our conversation full of excitement and anticipation. The following week and a half would be a challenge, trying to stay focused and not daydream about our date.

I did my best to keep my mind busy. I finished projects around the house, visited Mom and Dad, went for runs, studied, and did some more stuff. No matter what, time would ensure I learned the importance of patience. I couldn't clear my mind of spending time with this woman who intrigues me. Our period of becoming friends first gave us the unique opportunity to build a relationship without the interference of a misguided sexual fling that was based on physical attraction.

I hung up the phone feeling like a schoolgirl who met her first crush. I couldn't stop smiling. My walk had a significant bounce to it. I sang songs and acted them out like I was performing live on stage. The feeling was unreal. The thought of going on an actual date blew my mind. Luckily, I have school and studying to help pass the time. Although, all I did was daydream about Thursday morning. The anticipation was overwhelming. I have never felt like this before. The awaited morning could not get here soon enough.

The day has arrived. I awoke at zero-five hundred. I lay in my bed staring at my phone, checking the time. Slumber has betrayed me. Since I couldn't go back to sleep, I decided to go for a run to help relieve some anxiety. After three miles, I returned home and began getting ready. I stood in the bathroom mirror practicing how cool I would be on our date. I sounded suave and debonair. I laughed at myself. It felt like I was acting out a scene from an action thriller, and I was the tough guy leading man.

The time had come to head over to Shada. I placed my bag and chairs in my SUV. I hopped in the driver seat and took one final check in the rear-view mirror, "Outstanding." I stopped by the little breakfast spot on the corner a few blocks over; they have the best breakfast burritos. I purchased two, along with a couple of cups of hot chocolate.

I remembered Shada doesn't like the smell of coffee. I tried my best not to eat mine, but it kept calling me; it was ready to be devoured. My eagerness wouldn't allow me to sleep any longer. By five thirty, I was up. I straightened up my apartment, made some breakfast, and finished packing. I checked the window multiple times to see if Mason had arrived, it was only six thirty.

When everything was ready, I sat on the couch in the living room, staring at the clock. It stared back at me like, "what are you looking at." Now I know why a boiling pot doesn't like to be watched.

I arrived at Shada's apartment at zero seven forty-five. I didn't want to seem too eager, so I waited another six minutes before I made my way to her door. Before I knocked on her door, I took a deep breath and exhaled.

The firm knock on my door startled me at first. I almost jumped up and ran to answer it, but I didn't want to seem too zealous. I yelled out, "here I come," facing in the opposite direction of the door to give the illusion that I wasn't standing within arm's length of it. I gave a final check of my clothes and hair. 'Dang, I should have worn the blue blouse.' It was too late. I gave myself a 'you got this, girl.' Then, I opened the door.

"Hello, beautiful."

"Hello, handsome."

"You ready to go?"

"I am. Let me grab my bag."

I tried my hardest not to take a glance as she walked away, but it was to no avail, "Damn, she is wearing those jeans."

I knew he was checking me out as I walked away, so I put a little extra on it for him. I slowly bent down to retrieve my suitcase; I may have embellished my reach a little, but I'm sure he didn't mind.

"Let me get that for you."

"Oh, thank you. I appreciate that."

"I don't know if you've eaten breakfast yet, but I stopped and got us some breakfast burritos and hot chocolate.

"No, I haven't eaten. Thank you very much. That was so considerate of you."

"No, problem." We headed to the car. I placed our suitcases in the trunk and proceeded to the passenger door to open it for Shada. She had already begun getting in the truck. She looked surprised, "I think that's going to take me some getting used to."

"No worries."

He was more handsome today than he was when I last saw him. I hoped I could complement his gentleman ship by being the perfect lady. I have to shake the notion that I didn't deserve such treatment. I refused to let doubt creep in and spoil this perfect moment. As we got underway, I rolled the window down and tossed that notion out of my mind, I watched as it rolled and bumped down the road. "Is everything alright?"

"Everything is perfect. I just needed to get rid of something." We continued to our destination. Intertwined between conversation, laughter, and music, we enjoyed each other's company to the fullest. Our laughter was contagious. My jaws hurt from smiling and laughing so much. "You haven't eaten your burrito yet; you're not hungry?"

"Yes, I'm …I'm so excited I couldn't eat it yet." Mason gave me the side eye. "You already ate breakfast, didn't you?"

"Yes, I did. I didn't want to seem ungrateful or unappreciative."

"No worries, I have a cooler we can put it in when we stop."

Maybe I do know how to be a lady after all. I was so proud of myself. We drove for another forty-five minutes before we arrived at a small town at the base of the foothills. It reminded me of an old western movie. Everything was a throwback to an earlier time, even the train that waited for us at the rail station. "We're getting on that?"

"Yes, we are. Since we're here, I can fill you in with the details. I pulled out the pamphlet mailed to me when I made the reservation. We're taking this scenic rail train that runs along the base of the foothills for a couple of hours before it ascends into the mountains. All the passenger cars have big windows, so we'll have a great view of the mountains and terrain.

Our private room has two lounge chairs that recline, so we can stretch out and relax while we enjoy the scenery. We'll be having lunch and dinner in the panoramic dining car. They play smooth and contemporary jazz throughout the train. O yeah, dinner is enjoyed by candlelight. We have two stops along the way. Each stop is a small town that portrays life in the 1800s.

They put on little skits depicting the city's history and surrounding areas. The actors and actresses perform short sketches, reenacting what day-to-day life was like back then. There are gift and souvenir shops at each stop, and I think you can even take a ride in an old mind shaft.

But that's not all. When we get to the last stop on the trip, we'll stay in a five-star villa. Breakfast and dinner are included with the stay. The room is supposed to be super nice. It has two bedrooms, each with its own bathroom, and queen-sized beds. There is a jacuzzi on the back patio facing the forest, so we might be able to see some wild animals. The kitchen and the bar are fully stocked.

The town we'll be staying in has a music festival on Friday and Saturday: Smooth Jazz, old-school r & b, country, and soft rock. The lineup is impressive, some of the best in the business. So, what do you think?" I didn't know what to say. I was speechless. A part of me wanted to cry and scream, and the other half just wanted to get on the train.

"Mason, I can't believe this. I've never experienced anything like this before. It's hard to believe someone would do all this for me." I struggled to keep it together, "Thank you," is all I could get out. "It is my pleasure; I think you deserve this.

All we have to do now is wait for the boarding call." It wasn't long before we heard, "All aboard!" The beginning of our adventure had begun. Our room was in the middle of the train, and it was even better than I expected. I allowed Shada to go in first to see the card and roses that awaited her.

The complimentary bottle of champagne was chilling on ice, with two glasses engraved with our names. The large window was perfect for watching the world go by. The reclining chairs were extremely comfortable, especially if you put them on vibrate and warm massage. My first thought was, 'I need these for the house.'

We settled in and had our first celebratory toast. "To our first of many more dates, Cheers." We raised our glasses in salute. I could tell by Shada's smile she was feeling pretty good. "Hey, you want to go check out the observation car."

"Absolutely, if I can walk straight."

"Don't worry, I got you, but if you do fall, I promise I won't laugh until after I make sure you're ok."

"Alright then, and they say chivalry is dead."

We stumbled to the observation car, laughing at each other's calculated moves. We were both amazed at what we were looking at when we arrived. The car was decorated like an upscale saloon from the old west. The servers and bartenders were dressed in authentic costumes. There was even a guy playing the piano. We sat at one of the tables, admiring the beautiful scenery as it passed by. The only word I could think of to describe it was breathtaking.

Not long after we sat down, the waitress came by to take our order. "Good afternoon, welcome abord. Is this your first time traveling with us?"

I looked at Mason. "Yes, it is our first date."

"Really, well, that's a special occasion. What's your name?" We gave her our names and continued conversating. Mason did most of the talking. The view enthralled me. I still couldn't wrap my mind around the fact that I was having this experience.

Eventually, the waitress got around to taking our order. While we were waiting, a different waiter poured us some more champagne. Right after the drinks were poured, the man at the piano made an announcement. "Ladies and gentlemen, we have an exceptional couple here today.

Shada and Mason are celebrating their first date together. Let's give them a round of applause and raise our glasses in a toast."

Everyone in the car raised their glasses, cheered, and saluted. We extended our glasses in return. The man at the piano continued, "Shada and Mason, I dedicate this song to you." When the waitress returned with our food, we complemented her on her hospitality. The people that left the dining car gave us celebratory good luck on their way out.

I have never felt this special before. If this date ended right now, I would still be the happiest woman alive. This has been the most incredible day of my life, and it's only the start. About an hour later, we arrived at our first stop. It looked like an old mining town. We would be here for about two hours, enough time to see all the attractions.

We went on a cole mind ride that was scary but exciting. We visited the gift shops, the history theater, and every available attraction. Shada brought souvenirs, from shot glasses to matching t-shirts. She brought me a minor's hat that looked old and tattered. The craftsmanship was outstanding. We couldn't leave without getting some homemade caramel and fudge. They made it right in front of you.

When the time was up, we boarded the train. It would be another couple of hours before we reached our next stop. We started our climb upwards. The beauty of the foothills was one thing, but the majesty of the mountains differed altogether. "Are you alright over there?" Although I didn't want to miss anything, sleepiness had gotten the best of me. "Yes, I'm starting to get a little drowsy." Mason patted the seat next to him. "Come sit next to me to enjoy this view together."

The motion of the train and the sound of his beating heart put me fast asleep. His heart's melody had a rhythm that was music to my ears. Mason woke me up a few minutes before we arrived at the next stop. Of course, he tried to tease me about snoring, even though I don't snore. We pulled into the train depot; and exited the train. There was a familiarity associated with this town. We were introduced to the life of the black cowboy.

The sign in front of the log cabin that led into the town read, welcome to the land of the first settlers of the American frontier. This land was occupied by many formerly enslaved people who traveled west. When enslaved, they were expected to care for their former owners' crops, fields, and livestock. Once freed, they used what they learned to build a new life.

Shada and I quickly turned our heads toward each other. Our words mimicked each other's "Safety." I believe we both felt a sense of pride rush through us. Once we finished reading the sign, we checked out the rest of the attractions. There were memorials of some of the most famous black cowboys, like Bass Reeves, a formerly enslaved person that became a U.S Marshall.

He governed the territory that is now the state of Oklahoma. We learned about people we never knew existed and their accomplishments that would have gone unknown if not for places like this. It was good to see these pioneers recognized as the real heroes of the west.

Our souvenir collection grew tremendously. We purchased more this time than we did at the first stop. Shada was obsessed with the figurines and action figures of the black cowboys and their horses. She must have bought at least three of them. Before boarding the train, we purchased a few bags of homemade taffy and souvenir cups of freshly squeezed lemonade.

The remainder of the trip was as amazing as the first half. The sun began its descent behind the mountain terrain, and the trees glistened like decorated Christmas trees. The calm of the evening sky was on fire with the red and yellow rays of the sun. Shada and I were still pumped about the last stop when she unexpectedly jumped out of her seat, "Do you see that?" I was already fixated on what she saw.

A moose and her calf walked to the edge of the woods and waited for the train to pass. We were both astonished at how big and tall they were. "So, what do you think of the trip so far?" At first, she shook her head. "I can't put in words what I'm feeling right now. I've learned and seen more in the last few hours than in my adult life.

Mason, thank you for all of this." It felt great knowing she was enjoying herself. "It's my pleasure, I couldn't think of anyone else I would rather spend this time with." Her smile is like a sunrise after dark. "So, is this what life is like with you, full of excitement and adventure?"

I thought about how to answer her question. "I can't promise every day will be like this, but as long as were experiencing new things together, it will always be exciting and adventures." We gave each other a seductive stare. "I guess we better freshen up and join the rest of the guests in the dining car."

The panoramic view in the evening took on a romantic ambiance. Gliding along the backdrop of the mountains reminded me of how small we are. Although we were on this vast man-made train, it failed in comparison to God's great creations.

The dining car transformed into a sultry oasis of culinary enticement. The lights were dimmed as the candle flames flickered, illuminating the room with their sultry tango. I never had seafood before but was here for a new experience. At the suggestion of Mason, I ordered the shrimp alfredo and lobster tail. I truly mean it when I say it was the best dish I ever ate.

I was hooked from the first bite. Mason got the tomahawk steak and baked potato. I couldn't believe he ate that whole thing; it was huge. He was kind enough to let me taste it. After we ate dinner, we sat in the dining car, enjoying the mellow vibes. We were full and content until they brought the dessert cart around.

Somehow, we found room to enjoy some Bavarian cream rum cake topped with crushed pineapples and caramel drizzle. I knew I was getting closer to God because that cake was heaven. We let our food digest before we returned to the passenger car and gathered our things. It was about another hour before we arrived at the villa.

Once we were done, we sat down and enjoyed each other's conversation. We didn't get into anything too deep, but enough to open the door for future conversations. Once we arrived at the town, I could see the top of the snow-capped mountains. They looked like they were within walking distance even though they were miles away.

It amazed me we could be this close to the coldest area in the state, and it still is a calm sixty-five degrees. The village looked like a scene out of a Christmas story. It was summertime, but the village was lit with colored lights, decorations, and ornaments.

We checked in, dropped our stuff off at the room, and then returned to the town to catch the sights. The outdoor theater, where the concert would be held, was within walking distance of the villa. Everything felt magical. The walks, the views, and the conversations all blended in perfectly.

During our town tour, Mason eased in and took my hand. I felt like a love-struck teenager. The stores and shops closed at ten, so we headed back to the villa to put an ending to a wonderful day. Once we returned to the villa, we unpacked and met on the back patio to enjoy the moon-lit scenery. We relished the moon's glow while listening to the sounds of the night. I was eager to hear Shada's thoughts about the day. "What have you enjoyed the most so far?"

"Making memories with you" is what I wanted to say, but my mind overruled that statement because it was too soon to say such a thing. Before I could answer, I heard a rustling noise in the bushes across the yard. "Mason, do you hear that?"

"No, what do you hear." Three does, and six fawns came out of the forest's darkness. They looked around nervously before they started grazing on the grass. While the fawns ate, the does kept watch. They were there for about twenty minutes until the howl of coyotes startled them, and they ran off into the thick brush. "Where do you think they're going?" I pondered the question momentarily.

"I would imagine finding safety deeper in the woods so that they can protect the fawns." I could tell Shada had another question locked and loaded. The silence was thick with an enquiry. "Do you want kids?" That one caught me off guard. "Uhm, yeah, I think so, when the time is right." An even more thought-provoking silence followed my answer. "How will you know when the time is right?" I figured this topic was necessary, considering all that happened to her.

She never looked at me when asking the questions, she stared at the woods as if waiting for the deer to return. "Well, first, it would require getting to know her.

We would need to spend time together discovering each other's personalities, goals, beliefs, and plans for the future. That would call for some deep conversations and observations."

"What do you mean by observations?"

"I mean do they keep their word. Do they follow through with it if they say they will do something? Are they easily angered? Are they faithful? Do they place blame or take responsibility for their actions? It's easy for someone to say they will do those things, but actions speak louder than words."

"Sounds like you want someone perfect."

"Not at all. I'm imperfect, so I don't expect anyone else to be. But there are things that I'm willing to accept and certain things I'm not. That said, taking time to learn about the person I'm interested in is essential. I'm not looking to have a bunch of baby mamas running around. This time the silence was different. I couldn't figure out what it was, but I knew it was something. "Well, I think I'll turn in for the night."

"Ok, are you alright?"

"Yes, I'm fine. I'll see you in the morning."

"Ok, good night." I wasn't sure of what had just happened. I wondered if I said something out of line or inappropriate. I guess I won't know until tomorrow. I continued watching the nocturnal activities. It was amazing seeing the different animals come and go, it was like they were putting on a show. Towards the end of their performance, a bird in a nest above the patio began tweeting and whistling aggressively. I felt like my mother, or a drill sergeant was fusing me.

The continuous fretting of the bird initiated a bizarre thought. "If I could decipher what the bird was saying, would I know the answers to all of life's questions? After that thought, I knew it was time to go to bed, I was sitting out here contemplating a conversation with a bird.

I took a shower and fell fast asleep. Without the long day, I would have stayed up half the night thinking about Shada's abrupt departure. The next day I slept in until eight. Shada was already on the Balcony when I came out of my room. "Good morning."

"Good morning, did you sleep well?"

"I did. I awoke early, I wanted to watch the sun rise. This was my first time seeing such a beautiful event."

"Aw, you should have woken me up. I would have loved to share the moment with you. I'm glad you enjoyed it, though. Are you ready for breakfast? The concerts start at ten."

"Yes indeed." The rest of our day was filled with music, food, art, and culture. The artists that performed put on a great show. Shada was completely fascinated by their performances. "I didn't know I liked any other music besides R&B and hip hop. One thing is for sure, I love that smooth jazz. Those horns do something to me. Especially that sax a horn thing; it speaks to my soul. Country music isn't bad, either. It's like rap music without the cussing."

"Sometimes you must step outside your comfort zone and open your mind to new thoughts and ideas. You'll be surprised at what this world has to offer."

"I'm starting to realize that, and it doesn't hurt to have a special someone to guide your way." Shada was removed entirely from the life she used to know. It was satisfying seeing her enjoying herself at this level. She sang and danced to every song she knew, and if she didn't know it, it didn't matter, she still grooved on.

Once the concert concluded, we headed to the outside patio at the villa. It was nice and cozy. The fire pit had a warm and soothing blaze. The lights were dim, while slow music played softly in the background. The relaxed ambience of the night was amplified by the candles burning slowly on the tables.

The mood was set for a perfect romantic evening. We ordered a few drinks and dove into deep and revealing profound conversations. We laid out our expectations in detail. We were open and honest about what we both wanted: love with no limits. My personal goal was to help Shada overcome her past.

When all was said and done, we agreed to embrace the novelty of starting a relationship when we head back down the mountains tomorrow. The freshness of the morning filled the air. The sun manipulated its way above the crests of the mountains.

Meticulously it would ascend like a climber scaling the great peaks, asserting its dominance over the mountains and the earth. We would lay witness to this incredible spectacle. I was about to wake Shada when she opened her eyes. "Good, I didn't miss it."

"No, I was just about to awake you, and look, we have company." The deer from the other night joined us for this morning's ceremony. "I can't believe we slept out here all night."

"I think those drinks we consumed had a lot to do with keeping us warm."

"We did have a lot of them."

We! You, my dear, had a lot of them. I almost had to carry you to the room. I might add that you're funny when you're drunk and a little squirrely."

"Oh, no. What did I do?"

"Nothing too bad, but you were very suggestive about your erotic desires."

"I'm so embarrassed. Thank you for not taking advantage of my drunkenness."

"No problem, I understand your reasoning for wanting to wait, and I didn't want to violate your trust. I'm glad you felt comfortable enough to enjoy yourself completely. We did have a good time, though. You have a nice voice."

"How do you know that?"

"You don't remember doing karaoke? You sang three songs. Don't worry, I recorded all of it." We laughed at my embarrassing but enjoyable evening. We finished watching the sun rise into the sky and enjoyed our new friends, the deer, before we started packing to return to town. I couldn't thank Mason enough for all he has done and didn't do on this trip.

CHAPTER 2.

Family
Business

•●•

SAFETY FROM THE PAST

FREDRICK A. STEWART

I returned from the mountains with a new perspective. A whole new world has opened up before me that I desire to be a part of. What I've experienced this weekend I will hold near to my heart. But that alone won't be enough. My goal to be a better human will be displayed as I engage in a relationship for the first time. Regardless of the situation, I will allow patience to be my guide.

My words will not be sharp like a sword but comforting and well thought out. His peace will be my priority in good and troubled times. My presence will be his resting place when he is tired and weary.

Shada and I returned from our date ecstatic about our new relationship and the possibilities ahead. We found it difficult not seeing each other regularly because of the months I was away during recruitment training. At the same time, the absence allowed us to build a stable foundation to construct our future.

The excitement and anticipation of seeing each other between the training classes kept us engaged with priorities and potential. We used our time apart as a platform to work on the things essential to a productive future, trust, honesty, and commitment.

Statistics say it takes six to seven months before a man knows whether he wants to marry a woman. I would agree with that statement. Months after our first date, we were still floating in the atmosphere. We couldn't imagine life without each other.

There was no doubt it was meant to be. Every moment I wasn't on base, or she wasn't at school or work, we shared the enjoyment of each other's company. When I knew beyond a shadow of a doubt my attention for Shada, I called on the one person I knew with the knowledge and experience to guide me in the right direction. I called my dad. Some father and son time was long overdue, and this topic would be the perfect reason to get together.

His expertise in this field dates back fifty-plus years. I felt I was ready to take a major step in my life, and his knowledge would be vital in solidifying my decision. I picked Dad up from the diner and did what every father and son should do when they needed a tough and down-to-earth conversation; we went for drinks.

We went to Dad's favorite watering hole, a little sports bar downtown. This is his go-to place when he needs a break from the stresses of life, or mom, as he likes to say. I always tease him about it being his cheers because when he walks in, it's like everyone knows his name. He even has his table at the back of the bar where he usually sits. It's his VIP area. Over the years, he has counseled many people with wise and intelligent guidance at this table.

Before we took our seats, we stopped at the bar to order drinks. My dad has a favorite scotch that is reserved just for him. The bartender lit up when she saw Dad. "Hello, Mr. Barringer! I haven't seen you in a while." Braces accompanied the bartender's beautiful smile. Her complexion was like butter pecan ice cream. "Hello, Neveah. Yeah, the wife keeps me pretty busy."

The attractively small and dainty bartender agreed, "that's probably a good thing. Help keep you out of trouble." "Yeah, that's the same thing she says." The two shared a spontaneous laugh. "You remember my son, Mason?"

"Yes, I do. How are you today, Mason?" Her pleasant demeanor and soft voice were like a breath of fresh air. The first time I met her, I recalled thinking, "the biggest thing on her is her eyelashes."

"I'm good, nice to see you again."

"Likewise, what can I get for you, gentleman?"

"My dad responded, the usual for me."

"I'll start with a picture of beer, please."

"No problem. Would you like anything from the kitchen?

Simultaneously we replied, "Wings!"

"I got you; I'll get those going right away."

We sat at Dad's favorite table while we waited for the drinks and wings. Before my dad sat down, he made his way around the bar, saying hello to everyone he knew and those he didn't. That's how he's made. By the time he returned to the table, the drinks had arrived. My dad took that first sip. "Ahh yeah, that's that good stuff there.

"Alright, son, put your words on the table," as he slammed his massive paw down. The shear force caused the wood table to shake. I know it will be a deep and intriguing conversation whenever he says that. "Welp, Dad, it's like this; I think I'm ready to take the big step, I want to marry Shada." My Dad sat quietly for a few seconds.

My eyes were fixed on him while I drank my beer. My Dad picked up his drink, took a sip, and slowly sat it back down. He enclosed his fingers and looked at me with that stare of life and death.

"Son, "When contemplating marriage, you can't think that's what you want to do. You have to know that's what you want. You must be sure she is the person you want to spend the rest of your life with, through the good, bad, and ugly."

"Dad, I feel like that's what I want. I've excepted her past, I encourage her present, and I desire to be her future. I've watched her change from what she was to who she is pursuing to become. While I was at drill instructor school, she enrolled in college and started taking classes. She worked at the hospital and volunteered at the Veterans Affairs facility.

"Do you remember my partner, Jefferson?"

"Yea, I think I remember him, the one from New Jersey?"

"Yes, I talked to him the other day. He said he was sure he could help get her a job at the VA hospital. "That's good, son, but keep this in mind. When she becomes your wife, things are going to change."

"What do you mean by that."

"I mean, the expectations will change. Right now, what is her relationship to you?"

"She is my girlfriend."

"Right, when her name changes, so does her rank. It's like this, son, have you worked with someone, and they got promoted or made rank before you?

"Yeah, a few times."

Ok, how did they act after that?"

"Like they were running things."

"Marriage will be no different. She will no longer be Shada, Mason's girlfriend, she will be Mrs. Shada Barringer. That takes on a whole new meaning. You will see the change; it will be subtle at first. Then her walk will become a little sassier, and her words will have a little more snap to them. When she walks into a room, it will be like everybody is there to see her and her husband.

She won't have any problem making sure everybody puts some respect on her name, as the young kids say. But more importantly, son, what she expects from you will change. Once she becomes Mrs. Barringer, she will feel whole or complete. She will expect you to provide for her, cherish her, and protect her. She will expect you to listen to her and value her words."

"But Dad, I do all those things now."

"Ok, let's say you do, let's look at it this way. If someone gives you a gift, they are not giving you the gift out of obligation, it's more so admiration. When you marry a woman, you become obligated to do all those things and more. Some people say marriage is just a piece of paper, and that's not true.

The paper is a document showing that legally, you are bound by holy matrimony. However, when you stand before God and proclaim that you will forsake every other woman for her and that you will love and treasure her in sickness and health, for richer or poor."

"Even when she is a pain in the you know what, you have committed before God, and you have asked God to bless your marriage, and to be a part of that marriage till death do you part."

"I listened to the man who has been married for over fifty years and soaked up his knowledge and wisdom like a sponge. I contemplated, '*Could I make it last as long as he has?* That thought turned into a question. "Dad, have you ever not wanted to be married?"

My Dad finished his drink and gently placed it back on the table. He tilted the empty glass up and looked at the bottom as if searching for the answer to my question. He raised his head and looked me in my eyes, "more times than I care to admit. Your Mom and I have been together for a very long time, and through those years, we've come dangerously close to calling it quits.

About a year before your mother became pregnant with you, we had mostly given up on being married. We argued and disagreed all the time. We were young and immature. We didn't know anything about being married. We both were stuck in the useless cycle of trying to prove who was right and wrong.

She would have concerns about things, and I would ignore her and brush them off as nagging. This went on for quite some time, and it got to the point where I eventually stopped coming home, at least at a decent hour.

If I had to deal with conflict at work and then come home to it, I might as well stay at the bar and enjoy myself. There were times when your uncle Lance and I would put in eight hours at the job and then put in eight hours at the bar. This went on for a while, and eventually, we split up.

During that time, a series of events made us look at ourselves and evaluate what we wanted out of this marriage. So, to say we had our doubts would be an understatement. But I will say this, that woman puts the life in living for me, and if that's how you feel about Shada, then son, marry her." My Dad's words were like a song in my spirit.

We raised our glasses in salute. Dad stood up and proudly proclaimed to the patrons in the bar, "My son is getting married!" The cheers were loud and joyous. My Dad made his way around the bar beaming with joy. The next half hour was spent receiving celebratory congratulations and complimentary drinks.

I sat at the table watching my Dad enjoying this moment, and I'm sure I heard him mention something about grandkids. As much as I wanted to engage in the festivities, I was stuck in the paradox of whether I should or shouldn't. There is more I need to reveal to him. My conscience won't let me rest until I divulge what I have bound.

When Dad returned to the table, he was beaming with enjoyment. I could tell he was feeling no pain. He doesn't drink often, but when he does, he likes to get it in. He noticed I wasn't as joyous as I should have been.

"What's wrong, son? It seems I'm celebrating for the both of us."

"Dad, there's something else I need to talk to you about."

"Ok, what's going on?"

"Well, it's kind of a hard topic."

"This sound serious. I guess we better get another round, looks like we'll be here awhile." I put in our order and disclosed what was on my mind. Kings revere the council of a wise man. We spent the rest of the night in deep conversation and strong drinks. Our discussion was uninterrupted between the trips to the head and the occasional well-wishers stopping by the table to extend their congratulations. I laid my thoughts and concerns out on the table.

Dad gave constructive and non-judgmental feedback. We ran scenarios back and forth as if we were putting together a final play to secure the victory. I felt honored to be in his presence. His wisdom and knowledge were unprecedented. He never interrupted me when I was speaking. He listened until I finished before he gave his feedback.

After our discussion, my Dad seemed a little troubled. I figured I would lighten the mood, "Dad, are you ok? You haven't had too much to drink, have you?"

His chuckle was deep and raspy. "Don't worry, son, I can drink you under the table any time." I had no problem believing that was a true statement. "Son, everything happens for a reason. Our being here tonight is no different. I'm glad you shared with me what was aching you. Sometimes we carry our past with us for so long that we miss out on many beautiful events.

We go through life with that 'what if mentality.' And no matter how good life is, there's always that deliberation that makes you question if you made the right decision.

I felt my dad's statement wasn't completely about what I revealed to him. "What do you mean by that?" He exhaled loudly. Once again, he investigated the keep of his glass. But this time, it wasn't empty; it was full of the dark amber of truth.

The fermented past of malted barley accompanied him. His prolonged silence was concerning. I was used to him taking his time to gather his words, it was his trademark to think before he spoke, but this time was different. It was more than calculated thought. It was an anguish suppressed deep in his spirit that was yearning to be set free.

My Dad began revealing family secrets. "Son, there is something I've wanted to tell you for a very long time. I've kept it concealed in the shadows of my past for many years. I've come close on many occasions to breaking my oath of silence and revealing my one regret to you." I looked at my Dad with confused eyes. My mind was running various scenarios. I wasn't sure if I wanted to know the obscured secret within him.

I could feel my heart rate increasing with unbridled curiosity. I listened intently as my dad divulged his inner thoughts. When he finished, it felt like a hand grenade had exploded, and all I could hear was the high pitch ringing after the blast. I looked at the people all around me. I could see them talking and laughing, but there was no sound.

I stared at the bar and the people at it. They seemed to be enjoying themselves immensely. The bartender poured their drinks with skilled precision. Her smile and invigorating personality were welcoming. Shortly after, I could hear my Dad calling my name, "Mason, Mason, are you alright?" I did not know how to answer that question. "Does Mom know?"

"Yes, she does. We dealt with it when we decided to save our marriage all those years ago. I often wanted to tell you, but it never seemed the right time. Plus, your mother was dead set against you and Andrew knowing. It's been hard dealing with this all these years and facing the consequences of my actions."

Again, I had no words. I've always known my Dad to be an honorable man. Would this news change my perception of him? "I need to get some air."

I stood up and walked out the door. I posted in front of the bar, trying to understand what I was told. I gazed at the movement of the city. Cars drove by with their music up loud, some you couldn't hear at all. Traffic lights changed colors controlling the flow of cars maneuvering through the streets.

People strolled along the sidewalks enjoying the warmth of the summer evening. The world had not stopped spinning or come to an end. It was the same as when Dad and I walked in the front door of the bar, nothing had changed. The longer I stood there, the more I realized my unjustified judgement was not warranted.

Dad hadn't been critical or needed a break when I told him my news. I squared myself away and headed back into the bar. A person stopped me and asked if I could spare some change. I observed the person asking for help. His clothes were tattered and dirty. He was frail like he hadn't enjoyed meals regularly. I dug around in my pocket for some change.

All I had was a twenty-dollar bill. I handed it to the person. His eyes lit up in disbelief. He must have thought I was playing a trick on him because he didn't put his hand out to receive the money. "Here, I hope this will help."

"Yes, yes, it will. Thank you so much!" The man took the money and hurried off to the burger place across the street. Before I walked into the bar, I looked up towards the heavens, where my help comes from. I acknowledged his presence. "Yes, I know. I learned it from him."

When I turned around, a man was standing by the door. "You know that bum is just going to get drugs with that money." At first, I didn't want to entertain his drunken foolishness. "If that's the case is his drug use any different than your alcoholism?

My instructions are to help those in need." I entered the bar with a more profound admiration for my father. I stopped at the bar and asked Neveah for another round. "Sure, no problem." When she returned, Neveah seemed concerned, "Is everything ok? You looked troubled when you left." I contemplated for a second, "Yes, everything is fine."

"Great, in that case, this one is on me."

"Thank you." I smiled and went to have another round with Dad. I apologized to him for my rude behavior. His words of "no worries" were comforting. We planned on leaving the bar around nine. We enjoyed ourselves so much that we lost track of time and ended up shutting the bar down. "Dad, have you told her yet?"

"No, just like with you, I've come so close to saying something, and then I would freeze up. I definitely don't think tonight would be a good night considering we are not feeling any pain, and this is the only place I can get this delicious scotch from. Her mother started ordering this for me when she was born.

She knew scotch was my favorite drink, so that she would keep a bottle hidden for me. After her mother passed, the bar was closed for a while. When the bar reopened, I came here ready to wet my whistle with the best scotch in the world. I remember asking Neveah for a double shot that night.

She looked through all the bottles on the shelf but couldn't find it. I thought for a minute. I motioned for her to lean closer and whispered in her ear when she did. She looked at me like I had told her where Jimmy Hoffa was buried. She walked away and went to the back room.

When she returned she had the most beautiful dust-covered bottle I ever saw. The note that read, 'reserved for Mason Barringer, my dear friend,' was still attached. Since then, she has always kept a bottle on deck for me. Now and then, she'll have a shot with me."

"Wait a minute. She has had a drink with you before me?"

"Sorry, son, but yes, she has."

The betrayal was heartbreaking.

"I almost told her that night. She hinted around, asking if her mom and I had been involved. I deflected the inquiry and retreated to higher ground." Silence interrupted our conversation. There was a question I couldn't let die; it forced its way out of me. "Did you ever think her mom could have been the one?" I wasn't sure if I should have asked that question, but Dad gave his answer.

"Son, no doubt your mother was the right woman for me. But I will say this, her mother was a very close second."

As the night progressed, the bar began to empty. After things slowed down, Neveah joined us. For her being so petite she can definitely drink with the big boys. We drank, surrendered salutes, laughed, told jokes, and maybe even told a lie or two. Dad reminisced about his time in the Corps. Neveah, and I listened like two kids intrigued at their dads' adventures.

It felt like we were one happy family, even if everyone at the table didn't know it. We ended the night on such a high note we had to take a ride-share home. Neveah confiscated my car keys. "No drunk driving on my watch, gentleman, was her order." We both gave an inebriated, Aye, aye, ma'am and surrendered a intoxicated salute.

"Are you getting a ride share home?"

"No, I have a room in the back I designate for nights like these." Dad quickly jumped into parent protection mode. "Is that safe for you to be here by yourself?"

"Yes, I'll be fine. I'll turn on the alarm system after you leave. And I got some protection back there if I need it." I couldn't resist.

"Is it a nine, named Crazy?"

"No. It's a sawed-off named, wish I was Dead."

Dad and I looked at each other with teaming curiosity. In unison, we repeated, "Wish I was Dead?"

"Yea, I'm also a decorated markswoman. What I aim at is what I hit, and what I'm going to hit will make them wish they were dead."

"Oh, ok!" A concerning thought entered my mind, 'maybe you and Shada shouldn't meet.' It wasn't long before the rideshare pulled up. We gave Neveah hugs and departed into the car. The ride to my parent's house was serene. Before falling asleep, my dad conversed with the driver for a few minutes. I stared out the backseat window into the nocturnal sky as the lights of the downtown skyline disappeared behind us.

The highway was void of traffic except for a few other cars speeding to destinations unknown. Even in my intoxicated state of mind, I couldn't help replaying the topics my dad and I discussed. Our subjects of plans, and past transgressions, swirled around in my mind like a tsunami. Spending time with Dad was priceless, I wished Andrew could have been here with us.

Once we arrived at my parent's house, I attempted to wake my dad, which wasn't easy. When the big man closes his eyes and the snoring begins, it takes quite a bit to wake him. But that was the least of my concerns. I had to deal with the disgusted glares of the five-foot-four assassins standing at the door. I called my mother to let her know we were arriving.

I helped Dad out of the car and let the driver know I would be right back. I struggled to help Dad into the house, as my balance wasn't all that great either. I refused to make eye contact with the exasperated little woman waiting for us.

"Really, Mason!" Her words fired. "Hi, Mom."

"Put him on the couch!" I got my dad to the couch and helped him lay down. He had a sneaky grin, "what's funny?" he whispered, "She is pissed." We both laughed under our breath. "Goodnight, Dad."

"Good night, son. I had a great time. Love you."

"I love you too, Dad," were our parting words. I hugged my mother on the way out while still avoiding eye contact. I returned to the car and disappeared into the night. The following day, I called Shada and told her of our adventure. "I'm glad you both had a good time. Was your mom mad when you took your dad home?"

"O hell yes," that little lady can be very intimidating when she wants to be."

"I bet she can."

"Anyway, do you have any plans this weekend?"

"I was thinking about spending time with this handsome, strong, and sexy marine I met."

"O really! Well, he better outrank me, or there will be smoke in the city."

We both laughed vigorously. "You don't have to worry about that. You're the only person I'll take orders from."

"Copy that! I'll pick you up Saturday around noon."

"Ok, I can't wait to see you."

"Likewise, I'll talk to you later." I hung up the phone, feeling flushed. "Who is this woman that has me feeling this way? I am a United States Marine. My next step was to find an engagement ring suitable for my wife-to-be. I was like a kid in a candy store. I wanted to get her everything. I saw some beautiful pieces but couldn't make up my mind.

The lady that worked there noticed me struggling. "Do you need any help?" I was about to call my dad when the lady approached me. "Yes, I could definitely use some help." I spent an hour looking at different pieces. The lady was very patient and helpful while enlightening me, "you don't find the ring, it finds you." She was right.

The one I picked out outshined all the others, I knew it was the perfect unity circle. I left the store proud of my choice. I completed the first planning step, and now comes the hard part, carrying out the order. The rest of the week, I rehearsed how I would propose and what I would say. An assortment of ideas ran through my mind.

I laughed at myself. I thought about what my fellow marines suggested, skydiving. At least if she says no, I could forget to pull the cord and plummet to a quick death. After my thoughts wore me out, I headed to the diner to show Mom and Dad the ring. Dad and I agreed that I would tell them together, so Mom didn't get in her feelings about being told last.

I was underway when I received a call from the base. There was an issue that needed my attention. I wasn't too far away, so I headed in that direction. I arrived at the base expecting to be in and out, wishful thinking. By the time I left the base, it was evening. I decided to grab some food and head in for the night. The week drug on like a lazy cat on a hot day. My excitement and anticipation increased daily.

The hustle and bustle of Marine life kept my mind occupied. Saturday morning would arrive with expedited speed. I lay in my bed staring at the ceiling, anticipating my preparations for the day. I was still not sure how I was going to propose or what I was going to say. I officially adopted the marine's slogan, improvise, overcome, and adapt.

I remembered my dad's declaration that I had to be sure I wanted to marry this woman. For a moment, I allowed doubt to sneak in. I knew I wanted to marry her but was unsure of the unknown. Maybe it was cold feet or a case of nerves; either way, I had to shake the feeling. There's no turning back now, it's full steam ahead. Repeatedly, I rehearsed my proposal.

It changed every time. Different scenarios ran through my mind of how I would do it and what I would say. With so many different variables being considered, there was one notion I didn't have to give much thought to. There was only one place that could captivate the setting and supply the atmosphere that was needed.

We returned to where our lives first became intertwined, the place of new beginnings and spiritual awakening. It is where we learn to live again. Welcome to Safety. I picked Shada up at exactly twelve hundred hours. She was as radiant as I ever saw her. Her smile, walk, and physique blended like the perfect combination of grace and exquisiteness.

"Hello, beautiful lady."

"Hello, handsome man."

CHAPTER 3.

Special Day (Where Angels Tread)

•••

SAFETY FROM THE PAST

FREDRICK A. STEWART

"**A**re you ready for an amazing day?

"Yes, I am."

"Alright then, let's make it happen."

We left en route to Safety: no bad intentions, no Crazy the nine-millimeter, just me and my future wife. We drove the miles to Safety, full of enjoyment. We reminisced about the first time we went there and how different things have become. We both gave glory to God for allowing us to meet. I must have had a very noticeable smile on my face.

"What are you smiling so hard about?"

"Am I smiling? I didn't notice."

"Really, ok, what are you up to?"

"I'm not up to nothing. Can't I be happy spending time with my girl?"

"Yeah, I guess so?"

"But it looks like you have something devious on your mind."

"Naw, nothing at all. I'm the same old G."

"Ok, old school."

"You don't know nothing about that young lady." Are laughs were contagious. We continued to Safety, singing along to the old-school music that blared from the car stereo. We were oblivious to everything around us; we were the only ones on the planet, and for the time being, we were ok with that.

Before we knew it, we pulled off the exit onto the dirt road that led to Safety. It doesn't matter how many times I have been here before; the scenery never gets old; it will always remind me of a painting of a beautiful summer day. This was the first time we had returned to Safety since we met.

If this were a typical day, we would order food from the food hut. But today is different. Today I went to the trunk of my SUV and pulled out a blanket and basket. Shada looked at me with surprise. "What is that?"

"It's a picnic basket and a blanket."

"Ok, what's going on, Mason?"

"What do you mean, what's going on?"

"I was looking forward to getting a corned beef sandwich."

"Well, today I thought we would do something different, something we've never done before."

"Are you trying to be mannish, Mr. Barringer?

"What, no, I'm not, get your mind out of the gutter. I figured we would do something different since today was a special day."

"What's special about today."

"Every day we wake up is a special day."

"Ok, true, but what makes this day more special than any other day."

"You mean to tell me you don't know what today is"?

"No, I don't, should I?"

"Well, I hope you would."

I was getting a kick out of messing with her, I think it took the nervousness away from me. "Well, it's not your birthday, and I know it's not mine, so what else could it be?

"I tell you what, let's eat, and I'm sure it will present itself to you."

The confused look on her face was priceless. We crossed the bridge into the orchard and found a shady spot under the big fruit tree. I laid out the blanket and unpacked the basket. A massive gust of wind swept through the orchard, wrapped around us, and disappeared into the air. The land embraced us with a *"welcome back."*

The wind grabbed the scent of Shada's perfume and placed it directly in my path. I closed my eyes as I inhaled the wonderful aroma. While I was unpacking the basket, Shada sat down on the blanket. The tropical print sun dress she was wearing seemed as if it was custom-made just for her. It caressed her in all the right places and flowed perfectly in others.

The different hues of green leaves blended with the backdrop of Safety. Her freshly painted white fingernails and toes matched flawlessly with the white spaces on her dress. She was the true definition of elegance. Before I could react, Shada turned her head and caught me gazing at her. She blinked her enticing eyes and flashed a seductive smile before turning her head slowly.

Does she dare use her feminine wiles against me? I continued setting up the picnic when a sickening thought came to mind. What if she refuses my proposal? I considered my thinking for a second before concluding, *"the devil is a lie."* Shada asked whether I needed her to do anything. "No, but I must return to the car and grab something I forgot."

"Ok, I'll keep an eye on things." I walked back to the car hastily. Once I retrieved the ring box, I opened it and gave it a once over. The many carrots glistened from the reflection of the sun. I returned to the orchard feeling overwhelmed but in a good way. My stomach churned with anxiety. I tried to be as cool as possible, but I felt like it was the first day of school, and I was the new kid.

I checked my pockets often to make sure the ring was still present.

"Are you ready to eat?"

"Yes indeed, what are we having?"

"Let's see; I have some fresh fruit, an assortment of meat, cheese, crackers, a pasta salad, and a nice champagne to finish things off."

"That sounds delicious."

I did my best Houdini impersonation, removed the ring from my pocket, and put it in the basket with the champagne. I was so nervous I was shaking like a leaf in the wind. I was afraid Shada would hear my heart beating through my chest. I fixed Shada's plate and handed it to her.

"Thank you, sir."

Now all I had to do was find a way to put the ring in the glass without her hearing it. That's when I had to improvise. I poured the champagne into the glasses while they were still in the picnic basket and slowly dropped the ring into her glass. Before I took the glasses out, I looked at her.

"Shada, I would like to talk to you about something."

"Of course, is everything alright?"

"Yes, everything is fine. We have been seeing each other for some time now, and I can honestly say your presence in my life has been more than I ever expected.

I never imagined someone could bring so much change to my life. I love that your beauty is not just skin deep. I see it in your mind, soul, and spirit. I love your compassion and your encouragement. I especially love the way you have accepted God into your life.

And I want to say thank you for being that place of peace for me." She doesn't wear much makeup, some lip gloss, maybe a small amount of eyeliner. But right then, she looked like she had a complete makeover. Her skin glowed like the ambience of the summer sun.

"Wow, I wasn't expecting that. I hope I will always be able to live up to how you see me. Sometimes I feel like you see only the best in me, which motivates me to try harder to be a different person. Thank you for believing in me and allowing me to prove I could turn my life around."

"On that note, I propose a toast to our future together." I pulled her glass from the basket and handed it to her. My hand hid the ring from her sight. She held her glass up for a toast. "There is some… thing in it. Her eyes grew wide as she held the glass up to the sky.

The bubbles from the sparkling champagne, combined with the rays from the sun and the many precious stones, reflected through the glass. The trio of elements caused a light show that illuminated the orchard. "Mason, is that what I think it is, her voice quivered." Before I could answer, she quickly dumped the champagne into the grass while catching the ring midair.

I moved close to her and retrieved the ring. I placed one knee on the ground, took her hand, and slid the ring on her finger.

"Shada Shields, would you do me the honor of being my wife?" Her silence alarmed me for a moment until she tackled me with the force of an NFL linebacker. "Yes! Yes! I will marry you."

Her words were confirmation, her embrace solidified our new beginning. We stared into each other's eyes as we passionately embraced one another. We closed our eyes and embarked on our first kiss. It was the thing that dreams are made of. Her lips were soft and moist, her body warm and sensual. Her scent aroused my senses. I felt like I would become a willing prisoner of her love.

We lay on the ground of Safety under the big fruit tree for an extended time, discussing our future together as husband and wife. There was no turning back, we were full steam ahead. We lost ourselves in the majesty of our new beginning, time seemed to stand still. We lay embraced in each other's arms, basking in the amour of Safety.

Shada and I were lost in our own world when we heard someone approaching. They were whistling and humming a joyous tune. It was an older gentleman, probably in his late seventies or early eighties. "Oh, I'm sorry I didn't see you love birds sitting there." He had a distinguished look about him. He walked a little bent over and stepped carefully as he walked.

His skin was brown like a mature coconut. As fragile as he seemed, he maneuvered pretty well. He had a distinctive vibe about himself that suggested he was knowledgeable beyond his years.

"You're fine. We're enjoying this beautiful day. I'm Mason, and this is my fiancé, Shada."

"Well, very nice to meet you both. People call me Percy, I guess that's because it's my name, Percy." We all laughed in unison. "It's nice to meet you, Percy."

"Likewise, well, I'll get out of your way."

"You're not in our way, Safety is a place for everyone."

"Well, yeah, I reckon that's true, but I don't want to be a bother."

Before I could say anything, Shada confirmed, "You're not a bother at all. In fact, you are looking at the future Mr. and Mrs. Barenger as she presented her engagement ring."

"Well, Congratulations! Now that's cause for a celebration. In that case, I don't mind if I do take a load off." Mason realized it might be a little difficult for Percy to sit on the ground. "I can go get a folding chair in my truck for you."

"I would appreciate that, getting down there might be a bit of a chore."

"Ok, give me a minute, I'll be right back. Can I get you something to eat or drink while I'm upfront?"

"Well, I got me one of those corned beef sandwiches, but I forgot to get a drink."

"No problem, what would you like?"

"My doctor said I shouldn't be drinking them because of all the sugar in them, but I sure wouldn't mind one of those lemonade drinks they have up there."

"I'll tell you what, if you promise to take your time with it, I'll get you a large that should last you awhile."

"Well, I think I can abide by that."

"Ok, I'll be back in a minute."

Percy took a deep breath. "I sure do love this place. There's no place like it in the whole wide world. I would go as far as to say it's my favorite spot."

I agreed with a nod of my head. "I haven't been to many places outside the city, but honestly, this is my favorite place as well."

"You know, locals say that when angels come down from heaven, this is where they come before they go to their assignment. Can you imagine that we are purlieu where angels tread?"

"That does sound amazing. I don't know if it's true or not, but if it is, I can see why God would choose this place. Are you're from around here?"

"No, I'm not, but my wife was. She was raised a few miles east of here. I always loved coming here whenever I was on leave. We would often come back this way to visit her parents. One night the wife and I were sitting on the porch with her parents. It was a beautiful summer day, not a cloud in the sky. Out of nowhere I heard a rumbling in the far distance.

I looked out across the field and saw a strange cloud heading our way. It wasn't like any other cloud I've ever seen. It was massive, at least three to four miles wide. It moved like it had a purpose. The clouds rolled over each other like the tracks of a tank heading into battle.

The center of the cloud was inflamed like it was burning from the inside; sparks of red, yellow, and blue lit up the sky. It must have come within miles of us before it abruptly stopped. Everything went still. No wind blew, no birds chirped, and no sound could be heard. Suddenly, multiple shards of lightning rained down from the cloud, it lasted almost three minutes.

When it finished, a burst of wind swept across the plain in every direction. Trees were bent sideways, debris whirled around like it was caught up in twister wind. Then, the ground shook violently enough to capture your attention. I watched the cloud dissipate before my eyes, and then I heard a faint noise. It sounded like a large gathering. I wasn't sure but I thought I heard praising and singing.

I turned and looked at my wife and her parents in amazement, my heart was beating out of my chest, but they were unfaced. The smiles on their faces were like they had seen the sight before. I ran down the steps and stood in the front yard. I yelled at my in-laws and wife, "I have to see what that was. A voice entered my mind and spoke a language I've never heard, but I understood what it said."

"Peace, be still, and venture no further."

"That was my first introduction to Safety.

I've traveled to many different countries; I've sailed all four oceans and been to both north and south poles. I've seen some amazing places, but it's something about this patch of land that puts a shiver in my soul and a song in my spirit."

"What branch are you in?"

"United States Navy retired."

"Ok, my fiancé is a Sergeant Major in the Marines."

"A leather neck, hu! I didn't think the Corp allowed jarheads to marry such pretty women."

"Well, lucky for me, they do."

"I'm just messing, young lady. O, sergeant major seems to be pretty squared away.

"Yes, he proposed to me a little while ago, it was so romantic."

"He couldn't have picked a better place to pop the question. My late wife and I used to visit here often. Sometimes it's hard coming here without her, but we've had so many great memories it's hard to stay away." I could see the emotion overtaking Percy. I arose and hugged him. "I still get a little choked up when I think about her."

"How long has it been?"

"It will be a year in a couple of months. She gave cancer a run for its money for three years. I still recall her last words, 'baby, I'm tired. I'm ready to go home.' I believe she fought the good fight as long as she did because she didn't want me to be alone. We never had kids. By me being in the Navy and constantly on maneuvers, we decided against it.

I guess we were selfish that way. We enjoyed each other so much we didn't want to share with anyone else. I regret it some now that my love is gone."

"I understand. That feeling of being alone after you've lost someone is a hard one to deal with. Most days, you don't want to get out of bed. You lay there and wonder how you will make it through."

"You are absolutely right. Usually, I have to force myself to get up and keep living. I come to Safety to help me cope with being without her. For me, this place is magical; the history surrounding it and the resilience of the people who built and cultivated this land. They never gave up regardless of how many times they had to rebuild it.

I recall when my wife and I called ourselves giving up on our marriage. The stress of life and being a young married couple in the Navy had come to a boil. She didn't like me much then, and I wasn't too fond of her either. We came here full of anger and resentment. We weren't speaking to each other, at least nothing that carried any value.

Both of us blamed each other for the situation we were in. Neither of us was willing to give an inch toward compromise. As soon as we stepped on Safety's rich soil, the land had taken over. But it was the silence that I remember the most.

The land urged us to stop with our harsh words and stubbornness and listen to each other's hearts. It was dead silence for a moment, and then out of nowhere, you could hear remnants of the past. I closed my eyes and watched the scenes play out in my mind. I saw the people building, farming, and cultivating a new life with one another.

They enjoyed being free and living the life they always dreamed of. They trusted and believed in the vision that was Safety. Then I saw the red fire glowing in the night. I could hear the wailing of the children and the crackle of the fire and wood as homes and stores were burning to the ground. The yells and screams of those who fought and died echoed through the air.

When I opened my eyes, it was like the sun rising, and the people of Safety were already rebuilding what had been destroyed. I could hear the spiritual hymns and songs as they worked together on restoring what had been ruined. My wife and I walked over to the old bridge and walked across it. After I reached the other side, I realized my wife was still at the other end.

We stared at each other from opposite perspectives of the bridge. A strong wind blew in that caused a chill in the air. It started faint, but it grew in intensity. The leaves on the ground swirled in a circular pattern until they reached the bridge's center.

The wind spoke to us in a language we were not familiar with, but we understood what it said, *"bring your hearts to the center."* We started walking towards each other until we met at the bridge's center. After that moment, we never spoke about getting a divorce or quitting our love ever again. When things got rough, we always remembered to meet each other at the center of the bridge."

"Hey, when did you guys move over here? I thought you were still by the big fruit tree. I got the chair and the lemonade. Shada had a confused look on her face, like she didn't know where she was. "Babe, you, ok?"

"Yeah, I guess so."

"Ok, let's head back then."

We returned to the big fruit tree and pulled out the rest of our meal that we brought with us. Percy engaged in his sandwich and drank quite a bit of the lemonade. After a while, he needed to excuse himself to use the restroom. "Babe, are you sure you're ok? You seem a little bewildered."

"I'm ok, but can I ask you something."

"Of course."

"Do you… have you ever felt like you were in the presence of an angel?"

"Babe, I've fought in many conflicts and battles. I would like to believe I had some angels watching over me."

"No, I mean like." Before Shada could finish her sentence, Percy returned.

"Alright, now that we got that business out the way, where were we?"

"I was about to ask if this was your first time here at Safety?"

"Oh, no, like I was telling your fiancée, my wife and I often came here before she passed."

"I'm sorry to hear of your loss. I'm surprised I've never seen you before. As the old folks say, I have been coming to Safety since I was knee-high to a grasshopper."

"You may have seen me; I might have looked different then."

"Well, that's possible."

"Your lady tells me you're an old devil dog."

"Yes, but be careful, she doesn't like when people refer to me by that."

"I understand! My apologies. Sometimes it's hard for us old sea dogs to change our ways."

Shada's pleasant smile confirmed her words, "It's ok, I know you don't mean any harm."

"So, where were you stationed?"

Mason and Percy went on for hours discussing their tours of duty and getting underway. They were both so proud of their service, even as they took jabs at each other about which branch was the best. They concluded the Air Force was the worst. I sat and listened to them swap story for story.

I admired my engagement ring when I thought, 'I'm going to be a military wife.' The warmth of the Summer day began to cool as the evening air descended upon us. Reluctantly we began gathering everything together.

"Percy, do you have a ride to where you're heading? Percy looked at his watch and raised his eyebrows. "I normally catch the bus back to town but may have missed the last one. Percy tapped on the front of his watch. It looks like it stopped ticking an hour ago."

"That's no problem, we can give you a ride if you like."

"Well, that would be much appreciated. I live at a senior living facility on the east side of town."

"No problem at all. Shada, can you..." I stopped speaking when I noticed Shada admiring her engagement ring while striking different elegant poses.

I gently nudged Percy and motioned toward her. Percy smiled, "now that's alright right there." After Shada finished with her profiling, she realized we were watching her. "Oh, are yaw waiting on me?"

"Take your time, your majesty." It put a smile on my face seeing Shada hold her head up and prance off like royalty. When we passed by the food hut, she stopped and looked around. "What's the matter?"

"I don't know, it feels like something is missing. I walked over to my fiancé and wrapped my arms around her.

"Everything looks the same to me." She looked at the food hut, "yes, I guess so."

"So, did you enjoy your special day?"

"Oh, this is what you were talking about, she admired her ring some more. "Yes, I enjoyed this special day very much. I pray I'll enjoy it for the rest of my life."

"Hum, Mrs. Shada Barringer, I like that sound."

"Yes, it does have a nice ring to it."

We all entered the truck in agreement that today was a special day.

As we pulled off from Safety, I looked in the rearview mirror at Percy. He didn't have the same enthusiasm as before. He almost seemed sad. "Percy, you alright back there?" He didn't lift his head right away, when he did, we made eye contact in the mirror. "Thank you both for allowing me to share on your special day.

I don't come across too many young people that want to be bothered by an old-timer like me." I usually take the bus to and from Safety or around town. Most of the time, the younger generations don't have any respect or patience for me. They use all sorts of foul language and disrespectful behavior.

It saddens me to see future generations act that way after all we went through to give them the privileges they have now. I guess what hurts the most is that our people are usually the most disrespectful and mean."

"Percy, I humbly apologize that you have to experience that kind of behavior, you and our elders deserve better than that."

"Thank you. That means the world to me. We're living in different times compared to when I was a kid. Being disrespectful towards grownups would get you a good butt whopping by the adults and then by your parents when you got home.

Nowadays, these parents don't want anyone saying anything to their kids, even though they don't have any control over them. I heard a child cuss their mother out something terrible the other day, it broke my heart. We have lost the understanding that it takes a village.

CHAPTER 4.

Safety
Betrayed

•••

SAFETY FROM THE PAST

FREDRICK A. STEWART

I wish our youth could visit Safety, so they could plant their feet on its sacred ground and breathe the air of formerly enslaved people who fought and died, defending their right to be treated like humans and not property. Maybe then, the essences of our ancestors could speak to their existence and help them understand our survival is predicated on our will to care for one another, it is the blueprint to our survival.

Our history can't be only told in books, it has to be felt in our spirits and resonate in our souls. It must thrive in our hearts and minds and be displayed with engagements of love. We destroy ourselves from within due to the lack of knowledge.

Sometimes outsiders come to kill, still, and destroy, but if we could ever figure out how to unite, no weapon formed would prosper.

That reminds me of the time Safety was betrayed." Shada quickly turned around, "what do you mean?"

"Safety almost fell victim to one of our owns betrayal and evilness. The second battle with the Klan came at the doings of an outsider that Safety welcomed in with open arms. His wickedness and the previous conflict with the Klan were why the elders of Safety knew they needed to form a plan to protect themselves if they would survive.

You've never heard of the betrayal of Safety?"

"No, we haven't," we replied in unison, eager to hear the story. "Alright, let's see. My wife's great-grandparents settled in Safety. They migrated from the north. Some were led to believe there wasn't slavery in the North. It wasn't as prosperous as in the South, but that had more to do with the climate and economy than morality.

They were one of the first families that settled in Safety. They helped build her into the respectful place she was known to be. They set up roots and began raising a family. They lived, loved, and died on the ground we were standing on. Their names are carved in one of the trees of the orchard.

They were members of Safety during both battles. After the first conflict with the Klan, many people decided to move on and try and find refuge somewhere else. They had lost what little they had and didn't feel like rebuilding was safe. Luckily, enough members didn't see it that way and vowed to rebuild Safety better than before.

It was said the morning after the first raid, the pastor and the remaining members of Safety held a town meeting in front of the church while it was still smoldering. The pastor told the people one clear message, "If they burn it down, we'll keep building it up, this is our land!"

The resilience and determination of the people were the backbone of Safety. As it was told to me, a stranger wandered into Safety about eleven or twelve months after the first attack. A few houses had been rebuilt, and the church was almost completed. No one thought much of the stranger at first. "He wasn't much to look at.

He stood maybe five foot ten inches. His skin was brown like rust, and he was as scrawny as a hitching pole. His clothes were tattered and torn, but his shoes showed no evidence of ware, unlike the rest of his person. He had a scraggly mustache that connected with his beard. It draped down to his chest.

His hair was black as coal and matted as sheep wool. But none of that compared to the stench that resonated from him. It was told he had a following of flies that traveled with him wherever he went, like old friends out for a Sunday stroll."

Percy's story was interrupted by some raspy laughter and a few sips of lemonade. Once he cleared his throat several times, he continued with the story. "Most figured he likely escaped from a plantation and had been on the run looking for refuge. The people of Safety had all been in that predicament one way or the other, so they had no problem taking him in and giving him relief from his wandering. They supplied him with water and privacy so he could bathe in the river.

Food, clothes and a place to rest his head were also provided, all that was asked from him in return was to lend a hand and help rebuild Safety. It seemed like the perfect union. Things went well for a while. Most mornings, the people of Safety were up and at it before the rooster crows. If you weren't, you were either sick or caring for someone sick.

Every man, woman and child was expected to pull their load. Workdays started before the break of dawn and ended in the wee hours of the night. Raucus, the name he went by, was what the townspeople called an embellisher of the truth. He always had some amazing tale that kept people mesmerized and off task. It was said he did more storytelling than working.

Some days he wouldn't even show up to contribute. He would be smash faced from the night before. His thirst for corn whiskey was as strong as his lust for other men's wives. The elders of Safety didn't take kindly to Raucus's lack of luster behavior, but they believed in redemption and that everybody deserves a second chance.

Several times, situations became heated because of Raucus's continued disrespect for Safety and her values. The people of Safety had grown weary of him and wanted him thrown out, but he would always come up with some sob story about what he had been through and how he would change if given another chance. This went on for some time. Raucus would do well long enough to get the people's good graces, to turn around and do something worse than before.

Twice a year, on the third Saturday of the month, Safety would hold a trade exhibition. Neighboring towns and anyone who wanted to participate could come and trade goods. The trades included food, livestock, clothes, precious metals, or anything valuable. Two brothers came to Safety regularly for the trade exhibition. Often, they would stop in and rest during their travels.

They traded and traveled all over the country; they were regarded as men of honor, and good stature. Raucus was staggering around town as he habitually did on a Saturday afternoon. The brothers approached one of the elders, bewildered by what they saw. "When yaw start letting the likes of Raucus Radford be a member of Safety?"

The elder didn't understand why they were asking such a question but was intrigued by it. "He's been among us for a few months now, why do you ask? The brothers stood silently for a moment before one spoke up. "Be mindful of that one and keep an eye on him. Don't you trust him as far as you can see him?

And keep your woman folk as far away from him as possible, especially the young ones. If the traders had not been men in good accord and known to be honest and fair, the elder might have shrugged their words off as nonsense. But what he was being told caused an eerie feeling in his spirit.

"If I were you, I would get with the rest of the elders and kick him out of Safety before the sun set. He is bad news all the way around, snakes won't slither down the path he has tread on."

The traders finished loading up their wagon to head out, and one turned to the elder, "you be mindful of what we told you, and if that isn't enough, ask him about his boots." What the brothers told the elder weighed heavy on his mind.

Once the trading was done, the elder gathered the pastor and the other elders for an emergency meeting at the church. He relayed what the traders had informed him of and suggested they do as they advised. The elders deliberated in a heated discussion about what they should do. Things started coming out about Raucus that had been kept quiet and added some truth to the brothers' words.

One of the elders spoke up and divulged some shocking news. He confirmed that he had caught his wife and Raucus having relations down by the south end of Safety. No one ever went there because the ruff entrance to Safety was overgrown with thick brush, boulders, and enormous trees. He admitted he was too embarrassed to say anything and kept it to himself.

Others said things had started missing since his appearance at Safety. When the members asked about the missing items, he shrugged it off like he didn't know what they were discussing. All the babble stopped abruptly when Raucus entered the doors of the church. That was the first time he entered the church since he showed up at Safety. "What's going on in here? His tone and demeanors were sinister.

The pastor was the first to speak. "It has been brought to our attention that you may not be the person you have led us to believe you are, and you maybe apart of some shady dealings." Raucus eyes squinted, and a stern frown appeared on his face. "O' yeah, what shady dealing might that be?"

"Why don't you tell us and make things easier for all of us."

"Don't seem like nobody hears care, to hear my story, look like you made up your minds." It was obvious Raucus was stalling to give himself time to come up with a good enough lie. "Every man here is free, so everyone gets their say." The low tones of "Yes, that's right" went around the room. "I guess you have to forgive me for not seeing it that way, from the look on your faces, it looks like I'm set to be hung."

Elder Smith, distaste for Raucus was on display, "well, we do have some pretty good hanging trees down by the south end." The murmurs from the group grew louder. Raucus slowly moved towards elder Smith. "I understand why you would say that, but I bet your wife wouldn't like that."

Elder Smith lunged at Raucus with fists raised, "You dirty son of a... "Hey!" the pastor yelled, "this is still a house of God!" The other elders quickly grabbed Elder Smith and refrained from getting at Raucus.

Raucus smiled a menacing grin and retreated across the room. "There will be order in the lord's house," the pastor demanded. "House of the lord," Raucus mocked. "Well, it's obvious I have worn out my welcome here. If you, judgers of men, would allow me to rest one more night in your lovely town, I'll be on my way first light of day.

The townspeople heard the ruckus in the church and gathered around to see what was going on. "Yes, we all agree that it would be best if you leave first thing in the morning. The murmuring could be heard from inside and out, "he should leave tonight." Raucus's face turned to stone as he walked towards the church's doors and the crowd that gathered.

Right before he stepped out the door, the elder that spoke with the traders questioned, "Where did you get those boots? Raucus stopped in his tracks like he had stepped on a land mind. "That's my business!" he pushed through the crowd, stopping once to look at elders Smith's wife, who was standing in the back of the crowd with her head down.

The townspeople filed inside the church with the elders to discuss the events that had taken place. One of the ladies enquired why the elder asked Raucus about his boots. "Because there's a story behind them that's not good." A voice in the crowd rang out, "I know where he got them!" Everybody stopped and looked in the direction of the voice. It was a young man, maybe sixteen or seventeen years old.

He and his mother had come to Safety about three months before. They didn't congregate with the members of the town much. For the most part, they kept to themselves. Even at church, they would sit in the back pews. Right after church service was over, they would leave expeditiously.

They would only assemble with the town during Sunday gatherings when the whole town ate together. They never said much, but looking at them, you could sense a sadness accompanying them. When the young man spoke, it was the first time anyone heard him say anything other than good morning or hello.

His mother grabbed the young man's arm, "Ben, no!" The pastor told Ben, "Son, you and your mother come here." Ben looked at his mother, "It's okay, mama, they need to know." His mother reluctantly shook her head yes. They walked through the crowd like the red sea had opened. The pastor stood before Ben, "Son, what do you know about Raucus and those boots?"

The young man looked terrified. But he mustered up enough courage to give his testimony. "I know where he got those boots and what he did to get them. He got them from my little sister." His mother immediately broke down in tears. The ladies of Safety began consoling her. The pastor was confused, "Son, what do you mean he got them from your little sister?"

I, my Paw, my mother, and my little sister were the property of Master Radford's tobacco plantation in the next state over. Master Radford gave Raucus charge over us and the rest of his slaves. Raucus had no problem telling Master or the overseers if there was a murmuring in the camp.

"What do you mean, murmuring?"

"If there was any talk about escaping or if bad words were being spoken against the plantation, many men and women caught the whip or the hanging tree because of the poisonous words that came out of cottonmouth."

That's what we called him on the plantation, because his words were as deadly as a cottonmouth's venom. If you got on his bad side, he would lie to get you the lash or worse. Master gave him certain freedoms in exchange for the information. Mostly he would get drunk off corn whiskey and pass out, other times, he would...," Pastor put his hands on Ben's shoulder, "Go ahead, Ben, you can say it."

"He would have his way with the lady folk. He couldn't touch the younger ones because the master liked to keep them for himself.

He could do as he pleased with the married and older women. He enjoyed the fact that the husbands couldn't do anything to him because he had the protection of the Master and the overseers. One night when he was in his drunken state, he came knocking at our door.

My paw told him he would kill him if he touched his wife, Raucus knew my paw was a man of his word, so he slithered off. After a while, he came back. He had two overseers with him. One of them put a rifle to my paw's head while Raucus and the other overseer dragged my maw into the back of the outhouse. The overseer inside started taunting my paw.

"You hear that boy? It sounds like they are having a good time. Yaw hurries up so I can get me some." He started laughing that's when Paw rushed him. My Paw was a powerful man. He could carry four bales of tobacco on each shoulder at the same time.

He wrestled the rifle from the overseer and let out one shot. I had never seen so much blood before, it was everywhere. Where the overseer's face used to be was completely gone. The other overseer heard the shot and came running. Paw made it outside when the other overseer that was with Raucus came around the corner.

"Boy, what you doing with that rifle?" Finna kill all of you...,

Before he could get the words out of his mouth, another overseer shot him in the back. My Paw didn't die immediately, so they took him to the lynching tree. I watched my paw struggle until there was no more life in him. They left him up there for days until his body started to smell. Master was so mad that one of his overseers was killed, that he beat Raucus with the whip for three days straight.

Once Raucus healed enough to travel, he sold all of us to Master Bowls plantation down the road, for a couple of pairs of boots. Master Radford said we weren't any good for picking tobacco no more. At the new plantation, maw was made to work in the big house, cooking and cleaning. I worked in the barns cleaning the stables and feeding the livestock.

My little sister was left alone most of the day. One night we came home, and my little sister wasn't there. We looked all over for her until we found her. Her body was left to rot in the overgrown weeds by the swamp hole. She was skinned from the front and the back. We didn't see him do it, but everyone knew it was the work of Raucus.

He told Maw and me he was going to get us for getting him whipped. For about a month after my sister's death, Raucus was nowhere to be found. Then just like that, he was back on the plantation. I was cleaning the stables one day when I got a bit tired. I hid behind one of the feeding troughs to take a moment of rest.

If anyone had seen me resting, I would have been in trouble, so I covered myself well with straw and sat real still. I was fixing to get up when I heard Master and Raucus come into the barn. They were talking about why he was gone for so long. "You know why I sent you back to Master Radford for a while, don't you."

"Yes, Master Bowles, I know you wanted things to blow over about the little girl."

"Exactly, with you not here, no one could blame you for her death. And since you did such a good job with that, I have something for you." I could see what was going on through the slots between the boards. Master handed Raucus a pair of boots, the same boots he has on now. "Now, I expect you will be as helpful to me as you were to master Radford with information.

"Yes, Master Bowls, I will be."

"Good, I don't think you would want anyone to find out you were the one who killed that little girl and is wearing her skin on your feet."

"No sir, Master Bowles, I don't."

"Good, now remember, if you let me down, it will be your black ass swinging from the hanging tree skinned alive. I'm sure I could get a few good pairs of shoes from your hide; you got me, boy."

"Yes, Master bowels, I understand."

"Good! Now get your boots on and go find that boy and get him in here to clean this stable, it's a mess."

"Yes, Master Bowles."

Raucus walked over to the feeding trough I was hiding next to and sat down in front of it. He put those boots on and walked around the barn to get the feel of them, I guess. Before he walked out of the stable, he stopped and turned around. He looked like he heard something. I held my breath and didn't move a muscle. He stood there a minute before walking out of the stable.

I was so scared I almost wet myself lying on that ground. I couldn't move for quite a while. I was frozen in unbelief at what I had heard. I couldn't tell my maw until the night when she came home from working at master's house. My mother and I vowed not to speak of this to anyone because we knew it would mean death for both of us. This is the first time either of us has spoken of it.

When we arrived here and saw Raucus we were so scared he would kill us, so we kept to ourselves. We were heading to the buyers' market one day, and Raucus saw us. He said we better keep our mouths shut, or what happened to my little sister would happen to us. Before he walked away, he asked if we liked his boots."

"That settles it, he needs to go tonight," one of the members shouted out. The crowd's roar grew to a level not reached in any Sunday service. "Everyone, please calm down," the pastor pleaded.

"Pastor, this man has no place among us, he is a menace, a rapist, and a murderer of children, he belongs in hell!" The paster knew if he didn't get control of the crowd, something bad would happen, that Safety would not be able to return from.

"Brother, it is not our place to condemn his soul to hell, that is the Lord's dealings.

But you are right about one thing, he does not belong amongst us. Elders, we gave our word that he could rest tonight before he leaves in the morning, we will honor our word. We will wake him and escort him far from Safety in the morning. Everyone, please go back to your homes, and no one is to take matters of their own accord, he will pay for his sins, but our hands will not spill his blood. 'Vengeance is mine, I will repay,' says the lord."

The people of Safety slowly exited the church, their souls were wroth with anger. The elder that called the meeting approached the pastor.

"I pray the morning comes swiftly."

"Me as well, brother, me as well." Everyone returned to their homes except Ben's mother. She returned to the church to talk to the pastor. "Excuse me, pastor, can I have a moment of your time?"

"Of course, come in and have a seat. I was straightening up a little before I went home."

Ok, thank you."

"That is quite a burden that you have been carrying. I pray our Father will give you continued strength to bear that load."

"It's not the strength I need, it's forgiveness."

"What do you mean?" Just as the pastor asked that question, his wife entered the church. "Hey, love, I thought you would be on your way home by now."

"I was finishing things up here, and sister...."

"Ruth is my name."

"Came back to speak with me."

"Yes, I heard. Good news travels fast, worst news travels faster, but I am very sorry to hear of your loss." The pastor lifted his head towards the heavens and took a deep breath, "Seems I need to preach a sermon on spreading gossip at Sunday service."

"Well, I will let you get back to business, I'll see you when you get home."

"No," Ruth interrupted, "please stay."

Pastor nodded his head yes towards his wife.

"What I have to say I've spoken to no one about, not even my son. And I hope it won't go past the walls of this church."

"You have our word," the pastor assured.

Ruth lifted her head and looked at the pastor's wife. The pain in her eyes was unimaginable. It was the kind of pain only another mother could recognize.

"Do you have children?"

"Yes, we have a son and a daughter, they are older, but they are still our babies."

Ruth paused for a moment staring at the unfinished section of the church. "There is a space missing in me, just like that unfinished section of the church. I cover it up every day and night and go on with life. That section is covered up when it rains or at night to keep the critters out, but there is still an emptiness. When I was little, I lived way back off in the woods. It was just me and my paw. My mother died when I was young due to a fever. So, it was always me and my paw as far back as I can remember.

My paw taught me to hunt, fish, and catch various animals, vermin, and snakes. I was his only child, and since he didn't have any sons, everything he knew about the land he taught to me. My paw learned a lot of what he knew from a Sioux man called Fire in the Sky. He didn't like being called spirit man or medicine man, he said that was from the white man's language. He was referred to as Wicasa Wakan by his tribe. He and my paw were friends for many years.

Fire in the Sky taught paw and me about which plants and herbs were good for healing and could be used as medicines to help break fevers and sickness. He also taught us about the use of snake venom and how it can be used to heal, and also how it could be used to kill. I have caught and milked every poisonous serpent that crawls on the ground or falls from the trees. When they killed my husband and child, they didn't allow me time to mourn them.

They made sure every day I saw my husband's body swinging from that tree until he started to rot. Every day, I was still expected to serve the people responsible for killing him. One night, I returned to our shack later than normal. Ben was asleep when I arrived. I lay beside him when I felt uneasy, like something or someone was watching us.

I slowly turned my head in the opposite direction and locked eyes with a real cotton-mouth snake. I remembered my paw telling me to move slowly if they had eyes on me. I got off the floor and went to the fire pit to get the poker. The snake had curled up in the corner of the wall. When it saw me moving, it raised its head and fixed its body to strike.

I slowly moved back so as not to rile it any further. After some time and patience, I could maneuver closer to it. It only struck at me once, but it wasn't like it was trying to bite me, more so as a warning. I placed the split end of the fire stick over its head and pinned it to the ground. I picked it up at the back of its head so it couldn't turn and strike me.

My husband had made a wooden box with a top that we were going to use to put our freedom papers in. I got the box and sat it on the small table we used for supper. I slowly placed the tail and body in first before I let go of its head, then quickly placed the top on the box. Once I got it in the box, I could still see the slits of its eyes.

As I stared into them, I spoke words of vengeance, "you will do my bidding!"

I found an old nap sack and placed the box and cotton mouth in the sack. I tied it up well, so it couldn't get free. Every few days, I would catch a rodent or mouse to feed it. Once a week, I would milk it to extract its venom. I tore small pieces of cloth from my skirt or blanket and soaked the cloth in the venom. When I went to work in the big house, I would place a piece of cloth in their cooking water and some fungi that carried their own secret toxins.

The serpent's venom has a sweet taste, so it never tainted the flavor of the food. The fungi didn't have a taste. Most snake venom has to enter the bloodstream to do damage. If it's swallowed, it will take some time for the poison to have an effect. And that's just what I wanted. I didn't want them to die quickly, I wanted them to suffer, so I used small enough amounts so they would get sick over time.

My baby girl didn't die right away, she suffered. He gagged her and bound her hands, and only God knows what else he did to her before he skinned her and left her there to die slowly. I wanted them to feel the pain of watching their loved ones die slowly and painfully as my husband did. He didn't die from the gunshot wound.

He died desperately, gasping for air as they hung him and made us watch. About a month into my ordeal, there were signs that my intentions had started to take hold. The first one to get sick was Master. He was old, so his body couldn't fight off the poison well as the others. He lasted seven days after he became bedridden before he was dead.

The others took a little longer but met the same fate. Once Master died, I let Cottonmouth go. I let it out of the box into the sack. I untied the sack and laid it on the ground. It must have thought it was feeding time because it didn't come out immediately. After a while, it slowly slithered out of the bag into the tall brush.

Before it went about business, it stuck its head out of the overgrown grass, coiled up like it was ready to strike, and then opened its mouth, showing me the white flesh of its jaws. It kept that pose for a few minutes before it completely disappeared. Before Master got sick, he sent Raucus off somewhere. I never saw him again until I saw him here."

"What were your intentions for him?"

"I had none. During this whole ordeal, my womanly issue didn't happen. I knew when I had been with my husband last, compared to the date when Raucus and the overseer raped me, the times didn't add up. It wasn't my husband's child. When I figured that out, I took some of the stipes of cloth left over from cotton mouth, along with some wild mushrooms that grew under the shed, I ground them up and swallowed them.

It wasn't enough to kill me, although I'm not sure that wasn't my intention. But It was enough to make me sick and wish I was dead and enough to make me lose the child. With all the sickness and deaths going on, the whole plantation was auctioned off. We were sold to some fruit farmers miles away from the master's plantation. When they found out what we had been through, they seemed to pity us. After a couple of years of working on the farm, they set us free."

"You said earlier you haven't spoken about this to no one, so how did they find out about your ordeal?"

"Good news travels fast, bad news travels faster."

Pastor, I don't know much about God and his plans for me or what he expects since I did what I did. I don't want to shoulder this burden anymore. It broke my heart when I heard my son tell the townspeople about his sister and father. I was told that God would forgive me if I confessed my sins. Is that true?

"That is very true."

"Then how do I do that?"

"You… as the pastor was about to explain how to ask forgiveness, there was a loud commotion outside. "Honey, can you take sister Ruth and pray with her so I can attend to what's happening out here."

"Of course."

When the pastor went outside, the two brothers that were there earlier were pulling up to the church. The people of Safety had started coming out of their homes. "Sorry to disturb you, pastor, but we got something you might want to see." The traders had a horse tied to their wagon. "Isn't that elder's Smiths horse?"

"I believe something else belongs to Elder Smith in the wagon." The pastor went to the back of the wagon and pulled the tarp off. The expression on his face was one of bewilderment. In the wagon bed was Raucus, and Elder Smith's wife tied up together. "Seems they had been planning their little escape for quite a while. They had been hiding the goods at the South end of Safety. No one could see their stash amongst the thick brush, boulders, and huge trees."

As the townspeople gathered around the wagon, they started reclaiming the missing items. "Pastor, the lady may need some medical attention. When Raucus caught wind, we were on to him, he reared that steed and pushed her off so he could get away, and she hit the ground hard."

"Sisters, can you please help her out of there and attend to her wounds?" The ladies of Safety were reluctant to help but did what the pastor requested. "How did he catch up with yaw? Didn't I see you leaving Safety this morning?"

"After we spoke to the elder, we figured that might ruffle Raucus's feathers, and he is the scoundrel that he is, would try and get out of town as soon as possible. So, we made camp on the back side of Safety, and that's when we noticed the goods he was stashing. Unfortunately, this isn't the first town he's pulled this on." The men of Safety pulled Raucus out of the wagon.

"What are we going to do with him, Pastor?" The anger of the people was on display. "Hang him from the big fruit tree!" The wisdom of the pastor prevailed.

"Why should we taint the tree's fruit with spoiled bounty? Didn't everyone whose belongings were taken, have them returned?"

"Surely you're not going to let him stay amongst us."

"No, my brother, we are not. Since the first light of day is a short time away, I think he best departs Safety forever. The only thing he will leave with is what he came with." As the pastor finished speaking, Ruth and the pastor's wife came out of the church. "With all due respect, Pastor, those boots don't belong to him, they belong to my child he murdered."

The voice of the crowd grew rowdier and more hostile. Taunts of various unimaginable deaths were recommended. Ruth walked up to Raucus and stared directly into his eyes like she did the serpent cottonmouth. Without saying a word, she drew back and slapped him. The men of safety grabbed him as he lunged toward her. "That is for what you did to my child, my husband, and me. Your days have been numbered."

The pastor's command was carried out. "Brothers, remove those boots off his feet." The men holding Raucus forced him to the ground and removed the boots. They handed them to Ruth. The pastor concluded, "Raucus Radford, you are no longer welcome in the town of Safety. May God have mercy on your soul."

"You think you can do this to me? I'll see you again; there will be hell to pay."

Raucus continued cussing and fussing way past what the ear could hear. The brothers that brought him back to Safety tied his hands to the back of their wagon and escorted him out of Safety. They marched him across the rugged terrain until he collapsed. Where he fell is where they left him to the mercy of the land and the judgement of God.

A considerable amount of time passed before Raucus returned to Master Bowls plantation. He gave an account of what happened at Safety, which set in motion a series of events that led to the second conflict. Master Bowls held the title of Grand Dragon for the area he was over. The night before, the Klan set out to travel to Safety. Bowls through a party, complete with lots of corn whiskey. Raucus was unaware it was his farewell party. Bowls waited until Raucus was good and inebriated.

Bowls gave the order to take Raucus outside to the lynching tree, but hanging would not be his method of demise. The overseers bound his arms and legs. They tied the other ends to the reins of two plough horses facing opposite directions. Bowls said a few final words to Raucus.

"You brought your dumb ass back here without those boots and thought I would welcome you with open arms. You've got to be the dumbest plantation monkey I've ever met. Well, to hell with you! Bowls ordered the overseers to fire shots in the air to scare the horses. They both took off in opposite directions, tearing Raucus in half. The ground turned red with the blood of tainted bounty.

The members of Safety gathered with Ruth and Ben. They sang hymns and offered prayers of encouragement. Pastor over saw a proper funeral service for their loved ones. Ruth received the forgiveness she ached for. With the town's strength supporting them, they burned those boots and poured the ashes into the stream.

Afterwards, the pastor and elders held a meeting to discuss the future of Safety. They brainstormed for days until they were ready to present their ideas to the town.

"Brothers and sisters, a storm is coming.

We have to be prepared for whatever kind of evil comes our way. Whether it appears in the form of Raucus, the Klan, or something else, we must be ready. We can no longer walk amongst the grass and hope we don't stub our toe on a stone." That meeting was the beginning of a new Safety. They understood that freedom and peace weren't free, it had to be fought for.

CHAPTER 5.

Commanding Officer

•••

SAFETY FROM THE PAST

FREDRICK A. STEWART

Nothing else needed to be said after hearing the story of Safety's betrayal. We rode in silence, each having their own internal discussion. I reflected on the events of the day. It seemed surreal that I was engaged to be married. The foundation has been laid to embark on a new beginning. I also made a new friend who shares the same love for Safety as we do.

His history about the place that made Andrew and my childhood gratifying will forever be treasured. Nostalgia overcame me, 'These are the kinds of days authors write about.'

My thoughts were interrupted by the heavy breathing of my passengers enjoying their siestas. I laughed to myself and turned on some music to keep me company. As we pulled up to Percy's residents, Shada awoke. "Were here already?" I chuckled.

"Percy were here."

"Alright now, man, I sure needed that rest."

"Yeah, it seems like both of you did."

"Sorry about that, Sargent Major"

"No worries, the snoring kept me company." We all laughed in unison. "I appreciate your hospitality and giving me a ride home."

"No problem at all, Sir. As often, you Navy boys have given us a ride. It's the least I can do."

Ha! I'll let you have that one. You both take care, and congratulations."

"Thank you, and you take care of yourself."

"Copy that. If you're ever in the area, stop by and say hello. It would be nice to have some company."

"I'll do you one better. Let me get your number, and we'll call and check on you."

"That would be fine."

Percy and I exchanged numbers before he disappeared into the building.

"You know we didn't discuss a date for the wedding."

"Do you have one in mind?" She looked at me with that beautiful smile, "tomorrow would be nice." Her answer caught me off guard. "I'm kidding." I think there was some truth in her jesting. Before the awkward silence lingered any longer, I received a call. It was my mother.

"Hello, Mom."

"Mason! Where are you!"

"I'm driving mom, what's the matter?"

"Your Dad, were at the diner and he collapsed."

"Mom, call 911. I'm on my way." My mother's voice was frantic and shaky. "I called them; I can hear their sirens." I did my best to assure her everything was going to be fine. "I'll be there in a few minutes, don't worry." I drove to my parents dinner in a blind fury. Any red lights that could be run, I ran them. Stop signs became yield-and-go signs. I swerved in and out of traffic, disobeying all traffic laws.

Motorists angrily honked their horns in disagreement with my evasive actions. I pulled up to the diner to a distressing familiar scene of de ja vu. The paramedics were bringing my dad out on a stretcher. I hopped out of the car and ran towards him. "Wait, what's going on? The paramedics continued putting my dad in the ambulance. One of the firefighters on the scene was a regular at the diner.

"Mason, let them get him to the hospital. Your dad went into cardiac arrest and may have had a heart attack."

Although the night temperature was mild, I shivered severely due to the words that were spoken to me. The paramedics drove off with their lights flashing and sirens blaring. "Mason, let's go check on your mom." We went inside the diner. My mother was sitting in a chair. One of the other firefighters was kneeling beside her to keep her calm.

She threw her arms up when she saw me, eager for my embrace. I quickly wrapped my arms around her as she wept. Her tears emerged like water.

"Mason, I thought he was dead! They were pushing on his chest, and he wasn't responding." "Mom, he is going to be fine," I spoke those words, not knowing if it were true. After a while, I got my mother calm enough for us to head to the hospital. I helped her into the backseat and headed for the driver's side. Shada grasped my hands and removed the keys. "Sit back there with your mother, I'll drive."

"Thank you." I sat in the backseat, holding my mother close to me. During the ride to the hospital, my mother clutched my hand. "Mason, pray with me." I knew exactly what that meant.

Ever since I can remember, our parents taught us that when we pray, do not bombard God with our wants but trust Him and ask His will to be done. I knew that was my mother's way of preparing for the worst. As we pulled up to the hospital, fear gripped my heart.

Flashbacks of my dad being brought here for a gunshot wound a few years ago flashed before my eyes, as well as the unthinkable burden of telling my parents their youngest child was dead. I dreaded walking into this place. My heart fluttered uncontrollably, which caused pain in my chest. I wanted to turn and run. Seeing my mother gather herself and proceed into the sliding doors of the emergency entrance curtailed my evasive thoughts.

We checked in and had a seat in the waiting room. The look on Mother's face was heart-wrenching. The thought of losing my dad tortured me, I couldn't imagine what she was going through. As much as I watched my mother deal with her emotions, I couldn't help but wonder how Shada was doing. What should have been the happiest day of her life was abruptly interrupted.

Nonetheless, she was right there with us, extending her support. After an hour or so, the doctor tending to my dad came out to talk to us.

"Hello, are you the family of Mr. Barringer?"

"Yes, we are. He's my husband, and this is his son, Mason, and his girlfriend, Shada."

"Nice to meet you all. I'm trying to find a room to discuss Mr. Barringer's condition. So, if you can give me a minute or two, I'll be right with you." We agreed and sat back down, anticipating the news we would hear.

A few minutes later, the doctor returned and led us to a room down the hall. We entered the room and sat down. The doctor took his glasses off. "I wish I had better news for you, but as of now, Mr. Barringer is on life support. My mother reached over and took my hand. His heart failed in the ambulance, and the paramedics shocked him to regain a pulse.

He crashed again in the trauma room. He is on a ventilator, which is the only thing keeping him alive. I went through his charts, and there is a do-not-resuscitate order he put in place after his first heart attack.

"Yes, we discussed that a while ago. He made it clear he did not want to be on life support. "When it's my time to go, let me go in peace," was his order. The doctor shook his head in agreement.

"Can I go see my husband now?"

"Yes, ma'am, of course. We would need a few minutes to remove the tube and get things in order. After that, we will come to get you right away." The doctor left the room. I watched my mother rock back and forth, as she often did when something troubled her. I wrapped my arms around her, she laid her head on my shoulder.

"Oh, Mason," was all the words she could say. After a while, a nurse came to escort us to where my dad was. I walked down the emergency room corridor with my mother's arm intertwined with mine. Her walk was slow and shaky. I feared she might give out like she did when I informed her of Andrew's death. The walls seemed to close in on us. The pictures showed no concern for what we were facing, they laughed and pointed at our anguish. I heard the wicked snicker of life as it rubbed its hands together in a sinister circle.

We cautiously walked into the room. My eyes were fixated on the big man lying in the bed. The sensors and bags connected to him made it seem unreal. I approached the side of his bed and placed my hand on his chest, his heartbeat was slow and limited. As a child, my father would take my small hand and place it on his chest.

"Do you know what that is, son?" My reply of 'yes' was of childhood admiration. "This is the strength of a man. In his heart resides his desires, accomplishments, and dreams. What he gives and takes comes from the goodness of his heart. How he loves and treats others is encased in every chamber that pumps blood.

Son, always remember to live your life so that if anyone talks bad about you, no one will believe it." His words ran rampant through my mind. His eyes stayed fixed on me as if he was waiting for confirmation that I remembered his teachings.

I grasped his hand with both of mine and placed my head on them as acknowledgement. He slowly turned his head. On his right side was his wife of fifty-plus years, embracing his hand with hers, as they did all those years ago on their wedding day. Her tears shimmered as they cascaded down her face. They spoke no words as they stared at each other for the last time.

No words needed to be spoken. Their love for each other was proven through all the years of learning, accepting, and growing with each other. Their love had outlasted the hands of time as only death could do them part. My father gave his all to all that knew him, his family, friends, strangers, and the Corps. He put his heart and soul into everything he did, and now it was time for him to rest in peace.

As his heart prepared to retire from active duty, I knew he was in accord with his life. My father tilted his head back, his eyes looking upward. With his final exhale of breath, he gave up the ghost: - life no longer knows him.

The nurses rushed into the room to silence the alarms. I backed away. I looked across the room at my mother. Her eyes said he was gone, the nod of her head signified he lived a good life. The staff gave us time to say our last goodbyes. We stood holding each of his hands. My mother stared at the lifeless body of her beloved. Without lifting her head, she spoke, "Mason, can you give me a few moments with your father?" I laid my dad's hand beside him and exited the room.

I returned to the waiting room where Shada was. I did my best to hide my emotions from her, but it was written all over my face. "He is gone" are the only words I could speak. I struggled to keep it together, but I was no match for the pain that intensified inside me. I couldn't hold the line any longer. I broke down in heavy tears of sorrow. I wept soulfully while being held by the woman who had become my fiancé less than eight hours ago.

After my initial cry, Shada took me to the bathroom and washed the salty tears from my face. Her gentle caress gave me relief from my agony, even if it was for a short while. We returned to the waiting room. Memories of Andrew's death became fresh and new in my mind.

Once again, I watched everyone around me carry on. It didn't seem fair that I had to go through this pain all over again, that's when life whispered, "*I don't play fair.*" I closed my eyes and bowed my head in defeat.

While we waited for my mother to return, all sorts of scenarios ran through my mind. If I had known the night at the bar would be the last time I saw or talked to my dad, there would have been no last call.

I would have kept the rounds coming, our conversations would have never ended. I love you would have been shared a hundred more times. Goodbye, would have been a forbidden word.

As I snapped back to reality, I noticed my mother coming from the emergency room area. Her walk was unhurried. She walked closely alongside the wall for support. I rushed over to her. "Mom," she placed her hand on my chest. "I'm alright, son. I'm ready to go home."

"Yes, ma'am." I helped her over to where Shada was sitting. I walked out into the cool night to retrieve the car. I was immediately angered. No one cared that my father was gone. Everyone selfishly went on with their lives like it didn't matter. The chamber of the car was void of sound. No music played; no conversations were held. The ticking of the turn signal was the only noise, annoyingly enough.

We pulled up to my parent's home. "Mom are you sure you don't want to stay the night with me?"

"No baby, I want to stay at our house and sleep in our bed." I knew there was no changing her mind. I helped her out of the car and up the steps. "Do you want me to stay the night? Shada can take my car home."

"No, I want to be alone." I respected her decision, although I wasn't comfortable with it. "Good night, Mom."

"Good night, baby. Tell Shada I said thank you for being there for us."

I returned to the car and drove off. "Are you sure leaving her alone tonight is a good idea? "No, I don't, but she insisted she wants to be alone."

"I hope she will be okay."

"Yeah, me too. She told me to tell you thank you."

"Thank me for what?"

"For being there for us tonight."

"She doesn't have to think me for that, nor do you." I glanced at the beautiful woman sitting next to me, her words soothed my inner pain.

"Hell of a way to spend your engagement day."

"My engagement day was spent with the man I love. And whatever you go through, I will go through with you. Mason, I've never had a family. I don't know what it is like to celebrate a birthday, or holiday, with family. When Mama Moreen was alive, we celebrated holidays and special events together, but it was only us. We celebrated her kids' birthdays. They wouldn't answer or return her calls, so instead of watching her agonize over it, we would throw them a birthday party every year.

During Christmas, we would put up a tree and decorate it. We went Christmas shopping and brought gifts for each other and her kids. We wrapped and placed those gifts under that tree, hoping that maybe that would be the year they would come and see their mother. All the presents she brought over the years were still wrapped in her closet when she passed. Do you know when they came for her funeral, they went through those presents and took the stuff they wanted and left the rest?

I never wanted to introduce someone to Crazy as badly as I wanted to with them. Mama Moreen and I made do and believe me when I tell you we enjoyed ourselves, but we were both longing and hurting to be with the family that didn't want to be with us. Your parents have always treated me well, so I should thank them and you for seeing more than the dirt and grime that was my life." I took a glance at her, my beautiful diamond in the ruff.

"I think my Mom is dealing with more than Dad's death."

"What do you mean by that?"

"While at the bar, my Dad and I discussed a lot. I shared with him some things I needed him to know, and he told me things that caused me to see my parents in a different light."

"I don't understand. See them differently, how?"

"I mean, see them as people with a life that Andrew and I knew nothing about. We never saw our parents fight or argue. I can't even remember seeing them not talking to each other. They were well-oiled machines that never broke down or needed repairs. After all my dad shared with me, I realized that wasn't the case. A lot of family secrets came out of the closet that had been buried, along with the skeleton bones."

"Did your dad explain why they were hidden away?"

"Yes, he did. My mother didn't want us to know."

"Know what?"

"My dad has a daughter that is older than me." She was born while he and my mother were married."

"Your dad cheated on your mom?"

"Yeah, they separated when they were going through a rough patch early in their marriage. When they were apart, my dad became friends with the bar owner he visited. They hooked up one night after a party, and she became pregnant. When he found out she was pregnant, he and Mom were working on getting back together. Eventually, he told Mom he got another woman pregnant.

That didn't go well, especially since Mom learned she was pregnant with me. To make a long story short, Mom gave Dad an ultimatum: their marriage or his daughter. My dad's decision was made under duress. He helped his daughter's mother financially, but they both agreed that it would be best if Dad were not a visible part of their daughter's life.

Talking to my dad that night at the bar, I could tell he regretted his decision. There was a child without a father, a wife who lost trust in her husband, and a marriage in shambles."

"Wow, that is a lot. No wonder you two got smashed that night." I went silent, thinking about the rest of the conversations my dad and I had. Shada picked up on my quietness. "What's wrong? Your silence usually means there is something else on your mind."

She thinks she knows me.

"There is. I invited my dad to the bar to let him know I planned to ask you to marry me. I figured if I was going to do this, I should seek the wise counsel of someone who has been married and has some time under his belt. I valued my dad's opinion and was interested in his feedback."

"So, what did he say?"

"He gave me a lot of insightful information. He assured me that what I was getting into was not for the faint at heart and that what was expected of me would be more than I had ever imagined. He guaranteed me every day won't be a good day, but that's why it's God, you, and I. A threefold cord is not quickly broken. And I also…

"Also, what?"

I exhaled. "I told him about the diner."

"Mason, are you serious? Why would you tell him about that?

"Because Shada, I needed him to know."

"What else did you tell him?

"I told him everything, your past, your present, and our future."

"O, my God, I can't believe you told him all that about me."

"Shada, listen. I knew who I was talking to. Dad was not going to judge you or hold anything against you.

"I understand that, Mason, but you couldn't talk to me about it first."

"What was I supposed to say, 'Shada, I am going to ask you to marry me. Is it ok if I tell my Dad about your past?'

"That's not funny, Mason!"

"I'm sorry. Look, do you remember the conversations you had with my Dad?'

"Of course, I do."

"He told me he could tell there was something that you were struggling with, but he didn't want to push you to tell him. Shada, my dad is not... was not a stupid man. He was very inciteful and understanding."

"I know, I guess I didn't want his last thoughts about me to be of my past."

"That's not what his last thoughts of you were about. He was proud of you; for accepting God and turning your life around, being the person who accepts their mistakes instead of using them as excuses. His last thoughts about you were how you're going to be a good wife and mother."

"Mother!"

"Yes, he was expecting three or four grandbabies."

"Do you think he told your mom?"

"Oh, hell no! We both agreed it would be best if she didn't know." The rest of the drive to Shada's apartment was filled with silence. As we pulled up to her apartment, I could tell she was trying to come to terms with our discussion. "Are you going to be ok tonight?"

"I'll be fine," was my standard answer. "Ok, if you need me call, I'll probably be up for a while."

"Alright, I'm going to call and check on Mom and try and get some rest when I get home."

"Ok." She gave me a quick peck on the cheek and exited the car. Her reaction made me second guess myself, 'Maybe I should have asked her first.' I pulled off into the night. A mile down the road, liquid precipitation drops began falling on my windshield.

The splashes turned the once-dry surface of my car into a spotted mixture of dust and rain. Within a few minutes, the rain scattered and turned into a full downpour. My drive home was full of emotion and disbelief. The windshield wipers aggressively pushed the rain from side to side. I drifted into an imaginary world where reality was the deluge of water being pushed away from existence.

The horns from the oncoming traffic snatched me back into reality as I quickly swerved back into my lane. If a near-death experience wasn't enough, I realized I was at the intersection where I held my baby brother as he took his final breath.

As I pulled up to the light, a coldness caused me to shiver. It was the arctic stare of life gawking at me from across the road. Under the cover of darkness, it stood silent. The rain poured down heavily, but it was not affected. Its sinister apparel of black hat and black trench coat remained dry. I tried not to look in its direction, staring straight ahead, eager for the light to change. I wrenched my hands around the top of the steering wheel in anticipation.

When the light switched from red to green, life raised its arm and pointed to the middle of the street as a grim reminder of where my brother died. I cautiously drove by it, trying to make out a face. There was nothing but darkness. I sped off, taking a glance in my rearview mirror. Life stood in the middle of the street watching.

I decided to call my mother to help calm my nerves, but she didn't answer. I would have to rely on the melodies of music to help me refocus. I forced myself to believe my mother was alright and had gone to bed. When I arrived home, thoughts of my dad overtook my mind. Tears flowed like the downpour of rain earlier. Closing my eyes and taking some deep breaths allowed me to calm down enough, to exit the car and make it to the front door.

My hands shook fiercely, making putting the key into the lock difficult. Once the door opened, the bitter cold from before had returned. Reluctantly I turned around, and I could see life's shadow in the distance; it knows where I live.

My phone rang as I entered the house and locked the door, hopefully, it was my mother returning my call, but it was not.

"Hey, did you make it home yet?"

"Yes, I just walked in the door."

"Ok, I wanted to check on you. Did you talk to mom?"

"I called her, but she didn't answer. She probably cried herself to sleep."

"I can't imagine what she is going through."

"Yeah, it's going to be ruff on her."

"Listen, I want to apologize for earlier. I'm sorry for getting upset. I understand your reason for telling your dad. In a way, I'm glad you did. I know you valued his opinion. I guess I want that part of my life buried and forgotten like it never happened."

"Shada, I would never do anything to harm you, I told the one person I knew I could confide in. And ironic as it is, he took it to the grave with him." My conversation paused long enough for me to gather myself. "Mason, I love you, I trust you. I'm sorry you have to go through this."

"Dying is part of living, right," I told myself this truth, attempting to trick myself into accepting the harsh reality.

"I'm so sorry, I should be there with you."

"It's ok, love. Besides I'm vulnerable right now. I don't want you trying to take advantage of me."

"Ha! Take advantage of you! So, are you going back on an agreement to wait until we're married?

"Look, I'm in mourning, I can't be held responsible for my actions."

"Naw, you wouldn't be able to resist all this sweet, delicious goodness."

"Yeah, you're probably right about that. Besides, I think it's honorable that you want to wait. I wouldn't want to be the one who messes that up."

"I appreciate your understanding and not pressuring me into it as some men would. That means the world to me."

"Of course, my Queen. I'm going to turn it in for the night. I have to get up early to check on Mom and start the process."

"Ok, my love. I have a couple of classes in the morning, then I'll be available to you."

"Alright, you have a good night."

"You too. I'll see you tomorrow. Love you."

"Love you too."

After talking to Shada, I felt better. I could smile and laugh momentarily, which helped with my agony. Bedtime came with great anticipation. Closing my eyes didn't bring slumber right away, thoughts and memories appeared and disappeared. During my reflections, I remembered my dad's birthday was coming up. We planned a fishing trip for that weekend. As I lay there contemplating my thoughts, the grief that had me bound found its way back into existence.

It returned with the force of a heavy-weight boxer's punch. I refused to open my eyes until morning whispered, *Awake, my sweet.*

CHAPTER 6.

Follow Your Heart

•●•

SAFETY FROM THE PAST

FREDRICK A. STEWART

The next couple of weeks were hectic. Phone calls to Veterans Affairs and funeral arrangements were priorities. Reaching out to family and friends, updating them on my dad's passing, followed. There was so much to take care of. It was at a point that I couldn't remember when one day started and the other one ended. I tried to relieve my mother of as much responsibility as possible.

There were times when she seemed good, other times, she was completely overwhelmed. With a full plate and heavy heart, I charged forward. My mother and I reviewed insurance policies, filed claims, and filled out paperwork. I was willing to do whatever she needed me to do, but there was one thing I had to do that no one else could. Something my dad longed for in life that could now be rectified in his death.

I know my Dad would have wanted me to take care of this regardless of the turmoil it may stir up. I think I'm going to need a drink for this one.

I walked into the bar my dad and I visited a few weeks ago. The first thing I saw was my dad's favorite table. Memories of our times here swirled through my mind. The laughs, the talks, and the spirits brought a forgotten smile to my face. I proceeded to the table and took a seat. The place was empty except for some old-timers who seemed to live there.

"Hi, Mason," Neveah was coming from the back room when she noticed me sitting at the table.

"Hello, Neveah."

"I'm not used to seeing you hear without your dad."

"Yeah, that's why I'm here. Do you have a few minutes? I need to talk to you.

"Sure, it's not too busy right now. Can I get you a beer or something?"

"Yeah, that would be great." Neveah went to the bar and came back with a cold one. She sat down at the table with me. "Is everything ok?" I took a deep gulp of the beer, sat it down on the table, and tilted it towards me as if looking for the answer floating around amongst the foam.

"Unfortunately, no. Dad passed away."

"Oh no! Mason, I am so sorry. Is there anything I can do? Do you need help with anything?

"No, we have everything taken care of, but I need to talk to you about something."

"Of course, What is it?" The concerned look on her face made it even more difficult.

"When my Dad and I were here last, he confided in me that um, um."

"Mason, what!"

"He told me he was your dad." Neveah sat silently in her chair; a blank stare overtook her face. I don't think she even blinked. It was hard to tell if she was still breathing.

"Mason, I'm sorry, but my dad died fighting in the Vietnam War."

"Our dad fought in the Vietnam War. When he came home, he met my mom, and a year later, they married. Early in their marriage, they hit a rough patch and split up for a while, that's when he met your mom here at the bar. They started as friends. They spent a lot of time discussing Dad's marriage and what he could do to help it. Your mom through a new year's party here at the bar. There were many people, everyone was having a good time, they both had a lot to drink, and one thing led to another.

"So, you're saying I'm the product of a drunken affair, Great."

"From what Dad told me, your mom felt terrible about what happened. She suggested Dad not come to the bar anymore and focus on saving his marriage. Dad agreed, and they went their separate ways. A few months later, your mom found out she was pregnant. She told my uncle to ask Dad to come to the bar. When Dad came, your mom informed him that she was pregnant. Dad was shaken because my mom had told him a week before she was pregnant with me.

"Wow! That is a lot. Excuse me a minute; I need to get something." Neveah went to the bar, poured her a shot, and took it to the head. She returned to the table with the rest of the bottle of liquor. "I remember asking my mom about my dad, and all she would tell me is that she gets money from him being in the war."

"Well, when your mom found out that my parents were working things out and were expecting a child, she didn't want to cause issues, so all she asked of Dad was to help financially. Dad being the man he was, reluctantly told my mom. From his story and knowing my Mom, he went through hell for quite a while. Eventually, she accepted the fact that there was another child. She agreed to let him help financially but didn't want him to be involved in your life. That was a decision Dad regretted until the day he died."

"I think after your Mom met my Mom and got a dose of her rath, she was on board with Dad not being an active participant in your life."

"Mason, this is a lot to digest. Are you sure this is accurate?"

"Your mother's name was Angelina, right?"

"Yes."

I pulled an old, tattered Polaroid picture out of my pocket and slid it over to Neveah. Her eyes filled with tears instantly. "This was at my first birthday party." She stared at the picture of Angelina and Dad holding her together. "My Mom kept every picture she ever took of me. I remember seeing the other pictures of that day. She kept them in an old green photograph book. There was always an empty spot where a picture used to be. I asked my mom where that picture was, and all she would say was, "I gave it to your Dad.""

This is unbelievable. I've always looked at your dad as a father figure. All the counseling and sound advice he gave me was priceless. I was dealing with an ex, and your dad sat right here and talked to me for hours about what I was going through. If I had taken his advice, I wouldn't have gone through all the mess with that person. After that, anything he told me I would take to heart. He saved me from making some really bad decisions.

"Neveah, he was our Dad."

"I'm sorry, that's going to take some getting used to."

"I understand"

"But yeah, that was our dad. He was a walking gift of knowledge."

"Mason, how long have you known we were brother and sisters?"

"I found out the night we were here last. You also had another brother who passed away a few years ago."

"What was his name?"

"Andrew, that was my partner. We were thick as thieves."

"How did he die?"

"He got hit by a car. We were having a heated argument, when he jumped out at an intersection and got struck by a vehicle, trying to beat the light. I still struggle with his death, and now dad is gone."

"I'm so sorry for your loss. I know what you mean. I have weird dreams sometimes that I have to force myself to wake up from. Watching my mother die of cancer almost destroyed me. When she passed away a while ago, I inherited the bar. At first, I didn't want the responsibility. I wanted to sell it and go curl up in a ball somewhere. The more I thought about it, I realized this was my mom's life, her legacy, and I didn't want that in someone else's hands.

Now that I'm thinking about it, I remember Mason telling me about losing a son. I saw him more during that time than any other. The strange thing is he didn't come to drink, he would sit at this table and be available to whoever needed a listening ear. No one even knew he had lost a son. He didn't talk about it at all. He told me after three consecutive days of coming here. Even then, we didn't discuss it that much. Sometimes it seemed like he was trying to block it out by discussing everything else."

"My Mom didn't like talking about his death, so he probably came here to get things off his chest. Did Dad mention he got shot?

"No, he didn't! When did this happen?

"The same day Andrew died; it was the worst day of my life."

"O my God, Mason. You and your family have been going through it."

"It has been rough, but it has caused me to rely on God more and more, that's where my help comes from."

"Amen to that." We raised our glasses high in the air. "Salute! to the loved ones we've lost." The sound of our glasses clinking together rang throughout the bar." It felt good to have a sibling again. After we had our salute, Neveah looked somewhat distraught. "Are you ok?"

"Yeah, I'm contemplating what it would have been like having him in my life, full-time. Mason, please tell me about him, what was it like growing up with him as your father? Was he all that he seemed to be? Tell me the things that I missed growing up without him."

"I took another drink from the glass that had no answers. "What you saw is what you got with Dad. He didn't change up at home or around other people. I would have to say he was the most genuine man I ever met. He had an uncommon desire to help anyone that needed help. He always made time for those needing a listening ear. I'm pretty sure he talked some people out of hurting themselves. He owned his mistakes and shortcomings. He would tell you in a heartbeat, 'I'm not perfect, but I do my best.'

He was a man that led by example. That was his personality. As you know, physically, Dad was a tower of a man. Six-three and a solid three hundred pounds. His bronze-colored skin glistened like a lone star in a pitch-black sky. His gray pupils had a light blue ring around them. His body looked like it was carved from granite and hard earth. His stature was intimidating and fierce, but the heart that pumped blood through his veins was made of gold and precious materials.

If you dared look in his eyes, you could see what my mother called life and death. She would tell Andrew and me; she could always see the warrior in him by how he carried himself. If you stared long enough into the depths of his soul, you could tell he became a Marine, but he was born a soldier. I think that's what both our mothers saw in him. From what my aunt and uncle have told me, Vietnam changed him. He had a different outlook on life when he returned from that war. "What branch did he serve in?"

"Dad was a veteran of the United States Marine Corps. At seventeen, he was drafted to fight in the Vietnam War. He was among the youngest service members that fought in that war. It was a time in our history when men of color were expected to fight and die for a country that treated them like secondhand citizens, still, our father proudly served. My Dad told me it was his greatest honor to serve as a Marine.

Dad would light up with pride when he talked to me about his time in the Corp. He reminisced about how he loved waking up early in the morning for reveille, drilling and physical training, the friendship between him and his fellow bloods."

"He was in a gang?"

"No, that's what the black troops called themselves. Dad loved being a Marine, he considered it an honor. However, not all his memories of the Corps were revered. There was a pain associated with the rigors of fighting in that war. A pain he never shared with me until I told him I wanted to join the Corps."

"You're a Marine too?"

"Yeah, I've been in the Corps for about fourteen years, I'm at the rank of Sargent Major."

"Have you been in any wars?"

"I did a tour in Afghanistan and some other conflicts."

"O, my God, there is so much I want to know, okay finish telling me about Dad first."

"His demeanor constantly shifted when he reflected on all the brothers in arms lost in battle. Dad would say it was hard to make friends or get close to someone because one moment, they would be laughing or talking with one another, and the next moment, you might see them blown to pieces or torched beyond recognition.

As hard as that was to deal with, there was also the racism he endured from his commanding officers and some other soldiers who felt black soldiers were inferior to them. It didn't help that his black panther brothers back home labeled them flunkies for white America. He only discussed it when he would get together with the remaining bloods from his old platoon. As a little kid, I remember listening to them reminisce about their time in the country. During that time, about six or seven of them would get together yearly.

The numbers dwindled over time. A couple died from Vietnam-related things, and some by their own hands. They could never shake the horrible things they saw and the complicated orders they had to carry out. Dad said if it weren't for Mom, he probably wouldn't have made it himself. They always seemed to have a good time in the beginning. The laughter and spirited cadence combined with countless exciting stories. Towards the end, the memories would start getting the best of them.

With tears in their eyes, they would end the night with glasses raised to honour the brothers killed in action and the others they lost along the way. They would give a motivated Semper Fi in one accord, followed by a glorious Ooh Rah! About three months after Dad returned from his tour of duty, he met my mother, she was working as a waitress at a café on the other side of town. She worked there while attending college. They married a year after they met.

My most memorable moments with him was our time spent at Safety.

"What is Safety?"

"It's a place a few miles North of here. It's a place rich in history and culture. It has a fruit orchard, a creek, and an old church. It was a town built by freed and escaped enslaves."

"Wow, that sounds amazing."

"Maybe we can take a trip there after the funeral and once things calm down. That's where I proposed to my fiancée at."

"I would love that. I was going to ask, are you married and if I had any nieces and nephews?"

"No, I don't have any kids, but I did get engaged recently, so there may be some soon."

"Congratulations! What's her name?

"It's Shada. That's a pretty name."

"Yes, it is, and she is beautiful as her name. She has been through her ordeals in life but has stood fast in the midst of it all."

"How did y'all meet?"

"Well. We met at my mom and dad's diner."

"Was it love at first sight?

"No, it was actually Crazy."

"Ohh k." The confused look on Neveah's face was my escape route to a different topic.

"What about you? Anybody special in your life?"

"No, it's just me, no kids, no significant other. I've been focusing on myself and trying to keep the bar going. I want to make my mom proud of me."

"I'm sure she would be, she seems to have raised an amazing woman."

"Thank you, I'm doing my best."

Neveah and I chopped it up a couple more hours before I realized how late it had gotten. I reluctantly told her I had to go to check on Mom and touch down with Shada.

"It's been so cool getting to know you. I feel like we have a lot of catching up to do."

"Yes, we do. I can't wait to meet your fiancé."

"I'll see you at the funeral, right?"

"Um, do you think your mom would be ok with that?"

"It's not about that. It's about what Dad would want, and he would want you there."

"Then I'll be there…brother." We both flashed that Barringer smile that accompanied our dad throughout his life. I embraced my sister. I left the bar feeling better than I had in quite a while.

When I stepped outside, I expected to see the sinister shadow of life stalking me, but it was nowhere in sight. It must have found someone else to torment for the night. On my ride home, I called and checked on Mom.

"Hey lady, what you up to?"

"Nothing, I'm at the diner."

"Mom, what are you doing at the dinner this late?

"I wanted to stay here a little longer, I didn't feel like going home to that empty house."

"I understand, Mom. I know losing Dad has been hard on you."

"Mason, I was with that man for over fifty years, and there was hardly a night that we didn't come home to each other, and now he will never come home to me."

My mom's tears and sorrow tore at my soul. I hurried to try and find something to say to ease her suffering. "Mom, you and Dad had a great life together. You must treasure those moments when you feel overwhelmed by missing him."

"I know, baby, it will take some time to get used to. What are you doing out this late?" I wanted to tell my mother about going to the bar and talking to Neveah, but I wasn't sure if now was the right time or how she would react. "Shada and I went to the movies. I dropped her off and was about to head home."

"Ok, that's nice."

"What did you cook today?"

"Nothing, I didn't open the diner today. I gave everyone the day off. I wanted to be here by myself."

"I understand. Do you mind if I come to see you? I can give you a ride home after I raid the fridge."

"I thank there's some smothered chicken in there I can warm up for you."

"That sounds great, I'll be there in a few minutes."

"Ok, baby, I'll see you shortly."

I hung up from my Mom, feeling distraught. I haven't lied to her since I was a kid. I recalled eating a piece of pie she had made specifically for the diner. I told her I didn't know what happened to it. Of course, she knew I ate it. I must have washed a hundred dishes and swept and mopped the diner floor every ten minutes that day. It was a valuable lesson learned. I cleared my mind enough to call Shada before arriving at the diner.

"Hello, love, how are you doing?

"I'm good, and yourself?"

"I'm fine, on my way to pick up Mom from the diner."

"Ok, how is she holding up?"

"Not that good. She was at the diner all day but didn't open for business. I don't know what she did throughout the day, she probably reminisced. I don't think she can run the diner too much longer."

"Well, wait until after the funeral, after things have settled down, and see how she is doing then.

"Yeah, I guess so."

"How did your meeting with Neveah go?

"It went well. She was doubtful at first, which is to be expected. But after I showed her the picture and gave her some more details. She started putting things together, and it started making sense. We talked for hours about Dad, her mom, and our lives growing up. Knowing I still have a sibling to talk to and hang out with felt good. I have missed that since Andrew has been gone."

"That's great, I know you miss Andrew, and not that anyone could ever replace him, but it's good you have that piece of your life again. Is she coming to the funeral?"

"Yes, she said she would be there. I wanted to tell Mom about it, but after talking to her a little while ago, I'm unsure if that's a good idea."

"Now might not be the best time, but if you plan on building a relationship with your sister, she will have to know sooner or later."

"Yeah, well, I'll have to cross that bridge when I get there. There is something I need to discuss with you. Next week is Dad's birthday, and I want to do something special to remember him."

"Of course, what is it?"

I'm heading to the diner now, but I can pick you up tomorrow and take you to breakfast so we can discuss it."

"Do I get to go to my favorite spot?"

"Of course, spoiled woman."

"That's your fault, Mr. Barringer."

"I know."

"Tell Mom I asked about her."

"Will do. See you in the morning. Love you."

"Love you too."

I arrived at the diner a few minutes after hanging up with Shada. The smell of smothered chicken and fried potatoes greeted me as I entered the diner. "Mom, you in here?"

"Yes, I'm here."

"You got it smelling good in here, lady."

"Smothered chicken and fried potatoes were always your favorites. You would eat it every day if I let you."

"Nothing has changed, I still would if I could get away with it. It's not my fault you're the best cook this side of the Mississippi." I hugged the little lady and kissed her. She lit up like a light. She walked to the other side of the kitchen with her head raised and slightly smiling like she was thinking, "You better know it." To see her resembling her old self and in a good mood did my heart good, I didn't want it to end. "You know what would make this meal even better?"

"What?"

"A good western movie?"

"Oh yes, you know I love western movies."

"Well, there is a movie marathon going on tonight. We could wrap this delicious meal up, take it to my house, eat, and watch movies until we were fat and happy."

"Now, that does sound like a good idea. Your girlfriend won't mind you having another woman over your house, will she?"

"I think she will be alright with it this time."

She laughed slightly, "well, let's get this show on the road." We packed dinner, locked up the diner, and headed home to watch movies with my favorite girl. It was good to see Mom in good spirits. She had a pleasant smile that had been absent since Dad's passing. Her tone was lacking the drawl of heartbreak and pain that had been present with her since we left the hospital. It is enough to make an enjoyable memory, even if it's only for a little while.

We arrived at the house and unpacked everything. I fixed our plates so our mother and son date night could begin. She lasted forty-five minutes into the movie before I heard shallow and faint snoring. Seeing her resting comfortably was a welcome site. I placed a blanket over her and turned off the tv before I stepped outside on the back patio to call Shada.

"Hey, lady."

"Hello, my love. I wasn't expecting to hear from you again tonight."

"I know, my date ended short."

"Your date!"

"Yeah, Mom came home with me. We were supposed to have a movie night, but she fell asleep a few minutes later. I'm sure she hasn't been resting well or getting much sleep, so I didn't wake her."

"That's so cute. You do a good job caring for her. I know your dad would be proud of you. Have you told her about us being engaged?"

No, I haven't"

"Why not?"

"I don't know, it hasn't seemed like the right time with everything that's been going on."

"Mason, can I ask you something, and please be honest."

"Of course. What is it?"

"Do you really want to get married? Because if you don't, I would understand."

"Shada, why would you ask me that?"

"I don't know, it seems like nobody knows that we're engaged, and you haven't told your mom yet, I mean, I understand with your Dad passing, things have been hectic, I guess I thought it would be different."

"Shada, I am one hundred percent sure of what I want, and that is you."

"Mason!"

"Hey, let me call you back, Mom woke up."

"Ok, are we still going to breakfast in the morning?"

"Yes, I'll pick you up around nine."

"Ok, love you."

"Love you too."

I stepped back into the house. "Well, hello, lady, I thought you were out for the night."

"No, I was resting my eyes for a moment, taking a little power nap, I'm ready now."

"Ok, well, it's almost eleven thirty. I fixed the spare room so you can continue your nap."

"Oh, can't hang with the old lady, hu!"

"No, I'm going to retreat in defeat on this one, but there is something I've meant to tell you."

"What's that?"

"Well, with everything that's been going on, I didn't get a chance to let you know I proposed to Shada, and she said yes."

"Oh, really? Well, congratulations."

"Congratulations, that's it? I was hoping for a little more enthusiasm than that."

"I'm sorry, Mason, I guess with your father's funeral a few days away, I'm all out of enthusiasm. I think I'll turn in now, you have a good night."

I stood in my living room in disbelief as I watched my mother disappear down the hallway. I guess some of me expected the worst, while the rest hoped for the best. I immediately started making excuses for my mother's lack of jubilee, it was easier than excepting the truth. The next six hours of restless insomnia proved too much for me to conquer. I sat up on the side of the bed in deep thought. My mother's reaction concerned me.

I began taking on the assumption that my mother's apathy was a sign that I was not ready to get married or that Shada was not the one I should be marrying. The confusion pounded in my head like artillery rounds being fired off. I prepared myself to run in the cool breeze of the early dawn. I stepped outside into the hush of the new morning. Before I started my excursion, I entered into prayer.

I thanked my creator for the days of life he blessed me with. My prayer continued by asking for discernment, wisdom, and knowledge, *"In your son's name I pray, Amen."* Once I finished my prayer, I tuned in to the silence of the morning.

It was peaceful, it blocked out the confusion running ramped in my mind. The only sounds present were the seamless cadence of my stride and the conscious act of my controlled breathing. I ran about half a mile before the blissful silence was interrupted by the ignition of an automobile starting up. Toxic exhaust fumes quickly tainted the once crisp air.

Turning in the opposite direction of the vehicle aligned me with the rising sun. Its exuberant light became visible on the horizon. A flock of birds flew in its direction, seeking its rays' warmth. I had gone another couple of miles before changing my course and heading back to home base.

My return tour would not be as silent and peaceful as my initial voyage, the world has awakened. More vehicles were departing their driveways and entering the gray asphalt of the road. There were a few pedestrians that were out partaking in the blissful morning. The day was in full swing. About a mile from home, my mind shifted gears, and the thoughts I had escaped from earlier returned. I stopped at a stop sign. A city bus pulled up on my left, preparing to turn in front of me. Its blinker flashed brightly, although it made no noise, I could see its warning.

The capacity of the bus was half full. Everyone on the bus seemed to be gazing at me as I observed their presence. But it was not the people on the bus that caught my attention. The advertisement on the side of the bus is what had me captivated. The ad was for a local hospital that specialized in heart surgery.

The slogan covered the whole side of the bus. But it was the three words in the middle that had me entranced. They flashed harmoniously with the turn signal, ensuring it had my undivided attention. The words stood out from the rest as if intended for me. I read the three words repeatedly before the bus turned and continued on its journey.

As I finished my jaunt, the smile that overtook my face rejuvenated my spirit. I arrived at my front door, as sure as I had ever been about my plans for the day. Before I entered my house, I turned and looked out into the world. Still contemplating the words that reassured me, I spoke them out loud, "*Follow your heart.*"

I entered the house; Mom was in the kitchen making coffee. "Good morning, Mom."

"Morning dear, how was your run?"

"It was great, exactly what I needed."

"That's good, you always did enjoy your morning runs. Do you want me to make you something for breakfast?"

"No, that's ok. Shada and I are going out for breakfast."

"Oh, ok, well, you can drop me off at home first."

"Of course. Are you going to the dinner today?

"No, I think I'll try and get some of your father's stuff packed up and do some cleaning around the house."

"Ok, I can come by later and help."

"If you can find time, that will be fine."

I could sense the discord in her voice, but I refused to engage in the potential dispute at this time. I assured her I would stop by and continued to my room to shower and change. We left the house under the cover of silence. There was a thick layer of tension in the air. I tried to converse, but I was met with short deflective answers. We arrived at my parents' home. I helped my mother out of the car and to the front door.

"Ok, lady, I'll see you later." A slight grunt accepted my affirmation. I kissed the beautiful lady and watched her walk into the house. I returned to my car and headed to pick up Shada. Glancing in the rearview mirror, I noticed I had a smile on my face.

Thinking about the lady I would see caused me to beam with enjoyment. I pulled up to her apartment and exited my car, the verification I received earlier replayed in my mind, *follow your heart*.

CHAPTER 7.

Celebration of Life

●●●

SAFETY FROM THE PAST

FREDRICK A. STEWART

Iknocked on her apartment door. Her lovely voice greeted me. "coming." A moment later, the door opened. Every time I see her, she looks prettier than the last time I saw her. "You ready to go?"

"I am."

We left basking in the glow of each other's presence. Unlike my previous passenger, there was conversation and merriment. Our laughter was that of two people drunk off fermented grapes. We arrived at Shada's favorite breakfast spot. The waitress escorted us to a table that was close to the window. The scenery gave compliment to the newly rebuilt area. She gave us some time to review the menu before returning to take our order. It took me a little longer to decide on what I wanted.

Shada knew right away; she always got the same thing.

It wasn't long before our food arrived. The aroma was an added treat. We said grace and engaged in the wonderful meal. "So, what did you want to discuss? That got me a trip to my favorite eatery." I was about to engage her question when the waitress stopped by to check on us. "How is everything?"

"Everything is great," we both agreed.

"Ok, let me know if you need anything."

Although unsure how the topic I was about to take on would be received, I dove in headfirst. I laid it all out with military precision. I explained the pros and cons, as well as the rhyme and reason. When I finished my barrage of detailed particulars, I waited for her feedback, the moment of silence that followed caused a rush of uneasiness. When the lady spoke, her words were precise, her demands were reasonable and nonnegotiable.

Our willingness to compromise and understand each other's wants and needs was a good start to our plans for the future. Part of what we discussed would be put into play immediately, the rest at a date to be determined. I believe our compromise encouraged us to head into the unpredictable world of marriage. We left the restaurant feeling like we had taken a major step towards our future together. Now all we had to do was navigate through the land minds and tripwires that loomed before us.

In two days, it would be my Dad's birthday and funeral a few days later. I knew the wave of emotions accompanying the rest of this week would be unsettling as a boat being tossed around by turbulent seas. There will be highs and lows, laughter and tears, jubilee and mourning, all ready to be played out in the backdrop of the final days of summer. The closer it came to Dad's funeral, the harder it was for my mother to stay home alone. She worked at the diner during the day when she could muster up the strength to go. At night she would come and stay with me.

On Dad's birthday, I left the house early. When Shada and I returned home, Mom was sitting at the dining room table. She looked distraught with grief. "Good morning, Mom." I bent down and kissed her on the cheek." She closed her eyes and placed her hand on my face. "Good morning, son." Shada embraced her with a hug, "Good morning."

"Good morning, Shada, you smell nice."

"Thank you."

"Mason, you know it's your Dad's birthday today."

"Yes, Mom, I do. Dad and I were supposed to go to the river at Safety and do some fishing. I figured we all could go and make a day of it. It would be nice to get out of the city and get some fresh air while we celebrate Dad's birthday. What do you think, Mom?" She didn't say a word. She sat quietly. I looked at Shada, not knowing what else to say. "I think I would like that; I haven't been to Safety since I was there with your dad and Andrew. I breathed a sigh of relief.

"Great, I'll get the fishing equipment and load the truck. Shada, can you grab some blankets from the hallway closet."

"Of course."

"Mason, we need to stop by the diner on the way out, I made your dad's favorite rhubarb pie. We can't celebrate his birthday without that." It was good to see Mom perk up some. "Absolutely, Mom." We all loaded up in the truck and headed to Safety. The ride was enjoyable. "Mom, what would you like to listen to?"

"Oh, I don't know, anything as long as it's not that cursing and swearing rap stuff."

"Naw, we won't be listening to that."

"Oh, I know. Play 'I'm Ready' by Barbara Mason. Your Dad and I danced to that at our wedding." Shada and I got a kick out of Mom repeating, "now that's good music," as she bobbed her head and snapped her little fingers. Shada and I weren't quite familiar with the soulful singer, but it made Mom happy, so we grooved on. When we arrived at Safety, Mom was engaged in her memories.

There were times when she would flash a smile remembering the many Sundays we spent here as a family and then look as sad as I've ever seen her. I'm sure she thought about the two people who loved coming here as much as she did. The fishing spot was on the back side of Safety, a quarter mile or so behind the orchard. We ordered our sandwiches and drinks and sat on the old bench while waiting for our food.

I didn't want Mom to get too tired out, so I rented a golf cart to transport us to the fishing area. Mom wasted no time baiting her hook and getting to the business of catching some fish.

Shada didn't know anything about fishing. She did all right until it came time to put the worms on the hook, and then it was a no-go. She gave it a valiant effort until the worm started wiggling, that's when she screamed, dropped the pole, and took off running.

Mom and I fell out laughing. I had to go chase her down, she probably would have run back to town if I hadn't caught up with her. When we returned to the fishing hole, Mom had a devilish smirk on her face. "You're not going to catch no fish that way, sweetie, fish don't run." I think she rehearsed that line while we were gone.

"Mason, you better come on, I'm in the zone today." Mom had already caught a nice size fish. She tends to get very competitive when it comes to fishing. If she caught more fish than the rest of us, we would hear about it forever.

If she lost, it was because we got lucky. "Shada, come here so I can teach you how to catch some fish." The look on Shada's face was a silent cry for help. "Yes, Mam." The reluctance in her voice was felt. After a few minutes, Shada got the hang of casting her line. She was proud of herself. Mom aggressively instructed her to reel it in when she got her first bite. Things took a turn for the worse when the fish came out of the water.

"Shada! Grab the fish."

"I have to touch it!"

"Well, yes! How else will you take the hook out of its mouth, scrape the scales, and gut its insides?" The vomiting sound was my cue to grab the pole and remove Shada from the situation. "Babe, why don't you go to the orchard and grab some fruit from the trees?

"Ok, I can do that." After Shada left, I could see the devilish smirk on my mother's face had intensified. "Mom, you did that on purpose."

"Did what?"

"You know what."

"Hmm, I was trying to teach her how to prepare fish. Maybe you should rethink marrying her if she can't even handle a little worm or fish."

"Mom, whether or not she can fish isn't going to stop me from loving her and spending the rest of my life with her."

"You're talking like you're already married. I'm just saying, if she can't handle basic things, how will she handle the difficult times that will surely come."

"I don't see how that's a fair assessment, especially since you don't know what she has been through. Her life hasn't been easy. The things she's overcome are admirable. She desires to be better than she was, that's what draws me to her."

"Well, I hope you know what you're doing. The wrong woman can make your life a living hell."

"And the right one can make life worth living. Mom, I want to have your and Dad's kind of marriage. It wasn't always easy, but you both fought to make it work."

"What your dad and I had was different, it was special. It's starting to get cold and I'm ready to go. Maybe you should go get your fiancée."

"I'll go get my…never mind." Shada was sitting under the big fruit tree.

"You alright?

"Yeah, enjoying the serenity."

"I'm sorry about Mom and the fish. She can get a little carried away."

"It's ok. Did you tell her?"

"No, I almost did, but I don't think the words would have come out right."

"When the time is right, I'm sure you'll let her know."

"Yeah, well, we better be heading back, it's starting to get a little chilly."

"Hey, so do I get to sleep at your house tonight? In your bed, in your arms."

"Yes, Mrs. Barringer, that is affirmative."

We walked hand in hand back to where Mom was and started gathering the fishing equipment. The ride home was a little different than earlier. Mom fell asleep as soon as we got on the road. Shada and I listened to smooth jazz with affectionate touches and kisses every mile.

Each other's intoxicating desire enchanted us. I could feel the warmth of her body as it seductively whispered my name. We caressed each other's hands, vowing never to let go. We were tranced with love, and it felt amazing.

Once we arrived at the house, I woke Mom and began unloading the truck. Every time Shada would walk by me, I would bump into her or find some way to touch her. I was like a kid again. I guess Mom sensed something was afoot. "I didn't know you were having company tonight."

"Yes, Shada is staying over tonight."

"I see, well, you can take me home."

"Mom, you don't have to leave."

"It's alright, I have some things I need to take care of before the funeral."

"Mom, you don't have to leave."

"Mason, take me home, please."

"Yes, ma'am." I went inside to tell Shada I was taking Mom home. "You want me to come with you? I need to stop by the apartment and grab some clothes anyway, I don't have anything to put on."

"You don't have anything to wear, sounds good to me." We looked at each other with intriguing thoughts running through our minds. "I'll be back shortly; you can shower and put on one of my shirts. When I get back, we can watch a movie or something.

"Watch a movie, o no, you know what I want." She moved dangerously close to me, grabbed my shirt, and pulled me towards her as she raised her toes.

She planted a couple of tasty soft kisses on my lips. "I've waited a long time for this night, so hurry back, I've got plans for you." I couldn't take my eyes off her, I didn't want to let her go. I couldn't even remember my previous task. "Where am I going?

She smiled and gave me one more kiss. "You're taking your mother home."

"O, yeah. Ok, I'll be right back."

"Alright, I'll be waiting." She turned and slowly walked away. She put something extra on her departing walk that mesmerized me." *Whew! I didn't know it could get this hot in Autumn.* When I arrived at the truck, my mother had a disgusted look on her face. "Did you forget I was out here?"

"No, Mom, I didn't forget. Aunt Vivian and Uncle Charles get in tomorrow. I'll be picking them up from the airport around noon."

"Where are they staying?"

"They can stay with me."

"You're sure you have enough room?

"I'm sure, Mom."

"Well, in case you don't, I guess they can stay with me."

"I'll let them know the invitation was given."

"After you pick them up, we must go by the funeral home to drop your dad's uniform off and ensure everything is ready. There will be a lot of people at his funeral, he was loved by so many. It doesn't seem real that he isn't here anymore."

"I know, Mom, it's hard to accept that he is gone, but we must find a way to carry on. I know that's how he would want it."

"Yeah, you're right. He was a man of God and would always say, "God doesn't make mistakes. When it's your time, It's your time," we both recited in unison.

The next few days came and went. Time refused to stand still to allow me to grasp the reality of what I was dealing with, it pushed forward without a care.

Phone calls and visits from family, friends, and his brothers-in-arms were frantic. Everyone did their best to offer comfort, and although no words could ease the pain, I appreciated the attempts.

"Mason, are you there!"

"Mom, what's wrong? It's two o'clock in the morning."

"Mason, he is gone!" Who is gone?"

"Your   Dad, he's dead."

"Mom, what are you talking about?"

"Mason, he is gone, you killed him!

"What!"

"Why did you kill him?"

I didn't kill him!"

"Mason, baby, wake up! You're having a nightmare."

Shada's voice rescued me from the vivid nightmare that claimed me as its victim. *Ante merīdiem* has come, and I dread its arrival.

The reveille call has begun, but I will not be squared away. I will not be able to maneuver like a highly motivated Marine should, today has taken hold of me. Once again, I will face death, the one thing that is inevitable to all who draw breath. Today, I lay to rest the one person who has influenced my life from start to finish. He was my hero, role model, my commanding officer, but most of all, he was my father, Mason Andrew Barringer Sr.

My father demonstrated the essence of being a man by his actions and deeds. He taught me to live by the United States Marine Corps oath of God, family, country, and Corps. Today I will call upon God, my wife, and any that can share their support because not even my marine reserve will be enough.

As much as I dreaded the arrival of this day, I was glad it was here so that it could come and go. When Mom and I made Dad's arrangements, we purposely planned for an early morning service. We didn't want the day to drag long. The night before Dad's funeral, we stayed with Mom in the house I grew up in. So many memories were made between the four corners of this house.

We had an enjoyable night. My aunt and uncle told stories of growing up with my Dad and grandparents. Their stories reminded me of Andrew and me. Shada smiled as she sat in silence. Her childhood memories weren't fond recollections. I wish I could change the past for her, but I know I can't. All I can do is try and make memories that will be cherished in the future.

As expected, the funeral service was packed. Family and friends I haven't seen in years came to show their respect. My dad's brothers from his old platoon showed up in force. They all enlisted their service to be pallbearers. In one accord, they agreed, it would be an honor to carry their brother to his final resting place. I have been to countless funerals, but I can honestly say my dad's service was a celebration of life.

There was little or no time for tears. From the start, the pastor began with a story of how my dad counseled him during a rough period. Everything from the songs sung to the obituary reading was done so that you couldn't do anything but smile. The eulogies were the most entertaining. They all went over the allotted three minutes, but no one seemed to mind.

The laughter and enjoyable memories removed the sadness from the event. I closely watched my mother to see how she was holding up. I was so proud of her. Her face glowed. The smile on her face that had been absent for so long returned. I would catch her nodding in agreement when someone spoke highly of her late husband.

I scanned around the room at all the people that came to my dad's homegoing celebration, I was in awe. It was standing room only. How could one man have touched the lives of so many? I began looking for a specific face amongst the crowd.

It took me a minute, but about four rows back was the face I had been looking for. She didn't notice me at first, but when we made eye contact we flashed that trademark Barringer smile. Representatives from veteran's service performed taps, the folding of the flag and presentation to mom. Since Dad was being cremated, we didn't go to the cemetery.

We held the repast at the church. I watched the pallbearers load my dad's body in the hearse. I gave my final salute to my commanding officer. I took a moment and looked towards the heavens. I imagined God saying to my dad, *"Well done, good and faithful servant."*

After we left the church, a few close friends and family came by the house to continue in remembrance of Dad.

"How are you holding up, my love?"

"I'm doing well."

"Your dad was loved and admired by so many people."

"Yes, he was. He was a pillar of the community for a very long time. I wasn't expecting this many people to come by."

"It's alright, we've got some food left over from the repast, and I can throw something together to make sure everybody gets something to eat."

"I appreciate you for all the support you have given Mom and me through all these, you are a wonderful woman."

"I am a product of the love you have shown me." The touch of her hands on my face and her tender kiss drives me crazy.

"Now, go join your guests before you get something started."

"Copy that."

It felt good to have a family—people who loved you and wanted to be with you. I couldn't help but think about all those people at Mason Sr.'s funeral. Some people struggled with the loss, but most were able to recall memories that produced a laugh and smile in remembrance of an honorable man. Unfortunately, not everyone that stopped by was there to pay their respects.

Mason was in the backyard with his dads' marine brothers and other guests, he still loved hearing about their tour of duty in Nam. I was in the kitchen preparing food when someone leaned over my shoulder and whispered, "Hello, Shada." I quickly turned around to see Terry Salters standing danger close.

"Hello, Terry." Terry was one of Mason's high school friends who thought he was God's gift to women. He was handsome, but his personality and arrogance made him unattractive. His physical features got him a lot of attention.

He was almost six feet tall with a nice muscular build, curly salt and pepper hair, and brown skin. When he gawked at you with those seductive eyes, it was like he was undressing you. He had money from the multiple car dealerships he owned.

The deadly combination of looks and money led him to believe he could have any woman he wanted. He would soon find out that would not be the case. "How are you doing?"

"I'm well. All things being considered." My sarcastic tone was intentional. "Yes, I was very sorry to hear about Mason Sr.'s passing, he was a good man."

"Yes, he was."

"Is there anything I can do for you?"

"No, I'm fine!"

"Yes, you are," As he sneakily reached for my hand, I pulled it away. "Mason is outside in the back."

"I know, I want to make sure you are alright."

"I'm perfectly fine."

"Well, if you ever need anything, let me know, I can give you anything you want."

"You know what, I don't deserve all this special attention that you're so willing to share. But I have a very good friend I think you should meet."

"Is she as fine as you?"

"Well, everyone can't be that lucky. Stay right here, let me go get her for you."

"Alright, I hate to see you leave, but I love watching you walk away," The hissing sound from his split serpent tongue was annoying. When I returned, Terry was standing there with the silliest look. He was like a dog in heat. "Where is she?" I walked over to the counter. "She is down here, as I slowly moved my hand down towards my thigh. Terry's eyes grew big as saucers.

He almost lost his mind; I'm sure his pink thing came out. He moved closer to me. "Can I see her?" I moved my hand slowly toward the edge of my skirt. I gradually began lifting it. His eyes were fixated on the prize he thought he would receive. The silly smirk on his face quickly disappeared as he made eye contact with Problem Child, the newest edition of the Barringer family. Problem Child is a pink Glock with a bad attitude. Her Victoria pink frame and satin aluminum slide complement each other perfectly.

She is young and full of vigor. Her hair-trigger is quickly excited by the slightest touch. She is young, wild, and free, which makes her as dangerous as beautiful. She hangs out with her sixteen homegirls, who are just as rowdy and ratchet as she is. She is enticed by the pungent smell of her gunpowder, eager to give whomever the smoke, she may get her chance soon.

I pulled Problem Child out of my pink garter holster. The removal awoke her and aroused her interest. She began spewing explicit adjectives. Her threats are not to be taken lightly. I looked Terry in his deceitful eyes.

"If you ever come to my home and disrespect my husband, myself, or our marriage again, I will unleash six fire-breathing, soul-wrenching, demon spawns of hell into your body that will make you regret the day you got your first piece. And the only reason I wouldn't empty the whole nest is because you're not worth the price of replacing them.

Now, I thank it's time you leave."

The terrified look on Terry's face was exhilarating. He stumbled to get his words out. "I'll go say bye to Mason."

"No, you can leave." I could tell Terry had more to say, but something about the sound of an empty chamber being filled demanded silence. Terry slowly backed up towards the door. His facial expression said everything his mouth dared not speak.

I escorted him out the door and locked it. I returned to preparing food for our guests. A smile came over my face, I could hear Mama Moreen saying, *"That's my girl."*

CHAPTER 8.

Looking At Her Angel

•••

SAFETY FROM THE PAST

FREDRICK A. STEWART

The next two years flew by. A year after Dad's funeral, Mom closed the dinner. She would go there, but she wouldn't usually open for business. Her heart wasn't in it. Truthfully, I believe she lost the desire to run it without Dad. We convinced her to move in with us and convert her house into an Airbnb.

She was not too keen on someone else staying in her house. Eventually, she came to terms with it when she saw the income it generated, it put her in a better state of mind financially. Since we would have two new people living with us Shada and I, decided it was time to purchase our first home together. Not only was Mom going to be living with us, but we were also expecting our first child.

Shada was eight months pregnant. Mom was so excited about being a grandmother. She assumed that since it was her first grandchild and it would be a girl, we would name the baby after her. She was disappointed when we told her we would name her Moreen. We used her middle name, which cooled the flames a little. With a new house, a baby on the way, and Mom living with us, I needed to make some extra money.

When I wasn't on base, I worked on my side hustle as a rideshare driver. During an early morning run, I picked up an elderly lady named Cecilia. She was petite, maybe four feet ten inches tall. Her skin was the color of cocoa. Her hair was thin with grey and red tint braids. Her stature suggested she may have been in her early eighties.

Her face glowed and shimmered like satin without one wrinkle. I was amazed at how gracefully she moved. It was more like a slow glide. Her eyes had a sadness to them. Her beautiful smile overshadowed the sorrow in her eyes. "Are you Mason?" her voice was soft and kind. "Yes, ma'am, I am."

"Are you taking me to the airport?"

"Yes, ma'am."

"Ok." I opened the rear passenger door for her so she could get in. Once she was safe inside, I gently closed the door. I placed her small suitcase in the trunk and returned to the driver's seat. Once I entered the car, I checked my rear-view mirror and noticed Ms. Cecilia's smile. I asked her if everything was alright, "You have a nice car, and it smells good too."

"Thank you." I felt like I was in the presence of royalty, and I would provide a ride deserving of such distinction. I merged into traffic carefully, checking my speed regularly. I was steadfast and focused. I only took my eyes off the road when I glanced into my rearview mirror to check on my honored guest. She seemed to be enjoying the ride and the scenery.

Having Ms. Cecilia in the car reminded me of a story my dad told me. My dad was in no way a violent man. However, he did not stand for disrespect of our elders. He had a lengthy layover at the airport on his return from Vietnam. While he was waiting for his flight, he noticed an elderly lady had come into the sitting area. A younger lady accompanied her. They looked around for somewhere to sit. The elderly lady looked tired and worn out.

There were no empty seats anywhere. My dad walked over to the ladies. "Hello, I have a seat she can have." The little elderly lady looked up at my dad, he must have looked like a giant. "Thank you, I really would appreciate that." Dad extended his arm for her to hold on to as they returned to his seat. When they arrived, a man was sitting in his seat.

"Excuse me, sir, that's my seat, and I was going to let this lady sit there."

The man looked up, "I don't see your name on it, boy."

"Did you see my sea bag next to the chair? And I know you saw me sitting there."

"Look, boy, both of you niggers can go somewhere. My dad took the elderly lady's arm off his. He stood in front of the racist man sitting in his chair. "I am not a boy; I am a grown man. I am not a nigger; I am a United States Marine!"

"Get the fu...before the man could finish his sentence, my dad grabbed him by his shirt and snatched him out of the chair. The massive man had reached his boiling point. His bloodshot eyes confirmed his blood pressure had reached an uncomfortable high level. The frown on his face had an immediate reaction. The wrinkles in his forehead pushed downward as they forced his eyelids into a distinctive squint.

The tightness in his jaws could be easily seen on his clean-shaven face. The tension in his body elevated as his massive chest and huge arms pulsated with the heated blood of an ancient warrior. Nothing was worse than the words he did not speak. His silence was a fear factor all by itself. Obviously, he was not a person to be reckoned with or taken lightly.

The racist man pleaded okay! Okay! My dad gave the man a firm shove as he released him from the Kodiak bear grip that had the man's feet desperately searching for solid ground. My dad turned towards the elderly lady who looked at him with amazement. "Please have a seat" The lady sat down and immediately started weeping.

Her tears told her story as they slowly maneuvered through the pours and wrinkles on her face. They spoke of her childhood growing up in a segregated South. They divulged the abuse and heartbreak from former lovers and the tart bitterness of those who deemed her unworthy to be respected. They conveyed the trials of a mother raising a daughter in a male-dominated world.

But they also spoke of the victories. The triumphs over oppression, the rising from the ashes of defeat when all others assumed her death was imminent. *"She has earned this seat,"* her tears cried out. My Dad kneeled and asked her, "Why do you cry?"

The lady looked into my Dad's eyes. "No one has ever done anything like that for me before." The words from my Dad's mouth were placed in his heart by the almighty God himself. "Our father has left a few of us to watch over and protect you."

The elderly lady's tears slowed some. "Can I please give you a hug?" Dad stood tall at attention. "It would be my honor." My father kneeled on one knee before the elderly lady. Even on one knee, he towered above the seated matriarch. She placed her arms as best as she could around the neck of the massive man. After he received his hug, he stood up and turned towards the younger lady that accompanied his new friend.

"Is this your mother?"

"No, she is my grandmother."

"I don't have another seat for you, but you can use my sea bag."

"Thank you, that would be fine." My dad stood guard over the ladies for the rest of their time at the airport. When it was time to board the plane, my dad walked the ladies down the ramp. No one said anything about how long it took them to board the plane. He took the ladies to their seats and reassured them, "I'll be right back there if you need me," pointing to the back of the plane.

Dad proceeded to his seat. The man that he discussed with earlier was sitting a few seats behind the ladies. Dad stopped by his seat. No words were spoken. No stares were exchanged, but the mutual understanding was precedent. My dad told me he pulled guard duty many nights as a Marine, but that was the only time he felt that what he was guarding was worth dying for.

The memories of my dad were interrupted as I pulled up to the airport to drop off my distinguished guest. I exited my car, retrieved her suitcase from the trunk, and sat it on the curb. I opened the rear passenger door for her and extended my hand to help her out of the car. She took my hand and slowly exited the car. "Thank you for getting me here safely, I enjoyed the ride."

She took my hand and placed a five-dollar bill in it. I looked at the currency and smiled. I retrieved her tiny hand and placed the money back in hers. "It was my pleasure." Ms. Cecilia bowed her head and reached in to hug me. I embraced the beautiful woman gently. Without making eye contact, she released me, took hold of her suitcase, and proceeded to the airport.

I didn't want my mission to end. I wanted to escort her to her seat on the plane, but I knew that wasn't protocol. Instead, I watched her enter the airport and disappear among the passengers with unknown destinations. Before I could return to my car, my phone rang with a new ride request. I accepted the request and headed off to the other side of the airport for the pickup. When I arrived, I received a call from mom. "Mason, where are you?"

"I'm at the airport."

"You need to get to the hospital; Shada went into labor."

"I'm on my way." The passenger I was about to pick up stood at the curb, waiting for me to stop. He seemed shocked as I sped up and kept going. I yelled out the window, "sorry," and cancelled the ride. The drive to the hospital from the airport was about twenty-five minutes. I'm sure I did it in fifteen. So many thoughts rushed through my mind.

The most profound thought was, I was about to be a Dad. I arrived at the hospital in disarray. I pulled into a parking spot, moved the shifter to P, and jumped out of the car. I was a reasonable ten steps in before I realized I left the car running. I quickly returned to my car, turned it off, and grabbed my keys. I was a man on a mission.

I stopped at the front desk to find out where Shada was. All sorts of gibberish came out of my mouth. The attendant was a complete professional. "Sir, please, take a deep breath and calm down. What is the patient's name?"

"Um, Shada Barringer." The attendant made a few keystrokes on the computer. "Ok, so you must be Mason Barringer."

"I was! I do! I am!" The lady chuckled. "Ok, let's get you to the delivery room. Take those elevators over there to the fourth floor. When you exit the elevator take a left and an immediate right. The nurse's station will be on your left." When I arrived at the nurse's station the nurse at the desk was expecting me. She immediately took me to the delivery room.

I could hear Shada but couldn't see her due to the curtain being closed, she sounded like she was in a lot of pain. "Ok, the first thing I need you to do is scrub your hands and forearms, then put this gown and mask on." I scrubbed up and entered the curtain. Shada saw me and began crying harder. "You made it."

I smiled and kissed her on her forehead, "I wouldn't miss this for the world." I held her hand as she tried to bear the pain she inherited from Eve. A few hours passed before the doctor ordered, "It's time to push." I knew I was supposed to be at the head of the bed trying to support my wife, but I gradually made my way to the other end as I waited in anticipation of the arrival of our daughter.

I was in no way prepared for what I saw. The soldier in me yelled, "stand fast, Marine!" The rest of me was ready to holler, "man down!" But no matter what, A Marine never abandons his post. With one hand holding on to Shada, the rest of me was almost in the birth path. I watched in amazement as I observed the greatest event known to man, by the grace of God, I witnessed the birth of my baby girl, it was love at first sight.

The doctor cleared my daughter's airway and nostrils, clamped the umbilical cord, and handed me the scissors. "Would you like to do the honors?" I wasn't sure what she was asking me to do. "It's ok, cut in between the clamps." I made my cut, and it felt like I was cutting a rubber tube. The nurse wrapped our daughter in a blanket and laid her on my wife's chest. Shada was exhausted but still shined like a diamond.

She admired her labor momentarily before attempting to lift our child upward. I quickly began gently cradling my hands around this precious pearl. Shada could muster a few words, "here is your daughter."

Right away, I knew my life would not be the same. I stared at our blessing, captivated. When I could take my eyes off her, I looked back at Shada, who was fast asleep, she had earned the right to slumber. The nurse took our daughter to clean her up. I didn't want to relinquish control; I knew she was safe in my arms.

I sat in that hospital room, admiring my sleeping wife and reflecting on my new life and its responsibilities. Knowing I had a great teacher encouraged me. All that was left was putting those lessons into action. The next day we were eager to see our newest addition. The doctor came into the room and gave a report we were unprepared to hear. He informed us that our daughter had multiple complications that would require her to remain in the hospital for an extended period.

The first issue was she was born with a hole in her heart. They felt it was a situation that would heal itself over time as she grew. The second issue was her oxygen was dangerously low. She was already in the Pediatric Intensive Care Unit for constant monitoring. The third issue was they found traces of blood in her stomach that they couldn't figure out where it had come from.

Our daughter hadn't been in the world for twenty-four hours, and we were already facing a parent's worst fear. We asked the doctor when we could see her. "I'll get one of the nurses to take you to the PICU unit." I held my wife close. I could tell she feared the particulars of her past were the reason for our daughters' complications.

I refused to let those thoughts manipulate her thinking. "Love, this has nothing to do with what happened to you. Our daughter is going to be fine." My words were not only spoken to my wife but also to our father in heaven. A short time later, a nurse came to take us to see our daughter. Seeing her hooked up to wires, tubes, and monitors was painful.

The lights and beeping sounds were bothersome. The nurse brought us some chairs so that we could sit with her. Shada asked the nurse if she could hold her. The caring nurse adjusted the machinery so that she could be held in position. She informed us the oxygen tube and monitor had to stay in place.

My wife sat in the chair by the wall. The nurse removed Moreen from the cradle and handed her to her mother. Shada wanted to hold her close to her chest, but the clumsy tubes and wires wouldn't allow it. She immediately closed her eyes and began to rock. I'm pretty sure she was having a conversation with our father.

We took turns holding our daughter and falling in love with her. Three days later, Shada was discharged. We stayed at the hospital with our daughter as long as possible until the nurses strongly suggested we go home and rest. We returned to the hospital the following day. We received updates from the doctor as he performed his rounds.

All signs showed improvement. We waited patiently for the nurse to prepare our daughter to be held. Shada sat in the chair by the wall first. She laid Moreen on her chest and placed one hand on her back and one under her. After a while, our daughter awoke. Her eyes moved around like they were searching for something. She lifted her head from her mother's chest and stared at something behind her.

She stayed fixated for a few minutes. We looked at each other and did what most parents would do when their newborn did something so unique. We started having conversations about her being a genius and conquering the world. We didn't understand the ramifications of our daughter's action until she did it again while I held her.

In the same chair, with the same emptiness behind us, our daughter raised her head and fixed her eyes on what she saw. In unison, my wife and I agreed, "she is looking at her angel." We knew God had answered our prayers. Our daughter stayed in the hospital for about eight days in total.

When she came home, she still needed to be on oxygen. The joy and excitement she brought to our home were very much welcomed, it slowed the minor friction between Mom and Shada.

As beautiful as life can be, it hoards a sinister side. Again, it would grin an evil grin. Its thirst for anarchy is unbridled. Its narcissistic portrayal is embellished as it craves to play the victim. It finds enjoyment in the wreckage of unsuspected turmoil. Its menacing behavior is exhibited out of malice and the pompous pleasure of knowing it can.

CHAPTER 9.

Mama's Fury

•●•

SAFETY FROM THE PAST

FREDRICK A. STEWART

"**D**id you ever imagine we would be together like this?"

"What do you mean?"

"You know, a house, a child, married, in love."

"Honestly, I would have to say no! Considering the circumstances of how we met, I guess I'm happy to have made it out of the diner alive."

"Mason, don't say that!"

"I'm playing, babe."

"I know, but I was in a bad place. I didn't care if I lived or died when I walked into that diner. I was prepared for both."

"You know, when you approached me in the diner, I was sitting there contemplating my life. Seeing Andrew getting hit by that car and dying in my arms rocked me. Then dealing with Dad getting shot and Mom blaming me for Andrew's death caused me to question my faith in God. Even my time in the Marines didn't seem right. Seeing my brothers-in-arms lose their lives and almost being killed myself, I started questioning if it was all a lie.

There were times when I felt like God had abandoned me. Then he would show up and put all the pieces back together again. That's when I realized I made it through all I did because God was with me. It was no mistake or coincidence when you and Crazy came into the diner that I was there. I hadn't seen or spoken with my parents in years.

Out of the blue, my mother calls me and asks me to come to dinner. It was God's divine plan. Do you remember what you said to me when you approached me at the table?"

"Yeah, I said I need you to leave."

"Exactly. Babe, I had given up. I was done. I was tired of carrying the world's weight and being responsible for everyone else's burdens. At times during combat, I wished a round from my adversary's rifle would have found its mark and ended the misery that consumed me. When I asked if I could talk to you, I had no idea what I would say to keep you from robbing my parents' diner. All I knew was that if I didn't obey God, everyone stood to lose.

Before we headed out of the diner, God spoke to me. "We need you to stay!"

"What do you mean, we?"

"Not we, like he couldn't do it without me. It was more like we, my parents, you, and me. We were one together with him. Shada! Are you alright? What's the matter?" The look on my wife's face was alarming. It was as if she had been frozen right before my eyes. I put my hands on her shoulders and pulled her close to me. "Shada! what's wrong?" It wasn't until I heard my name being called in full verbatim that I realized the source of her petrified state.

"Mason Andrew Barringer!" I slowly turned around to lock eyes with the woman who gave birth to me. The expression on her face was terror and disbelief. She was not intimidating in stature but had a fierceness that was only unleashed at times like these.

"Are you serious!" her voice trembled. Her petite body shook with anger. Her breathing was short and uncontrolled. Even her skin had become red, like it was filled with fire.

"Mom, please listen."

"No! 'I have heard enough. How could you? How could you bring this person into our lives? Wasn't your father getting shot enough? They put a gun in my face, they could have killed us, and you go and marry one of them."

"Mom Shada had nothing to do with that."

"She is no different from those thugs that shot your dad. Too sorry to work for anything, so instead, they take from others who have spent their whole life trying to have something.

"Mom, you don't understand Shada is not like that anymore."

"Mason, a leopard never changes its spots."

"Mom, she is not a leopard, and she is not a thug."

"I don't give a dam what she is. How could you betray your parents for this?"

"Mom, I would never disrespect you, but you are talking about my wife."

"Your wife! Your father would be so disappointed in you."

"You know what, Mom, he wouldn't."

"What are you talking about, Mason? "I talked to Dad before I asked Shada to marry me. I explained everything to him. I told him about the dinner and why I took her to Safety. We discussed her past and the things she has been through."

"Your father wouldn't keep something like that from me."

"I asked him not to tell you."

"Why would you do that?"

"Mom, look at how you're reacting now."

"How I'm reacting! I'm the one who just found out she was going to rob the diner, and you and your dad kept it from me."

"Mom, I've had to overcome a lot in the last few years. I've had to learn to live without Andrew, accept that you blamed me for his death, and now Dad."

"I don't want to talk about that, Mason."

"I know you don't, Mom, but I need to discuss it. I need closure to find the peace that has eluded me all these years. I've fought those demons; I've had to force myself to wear a smile that wasn't there. Pretending to go on with life like everything was okay, when inside, I was fighting a battle I couldn't win.

I had to make amends with myself, but it wasn't until Shada came into my life that I realized I had to learn how to forgive. First, I had to learn how to forgive myself for accepting the unjust blame of Andrews's death, and more so, I had to learn how to forgive you."

"What do you mean forgive me?"

"Mom, you blamed me for Andrew's death. You placed a burden on me that was too heavy to bear. It felt like you used my love for my brother against me. You allowed me to carry that guilt around for years, not even caring how much it destroyed me. You shut me out of your and Dad's lives, and not once have you apologized for that.

The biggest moments of my life you weren't present for. When I graduated from boot camp, you were not there, when I made rank, you were not there. You are the reason I volunteered to go to Afghanistan. So many times, while I was over there, I hoped I wouldn't make it back alive so that you could see what it was like to carry that burden.

The truth is, Mom, you blamed me because of your guilt for not being there for Andrew and me. You placed the responsibility of raising Andrew firmly on my shoulders. And when he died, you did not ask how I was doing, but I'll tell you. I was dying inside."

"Mason, how could you talk to me like that? How could you say those terrible things to me? I'm your mother. Your father and I did our best to ensure you and Andrew never wanted anything. We spent years trying to build a legacy for you and Andrew. Don't you think we sacrificed? We wanted to be at your and Andrew's school functions and events.

We wanted to be there, but we also knew the lifestyle we were trying to provide you would require us to miss out on some things, so we chose to give you and your brother a life without want."

"Mom, I appreciate what you and Dad did for us, and I did the best I could raising my little brother. I have no regrets about the role I played in his life, but there is not a day that goes by that I don't think about him and wish I could change what happened. But the truth is I can't change anything. All I can do is live with this hole in my heart where my little brother used to be.

And I needed someone like Shada, someone dealing with as much pain and anguish as I was, so we could heal together and learn how to live again."

"If that's what you call living, then you go ahead and live that lie. She is no different from any other thug, murderer, or thief that runs the streets—praying on others for their own gratification and using excuses to justify their behavior. And you had the nerve to keep that from us.

"Well, Mom, I guess I got it honest."

"You got what, honestly, Mason?"

"Keeping secrets."

"And what is that supposed to mean."

"You know what it means. But in case you've forgotten, I know how bad your memory can be. What about Neveah? And how you wouldn't allow Dad to be a part of her life."

"You don't know what you're talking about."

"I know my dad has a daughter, and Andrew and I have a sister that if it were up to you, we would have never met."

"Your dad cheated on me and got that woman pregnant."

"So, you made him choose between his family and his daughter. Did you ever stop to think about how that affected Dad? How much he regretted not being a part of her life. Did it ever occur to you that maybe, just maybe, Andrew and I wanted to grow up knowing our sister? Mom, the only time we were a family was at Safety. Somethings can't be aborted."

"What did you say?"

"Yes, I know about that too."

"Well, your Dad's loose lips seemed to have leaked all sorts of information."

"Dad didn't mention that. When he told me about Neveah, he left that part out. It wasn't until after Dad died and I was at the house helping you pack up his things that I ran across a box with some pictures, letters, and documents. That's when I came across your discharge papers from the clinic."

"I made a sacrifice as well. I chose our family over my child. At least he was still able to see his mistake."

"They weren't mistakes, Mom, they are and were people. They were as much part of this family as Andrew and me."

"Well, I'm glad you have all the answers, Mason. I'm glad you can make all the tuff decisions without blinking an eye or giving it a second thought. But you heed this, if I had not made those difficult decisions, there might not have been you or Andrew."

I couldn't stand hearing my husband and mother-in-law going after each other like that. It tore at the very fibers of my soul to hear Mason having to defend me from my reckless past. Out of all the people on this earth, he is the last one that should have to carry that burden.

"Mason, please let it go."

"No, Shada, I can't let it go. Let her start with her own if she wants to hold someone's past against them."

"How dare you talk to me like that. You think you know so much, little boy, you don't know anything. You think you got all the answers. Until you've put in some time being married and understanding what it takes to continue to love someone when that flame starts to flicker out, and those hard times come and trust me, they will come.

Wait until you've repeatedly dealt with that person's shortcomings, faults, and failures until you start to rethink your vows of till death do us part. Or when that spark isn't there anymore, and you can barely stand to look at that person, let alone breathe the same air or be in the same area with them for more than a few minutes.

Wait till you have to make difficult decisions that other people get to sit back and judge you on. Because until you've spent 10, 30, 50, plus years of your life with the same person, giving and taking all that you have, trying your hardest to make your marriage and family work, I don't give a dam about what you think you know. Because you don't know shit!

"Mama Barringer, I am so sorry, please forgive me."

"My name is Marie Barringer."

The tension had become too much. I grabbed my coat and rushed out the door. "Shada, where are you going?"

"You don't have to leave, this is you and your husband's house, I'll leave."

"Shada, wait."

"Mason, I asked you to let it go. Now look at everything. I have to go."

I left our house distraught. It was all my fault that Mason and his mother had such a terrible argument.

No matter what, I can't run from my past, it always finds a way of catching up with me. I walked out the door in tears. The feeling that accompanies me is dreadful. I reached the sidewalk when two men in suits approached me. "Excuse me, does Shada Barringer live here?"

"Whose asking?"

"I'm Detective Dean, and this is my partner Detective McAfee." They both showed me their credentials. "We were hoping we could ask her a few questions."

"Question about what?"

"Where gathering information about some homicides that happened a few years ago, and we hoped she could help us with them. Are you Shada Barringer?

"I am, but I don't know anything about homicides."

"Well, you may have known the victims, which may help find out who was responsible for their murders."

"Why do you think I know the victims?" Um, well, we received some information that they were your friends.

"You received information from who?"

"The person asked to stay anonymous.

"Really, well, maybe that's who you should be asking questions."

Ms. Barringer, we're not trying to harass you or anything, we're trying to gather information that may help the investigation."

"Well, right now is not a good time."

I understand, maybe we could stop by tomorrow.

"I don't think so."

"I tell you what, here is my card. If you can call me when the timing is better, we can set up a time for you to stop by the precinct. I promise it won't take long. You can call me whenever you're free, and we'll make ourselves available."

"Sure."

"Have a nice day, and thanks for your time."

I continued on my way, struggling immensely with my emotions. I fought fiercely to contain my sorrow, doing all I could not to succumb to the murmuring that had begun as a faint undertone. Gradually the clamor rose to a robust uproar.

I could hear my past speaking slanderous words against me. In dark places void of light, it declared foul words filled with hate. Behind my back it told stories about my transgressions, while embellishing its own sinister versions.

My past is an evil enslaver that refuses to set me free. It wants to keep me imprisoned in a lifetime of misery. Shackled, it parades me around for all to see my nakedness and shame. It still longs to strip me of my dignity while continuously reminding me I am not from this land, but I will be forced into cruel punishment to till its soil.

Even the air I breathe, it doesn't want me to partake in. It is a heartless mistress that longs for the day I return to the dust I was created from. But my past does not know who I've become. It is clueless to the transformation that has taken place.

By the will of God, it will not have its way with me. It will sit mute alone in a cold, dark empty dungeon, with only diseased rats as company. Its tongue severed from its mouth, so it can no longer speak atrocities against me. Its eyes, plucked from its skull by the crows of the field. Its disease-ridden body will wither away malnourished and frail.

I have committed many sins, and foul acts, but my repentance has given me a new life. My Creator is righteous, He is not a man, that He should lie. I continued my walk, ignoring the many calls from my husband. I needed to regain the peace that eluded me, alone with my thoughts was my only conclusion.

A few hours later, I returned home. When I entered the door, Mason was sitting in the living room with his head in his hands. He immediately rushed over to me. "Where have you been? I have been calling you for hours."

"I know, and I'm sorry I didn't answer. But I was trying to clear my mind and figure some things out."

"I wish you would have at least let me know you were ok."

"Your right, I should have, and I apologize for not answering. I have a lot on my mind. Where's your mom?"

"She went to her room and hasn't come out."

"Babe, I'm sorry about all this. I'm sorry you have to go through this because of me. You don't deserve that."

"Shada, this isn't about you. And it's not your fault. It needed to be addressed, I wish it didn't happen the way it did, but I'm glad it's out in the open. It's getting Mom to accept it, which will be the hard part."

Ok, I'm going to go check on the baby." As I started to walk away, Mason gently took ahold of my arm, "Are you sure you're ok?"

"Yes, my love, I'm fine." I felt like I had lied to my husband. I wanted to tell him about the detectives and their wanting to question me about the murders. But how could I bring that up after what happened with Marie? I entered our daughter's nursery. She was sleeping peacefully, without a care in the world. A question arose in my mind. 'Would I ever tell her about my past and the wrong I committed?' Suddenly, Marie's point of view became a lot more understandable.

Over the next few days, I received multiple phone calls from the two detectives that stopped by. I knew they wouldn't go away, so I called them and let them know when I would be coming in for questioning. Since I could not get around this, I decided it would be done my way, on my terms.

"Hello, I have an appointment with Detectives Dean and MacAfee."

"Your name is?"

"Shada Barringer."

"Hold on, let me see if I can find them."

The desk Sargent made a phone call. I looked around the precinct, thinking, 'this is the last place on earth I want to be.'

"You can sit over there; they should be with you soon." I looked in the direction that the Sargent was pointing, it looked like I was being sent to time out. I sat in the waiting area, watching the clock slowly pass by. A half hour had passed before I started getting heated. I approached the Sargent again. "Can you please check and see if they are still coming?"

"Ma'am, they said they would be available soon."

"Yes, I know, that was over a half hour ago."

"I'm sorry, I don't know what else to tell you."

I took a deep breath, "is there a restroom I can use?"

"Down the hall on the left."

"Thank you." I proceeded towards the restroom. I could feel my anxiety and anger starting to rise. Once I entered the bathroom and looked around, I decided I could hold it. I went to the sink to wash my hands, when I looked in the mirror, the ugly in me was not there. My reflection didn't turn away disgusted. I closed my eyes for a moment, then I heard a familiar voice. It was the voice I missed badly. I listened to the words that were spoken. When I opened my eyes, there was a smile on my face.

My heartbeat raced with exhilaration. 'She is still with me.' I left the restroom renewed. Walking down the hallway, I could see the detectives waiting for me. My smile grew more significant because I knew I was not alone.

"Hello, Mrs. Barringer, I apologize for keeping you waiting so long."

"It's ok, it gave me time to catch up with an old friend." Both of the detectives had confused looks on their faces. They stared at each other, baffled. "Ok, well, let's get started. Detective Dean escorted me to an interrogation room. Detective MacAfee went and had a conversation with the desk Sargent.

After a while, he joined us. So, Mrs. Barringer, we want to talk to you about the murders of Sidney Jones, Craig Williams, and Darrius Snyder."

"Who?"

"Sidney Jones, Craig Williams, and Darrius Snyder, weren't they acquaintances of yours?" "No, they weren't."

"Are you saying you don't know these people?"

"I'm saying that I don't know a Craig Williams and Darrius Snyder."

"I'm sorry I'm a little confused, but didn't you use to hang out with them a few years ago? I didn't say anything immediately because it had become obvious they didn't know as much as they thought. I smirked a little bit. "Mrs. Barringer, is something funny?"

"Yes, it is. How long have you been detectives?"

"Mrs. Barringer, what does that have to do with anything?"

"A lot, you asked me did I know Craig Williams and Darrius Snyder, correct."

"Yes."

"And I told you I didn't know them correct."

"Yes, that's correct."

"Well, that's because the Craig and Darrius I knew were Craig Snyder and Darrius Williams." I couldn't help but draw enjoyment from seeing the detectives rubbing their foreheads and looking up at the ceiling with their hands over their mouths. "Detectives, is that all you needed from me?"

"No, we have a few more questions for you, if you don't mind." They sounded like someone had let the air out of their balloons. "How well did you know the deceased?"

"They were friends of a friend."

"Which friend might that be?"

Detectives, I'm sure you know what, friend, I'm sure you know what she did and what happened to her, so why are we playing whose who? I came down here on goodwill, and you're trying to implement me in these murders.

Mrs. Barringer were trying to get some answers. And…"

"You know what, Dean; I think we have been more than accommodating with Mrs. Barringer, and she hasn't given us anything."

"I can't give you what I don't have."

"Well, how about we try this? When was the last time you saw Craig Williams?"

"Before he died."

"Do you think this is a game?"

"By no means do I think this is a game or funny. It's sad that you still haven't found out who is responsible for their deaths after all these years. And now you are grasping at straws, trying to find someone to place the blame on."

"Hum, well, maybe you can explain what you were doing at Craig's place the night he was killed."

"I don't know which night he was killed, so I can't answer that either."

"That's interesting because we checked his phone, and there was a text from Mr. Snyder to Mr. Jones saying that you were there, and he was about to hit it."

"That's quite possible, but he didn't hit it. I saw Craig on the train on my way to a friend's house. He asked me to come by and chill for a minute. I hadn't seen him in over three years, so I agreed.

We were chilling and having a good time when he flipped the switch. He started making sexual comments while trying to feel me up. He kept saying how bad he wanted to get with me, but that wouldn't happen because he was seeing Karmen."

"He was high and had been drinking. I recalled how rough he would get with Karmen when he was like that, so I told him I had to go. He kept insisting that I stay. It wasn't until I told him I was on my period that he was ok with me leaving. That's the last time I saw him."

"Don't you think it's more than coincidence that you were the last to see him alive?"

"How do you know I was the last person? You just said he texted Sidney and told him I was there. Sidney had a crush on me as well."

"So, you're saying that Sidney may have killed Craig."

No, I'm not saying that at all. I am saying it's possible that I was not the last to see him alive. Gentleman, it's getting late, I still need to go grocery shopping and have been here longer than expected. So, if there are no further questions, I would like to leave."

"Of course, if we have any more questions, we'll call you."

"Ok."

"Oh, one more thing. Why did you stop hanging out with them?"

"I grew up. Good night, gentlemen." I eagerly left the precinct. It felt like a million pairs of eyes were gazing upon me. Questioning my integrity, looking to find a flaw in my story so they could pounce upon me like unexpecting prey.

"So, what do you think?"

"I'm not sure if she did it, but I think she knows more than she lets on. Unfortunately, the people who could shed some light on the situation are dead. We'll stay in touch with her, if she knows something, she'll slip up. Why don't you check with your friend again, if his statement is true, she's not as innocent as she lets on."

"Copy that."

I began unloading the groceries from the car when Mason arrived home. He and the baby were returning from dropping Marie off at the airport. She wanted to stay with her sister out of state for a while. She was still struggling with the thought that her son married a criminal. With her not here, telling Mason about the investigation should be easier. "Hey, love, how was your day?"

"Better now that my two most favorite people are home. "How's mamas baby doing?" The smile from the beautiful baby staring back at me was priceless.

"You know she's going to be a daddy's girl, right." Taken back by my husband's comment, I rolled my eyes slightly. "O, really, and what makes you think that?"

"Well, we had a long conversation on the way back from the airport. We discussed all the things I was going to teach her. Like fishing and shooting, oh, and which sports team to root for, four nine for life, I told her that one was non-negotiable. Yeah, we had a good conversation.

"Baby, you know we can make another one, and you can teach all that to your son." My husband moved in close and placed his hands on my waist.

"Make another one, I think we should embark on that mission immediately."

"How about you finish unloading the groceries, and I'll take our little princess inside and get her ready for bed."

"Copy that. Oh! We agreed she wouldn't date until she was in her thirties."

"Good luck with that one, my love." Hearing my husband's cute but misguided conversation with our daughter was funny.

I thought about the discussion I planned on having later and how I was not looking forward to it. I don't like being the one that destroys the peace in our home or causes conflict. Unfortunately, that has been the case for the last few weeks. My life is so much different now than it was years ago. I would hate for my past to destroy the beautiful family that we have worked so hard to have.

Regardless, I refuse to keep this from my husband any longer. I told him I would be open and transparent with him, and I will do that. The cool breeze of the autumn air had settled upon us. Nights on the back patio were accompanied by the roaring blaze of the fire pit and a large blanket that was big enough for the both of us to snuggle under together.

The full moon in the clear sky helped illuminate the evening's nocturnal persona. What should have been a romantic night, teeming with unbridled passion, will be marred with the reality of a life long ago.

I hope the glasses of fermented grapes will give me the courage to embark on the unpleasant discussion. "I finally got baby girl to sleep, she was acting like she wanted to stay up and hang out with the grown folks. I brought her monitor with me in case she wakes up."

"Alright, you ready for a glass?"

"Definitely. Did you and Mom work things out on the way to the airport?"

"No, she was still being stubborn and combative. She called her self-going to take a ride share to the airport until she saw how much it was going to be. I hope she can get over it, the past is the past."

"You know, Mason, maybe you should be more sympathetic to what she is going through. That was a lot to spring on her. I know she had to be scared when those guys pulled a gun on her and seeing Mason Sr. shot had to be traumatic."

"I'm sure it was a lot, but that had nothing to do with you. That's what I was trying to get her to understand. We all make mistakes and have done things in the past that we were not proud of. But forgiveness is the only way to resolve the issue. My parents taught us those values growing up, and to see her act like none of that matters now is frustrating."

"I understand, but it's not like I wasn't planning on robbing the diner. Anything could have gone wrong, which could have been completely different."

"Ok, Shada, what's going on? I've never heard you talk like that before." I closed my eyes and placed my face in my hands. I could hear my heart rapidly beating in my chest. The strength of my husband's hands caressing me and pulling me closer to him made conveying it easier.

"The day everything came out about the diner, you and Marie were going at it pretty hard. I felt like it was all my fault. Two detectives came up the walkway as I was leaving the house. They wanted to question me about the deaths of the guys who raped me. I told them I didn't know anything about murders, and then it was not a good time to talk. They asked if they could return later, and I told them no, but I would contact them when I could come to the precinct. Today I went and talked to them.

They wanted to know what my relationship with the guys was."

"What did you tell them?"

"I told them that they were friends of a friend. Craig supposedly sent Sydney a text telling him I was over there, and we were about to hook up. So, the detectives believed I was the last person to see Craig alive."

"Something doesn't sound right. Why are they questioning you now if they thought you were a suspect."

"The detectives said they received a tip that I might know something about the deaths that could help them investigate. It felt like they were trying to get me to say something that would incriminate me. I explained I hadn't been in contact with any of them before their deaths."

"Shada, why didn't you tell me about this sooner?"

"Because with everything happening with Marie finding out about the diner, I didn't want to add fuel to the fire. Babe, I feel like my past will always haunt me, I can't find any peace in it. And even more, I've involved you in this mess."

"Shada, you told me about your past, and I've accepted that it may show up occasionally. But babe, we are in this together. The good, the bad, and the ugly, its team us, till death do us part."

"Mason, I need you to promise me something."

"What's that?"

"If this ever gets to the point where I'm facing time, please tell them you knew nothing about this, that I never told you about any of it. I don't want them coming after you."

"To deny I knew about your past is to deny you. I won't do that."

"Mason, it's bigger than us. I grew up without my parents, I don't want our daughter to grow up without hers. She will need you to raise and protect her from the wolves."

"We will get through this together, and what we can't do, our father can. He didn't bring you this far to abandon you."

"When all that stuff happened with Karmen and her crew, I stopped caring about life. When I lost the twins, and Mama Moreen died, it was like I had reached the end of my rope. All that resided in me was hurt and pain. I was a miserable soul, walking upon this planet, going to and from. I was not a good person. My heart was black, and my thoughts were evil. Hurt and anguish were my only companions; they didn't want to be around me half the time.

Now, I feel like I have something to live for. I have a family and people that love me, and that's all that matters to me now. That's all I ever wanted was someone to love me truly. I know God has forgiven me for my sins, he's probably tired of me asking, but it's times like these I question if I've forgiven myself."

I didn't try and comfort my wife with words. I held her close. She didn't confide in me her thoughts so I could fix the problem, she needed me to listen and understand, I gave her my undivided attention. As the night progressed, the chill of the night air became bitter. Not even the roaring flames of the fire pit brought enough warmth to remain outside.

We checked on our daughter asleep in her room. We gave her kisses, covered her in prayer, and thanked our Father in Heaven for our Precious Pearl. We proceeded to our room. We said goodnight to this day and prepared ourselves for tomorrow's arrival. The next few weeks were rather enjoyable, other than the occasional calls from the detectives who seemed to have no real reason for calling, our home was filled with joy and laughter.

CHAPTER 10.

Peace Restored

•••

SAFETY FROM THE PAST

FREDRICK A. STEWART

Marie had been with her sister out of town for the last three weeks but was coming home this weekend. I had mixed emotions about her return. The peace has been rejuvenated throughout the house. I did not want it to come to an end. I was reluctant to bring it up to Mason at first.

Then I realized I couldn't walk in fear when something bothered me. I needed to learn to communicate with my husband, even when I didn't think it would go well. Letting go of how I used to do things was a work in progress. I'm still learning how to trust and believe in another person.

Especially since my husband has been nothing but understanding and supportive since we met, if I didn't know how to address things with him, it was as if I was saying I don't have faith in him, which is the furthest thing from the truth.

It's times like these the wise counsel of Mama Moreen feels my mind, "Baby, it's not always what you say, but how you say it." I love and miss her so much, even in death, she gives me jewels. During the months I've been married, I've learned that bombarding my husband with issues as soon as he walks into the house is not the best practice.

I need to give him time to relax and shake the day's stress off. Be his peace and not his problem is another of Mama Moreens' jewels.' I wish she and Mason could have met.

Usually, when Mason comes home from work, his first objective is to find Daddy's baby, as he likes to call her. Sometimes, she gets kisses before I do, we'll have to work on that. Today his little princess was asleep, and she still got kisses before me. I stood at the entrance of our daughter's room, watching this big man become like a child in the presence of this baby.

It feels my heart with joy when I see their interaction. I knew he thought of waking her up, so I quickly intervened.

"No, do not wake her up!"

"How long has she been sleeping?

"Not long enough, come on out of here, she gets cranky like you when she doesn't get enough sleep." His grunt of disapproval was noted.

We left our daughter's room and gently closed the door behind us. When we entered the hallway, I pulled my husband close to me. "You know that little girl gets kisses before your wife when you come home."

"Before my wife! Oh, so you play the wifey card?"

"I pulled, kissed, played, kissed, and won with it!"

"I see, well I guess I better change my behavior than."

"Yes, you should, my love. Now go get changed, dinner is almost ready." As I sashayed away, I put something extra on it for him, I could feel his eyes admiring the view. After a short time, Mason returned from the bedroom. He changed out of his uniform and took a shower, he smelled wonderful.

The thought crossed my mind to have him for dinner, but I decided to wait. I'll have him as a late-night snack later. We sat down to dinner, said our prayers and made conversation about our day.

"What time does Marie's flight get in tomorrow?"

"She gets in late, her plane lands at seven twenty."

"Ok, well I want to talk to you about that. Things were intense when she left, and it's been peaceful since she was gone.

If we're all going to live in harmony together, we have to find a way to address the issue, without it becoming an argument. I don't want to walk around on eggshells or want her to feel uncomfortable either."

"Yeah, I've been thinking about that. Mom can be stubborn at times. It's hard to get her to see anything except what she wants when she gets like that. She has been that way as far back as I can remember. But you're right, this is your home, and you shouldn't have to live like that. I'll talk to her about it when I pick her up from the airport. Hopefully, the time away has calmed her nerves some."

"Well, I have a different idea. I want to pick her up from the airport. Maybe, if we have a moment together, she will allow me to explain what caused my reckless behavior. If she can get a glimpse into my past, she will have a better understanding, and hopefully, we'll be able to reconcile, and she can find it in her heart to forgive me."

It was hard to decipher the look on Mason's face, accompanied by the words he didn't speak. I could tell he was running different scenarios, calculating possible outcomes. "Well, what do you think?"

"If you're sure that's what you want to do, it's fine with me."

"I think it's the only way we'll get through this. She has been the only woman in your life. Now that there is another, it may be a hard adjustment for her."

"Ok, looks like the baby, and I will have to find something to get into."

"I hope to take her with me, in case things don't go the way I plan. Her being in the car may reduce the yelling and foul language."

"Alright, I guess I'll go see Neveah tomorrow. I talked to her the other day, I told her I would come to hang out with her for a while, we haven't seen each other since the funeral."

"Ok, sounds like your princess is awake. I'll go get her."

"Not, I'll go get daddy's girl."

"Alright. Well, make sure you change her diaper."

"Copy that. Hey, could you do me a favor? When you go pick Mom up, make sure you leave Crazy and Problem Child here."

"Really, Mason, I should be more concerned about what she has in her purse."

"Yeah, you're probably right about that. Daddy is coming, princess."

The drive to the airport was tedious. The rush hour traffic was starting to clear up, but there were still enough cars on the road to slow traffic. I'm beginning to learn the significance of when you are faced with a difficult situation, giving it to God first before you confront it.

"Hello, Marie."

"There's grandma's baby!" I thought Mason was picking me up."

"He was, but I asked him If I could, so we could talk."

"Talk about what?"

"About what happened at the diner and what happened before the diner. I want to give you some insight into my life before I met Mason and how much it has changed since then."

"We don't need to discuss that."

"Marie, please, it's not fair you are holding my past against me, without knowing the circumstances. I'm not making excuses for what I did, I need you to understand what I was going through at that time in my life."

"Fine. I need to stop and get something to eat, I haven't eaten in a while."

"Of course," where would you like to go?"

"There's a place on the thirty-second street I like." I had the feeling this conversation would cost me more than just me bearing my soul.

As much as I wanted to see and spend time with my sister, it didn't seem right to go to the bar without Dad. I thought about meeting her somewhere else, but that made no sense, he loved this place, plus they have the best wings in town. I took a deep breath and walked in the door; Neveah was at the bar serving drinks. When she saw me, she waived me over. She quickly came from behind the bar to hug me. I can see dads smile in her more now than before.

"Hey, brother."

"What's up, sis."

"I thought you were going to bring your wife, so I could meet her."

"I was, but she has embarked on a noble adventure, I'll tell you about it later.

"Alright, well, wait right here. I have a surprise for you. Sharon put his drinks on my tab. Go ahead and order something to drink, I'll be right back."

Neveah returned in a few minutes with a frame in her hand. "Ok, come on over to the table." Dad's favorite table looked different. When I got close to it, I was amazed. Neveah had it resurfaced and lacquered, with the words, Honorary Table of Mason Andrew Barringer, A great man, and wonderful father, was branded into it. "I've been waiting for you to come to the bar so we could hang this up together."

She showed me the picture she had in her hand. It was the picture of Dad with Andrew and I photoshopped into it.

We embraced each other and hung the picture up by Dad's table. I sat down with my sister. "So why my sister-in-law couldn't come," I explained why Shada hadn't joined me. She was impressed by Shada's resilience. "I'm looking forward to meeting her, and my niece."

"Why didn't you come to the repast after Dad's funeral? I looked for you after the service."

"Mason, it didn't feel right. I didn't know anyone there but you. No one knew who I was, or that he was my dad."

"I understand. I wanted you there so bad, I didn't stop to think how it would make you feel, I'm sorry."

"No, no reason to be sorry. I wanted to be there, I guess, I felt out of place."

"Well, we'll have to figure out how to correct that."

"I'm sure we will, but until then you're always welcome here." We raised our glasses in cheers. The rest of our time was spent laughing, talking, and sharing stories. We made plans for the future. We promised to keep in touch with each other, better than we have since Dad's funeral. We enjoyed each other's company like we grew up together. At times it got emotional, but we knew our thoughts about our father were shared in love.

Before I knew it, time had rushed, and goodbye was in order. With one last embrace, I departed the bar. I hopped in a rideshare and headed home. With a smile, I relished the time spent with my sister. I wasn't sure what I was walking into when I arrived home. I almost expected to open the door and see tables thrown around and the house torn apart.

That may have been a bit of an exaggeration, but I prepared myself for anything. What I saw was a relief. Mom and Shada were sitting together on the couch. Mom was holding baby Moreen. It seems they were enjoying a bottle of wine. "Hi, mom."

"Hey, baby." The little slur in her voice assured me she was feeling alright. How was your trip? Oh, it was lovely. I had a good time with your aunt. She sends her love."

"Alright, is everything good here?"

"Yes, everything is good. I noticed Mom had reached over and taken hold of Shada's hand. Shada looked at me and gave me a nonverbal confirmation. My heart raced with happiness. "Mom, you're holding the baby and drinking wine?"

"Boy, please. I used to have a couple of glasses of wine while carrying you." A shocked realization overtook my happiness. The two half-drunk ladies must have thought that was funny as they laughed.

"Come get this baby and put her to bed while my daughter and I finish our girl time." I did as I was instructed and left them to their business. It was good to hear them enjoying each other's company again. A few hours later, I could hear Shada helping my mother to her room.

It was like hearing two little schoolgirls giggling and snickering amongst themselves. Once Shada got Mom safely into bed, she staggered down the stairs. Luckily, the walls were sturdy enough to withstand the constant banging they endured as she made her way to our room.

She entered our bedroom like a lioness, searching for a late-night snack. Her drunken growls and purrs were stimulating. Her inebriated call of, "Mason, where are you?" was intriguing. She made no quarrel about her intentions. She was unwavering in her objective. I became her willing quarry, eager to be devoured in the ecstasy of her desire. Morning need not rush to arrive. The night belonged to us.

"Good morning, my love."

"Good morning, how are you feeling?"

"Wonderful."

"I see you broke out some new stuff last night. Where did you learn them from?" The devious smile on her face made me rethink my enquiry. She looked at me like she had been eagerly awaiting this moment. "Her sultry answer of "your mama" removed the slight smile from my face. "That's not funny, Shada." Her hysterical laughter accompanied her into the bathroom. I ventured downstairs to grab some coffee before I left for work.

Mom was at the kitchen table feeding the baby. "Good morning, Mom." I couldn't even make eye contact with her.

"Good morning, Mason, how was your night? My reply was quick. "It was fine."

"Uhm, I heard." I didn't say a word, I buried my face into the empty cup of coffee. Shada appeared from our room. She still had that devious smirk on her face. I could hear them whispering, gossiping and giggling behind my back. I think even the baby girl was laughing at her dad's embarrassment. "Alright, I'll see you all later." I moved expeditiously towards the door. In unison, they both replied, "Bye, babe."

I rushed to the car. Out of my peripheral vision, I could see both of them standing in the window, I refused to make eye contact. I was down the street before my complexion returned to normal. I looked in my rear-view mirror, and a huge smile appeared when I realized that peace had returned to our home. Around noon I called home to check on the family.

"Hello?"

"Hey, love, what's going on?

"I just got your daughter to lay down for a nap, she has been extra fussy today."

"She missing her daddy, that's all."

"I was ready to bring her to her daddy so that he can deal with her."

"How's mom.?"

She went out to lunch with one of her friends from church."

"Seems like your idea worked to get things back in order."

"It didn't start well. At first, she didn't want to discuss it at all. You know how she is when she doesn't want to discuss something. Once she was willing to listen, she said she hadn't eaten and was hungry, so we stopped at this seafood place on 36th street."

"Wait, you took her to Shells on 36 Street."

"Yeah, how do you know that?"

"She got you, babe."

"What do you mean?"

"That was her and Dad's favorite spot. I took them there one year for their anniversary, and they fell in love with it."

"That makes sense now, it seemed like she knew the menu too well."

"Yeah, she got you."

"Well, wait until you see the credit card bill."

"Aw, shoot."

"When we arrived at the restaurant, her focus was entirely on the baby, I'm pretty sure she was trying to ignore me, but I wasn't about to let that happen. We ordered our drinks; I think that helped loosen her up. Once she took a few sips of wine, she became more attentive. After that, I gave her the rundown of my life and the events that led up to the dinner.

When I was done, she sat quietly for a few minutes. Eventually, she excused herself and went to the restroom. When she returned, she took a minute to gather herself and apologized."

"Wait! Mom apologized?"

"Yes.

"My mother apologized?"

"Yes, she apologized for how she treated me, what she said, and everything that happened to me. She did mention she wished you would have talked to her about it. I told her you wanted to, but you didn't think she would handle it well. She agreed it was probably best that you told your dad first.

I guess that's one of the things she and her sister had a heated discussion about. Mom was ready to leave because she didn't want to hear anymore, and your aunt told her she wasn't going anywhere until she faced some truths."

"Wow, that's hard to grasp, someone making my mom do something she didn't want to do. Did you tell her about the investigation?"

No, I left that part out. I don't want her involved in that. But you know your mom got some thug in her."

"Why did you say that?"

"After I told her what Karmen and her crew did to me, she sounded ready to ride, find them, and put in work. She started talking about cutting off certain body parts. I think she scared the waiter because he wouldn't come back to the table, he would stand at a distance and give me the thumbs up to see if we needed anything.

I want to send your aunt a gift. Last night may not have gone as well without her input. We talked about a lot of things. Mason, she is really struggling with losing your dad."

"I'm sure she is."

"Did you know she cries herself to sleep every night because she misses him so much?"

"No, I didn't know that."

"She is trying to be strong for you. She doesn't want you to see her unhappy. She said she didn't want to leave her house because she was waiting to die in their home, but God kept waking her up every morning. She said she would rather be with your Dad in death than alive without him. She feels all alone. We have started our family, and she sometimes feels like a burden on us. I assured her she wasn't and asked if there was anything we could do to make her feel different, she said no, unless I can bring her husband back.

They planned on selling the diner this year, so they could travel and spend their remaining time enjoying each other. When baby Moreen was born, that helped her some. She felt like she had a sense of purpose again. She wants to feel needed, but more than that, she wants to make up for not being there for you and Andrew.

She did ask me why we named the baby Moreen. I told her about Mama Moreen and all that she did for me. She was like, "That's my kind of girl." I think they would have gotten along well; they both have that same fire."

"Wow, I didn't know all that. I feel terrible about everything I said to her during that argument. I didn't realize she was dealing with so much."

"Yeah, she was hurt, but she said it helped open her eyes and look at things differently. Along with your aunt's tuff love, she could see the era of her ways. All she wants now is to reconcile and enjoy her grandbaby. She wants to be at peace with her life, and everyone in it."

"I can understand that. Shada, thank you for putting yourself out there, and being vulnerable with Mom, I know it's not easy having to relive those events repeatedly. It means a lot to me that you did that for our family."

"You're welcome, I'm glad it worked out the way it did. I got to see a side of Mom that I probably wouldn't have seen any other way. I enjoyed spending last night with her. She wants to do girls' night at least twice a month."

"Uh oh, well, if that's what it takes to make my girls happy, then so be it. Hey, I have to go, I'll see you this evening. Kiss my baby for me."

"Will do, I love you!"

"I love you too."

The fall nights have given way to the grip of the colder-than-normal winter months. The frost on the trees and roads seemed to be permanent fixtures. The temperature played tricks regularly, leaving us longing for the thaw of Spring. We enjoyed the many firsts that presented themselves as the Christmas season approached.

Our daughter's first Christmas was the buzz of the house. It was my mother's first Christmas as a grandmother and Shada and I's first Christmas as parents. It was sometimes difficult for Mom to deal with Dad not being present.

She constantly wiped tears from her eyes while helping put up the tree. Christmas was their favorite holiday and time of the year. Shada or I would comfort her with a hug, and if all else failed, a glass of egg nogg did the trick. We made sure we took plenty of pictures with her and baby Moreen.

Mom ensured that the baby girl had the cutest outfits on at all times so that she would be ready for any photo shoot. The first ornament hung on the tree was a porcelain Winnie the Pooh, sitting on a rocking horse that read, "Baby's first Christmas." Eighty per cent of the gifts under the tree were for baby Moreen.

She received gifts from all over, family and friends, near and far, my brothers at the base, and Mom's friends from the church. It seems like she got gifts from people we didn't even no. We knew at four months she didn't understand what this was all about, but her mother and I vowed to teach her the real meaning of the presents and the true reason for the season.

Shada brought Mama Moreen a purple heart plant, which was her tradition. Out of all the many gifts that were brought, received, and would be exchanged, the greatest gift was yet to come.

"Shada, what do you think Mason would like for Christmas? I want to get him something special."

"Mama Barringer, you know your child is the hardest man to shop for. Whenever I ask him what he would like, I get the same response, "I have everything I need, so I don't want anything.""

"Oh, lord. That sounds just like his daddy. I would get frustrated with Mason Sr. trying to get him a gift for his birthday or Christmas. After a while, I gave up and brought him what I thought he would like. He never complained about anything I brought for him. He would always wear it or use it. I brought him this ugly sweater one year to see if he would say anything. Of course, he didn't, his friends talked so bad about that sweater, I made him go and take it off."

"I know what you mean. Do you remember what happened when we took him out for his birthday? We told him he could get whatever he wanted, and what happened? we came back with stuff for the baby."

"I guess we're looking at it wrong. What they wanted and want is to care for and provide for us. For them, that is the only gift that matters."

"Mama Barringer, You're on point with that one. This man has clothes from about ten years ago. I asked him when the last time he brought himself some new clothes, he couldn't even remember. I ended up taking him to the store and buying him some new stuff, even then, he was more concerned about getting me something. Well, I did get these adorable shoes, and of course, I had to have the matching purse."

"What you two in her laughing about?"

"Oh, nothing having a little girl talk."

"Uh oh, where the wine at?"

"Hey now, that sounds like a good idea, Shada, shall we?

"Mama Barringer, we shall."

I watched the two prance away with their bottle of wine and wine glasses. All I could do was shake my head, "what have I gotten myself into." I had to admit I enjoyed seeing their relationship blossom, it was better than I ever hoped. I finished getting chairs and tables from the garage and basement.

Christmas dinner was at our house this year, and by the replies we received, there were going to be many people attending. I figured with all the family and friends present, it would soften the blow of Dad not being with us.

"Mama Moreen, I'm sorry, Mama Barringer."

"It's ok child, I know what it's like to miss someone so much, you have to say their name now and then."

"Yeah, I think about her often. For so long, she was the only family I knew. That's why I'm so excited about having my own family. It's a feeling I will always treasure.

It tears me apart knowing I have a family that doesn't want anything to do with me. I wouldn't want anyone to have to go through that."

I looked at Mama Barringer. She had a look on her face like she was deep in thought. "Mama Barringer, are you alright?"

CHAPTER 11.

Reconcile

•●•

SAFETY FROM THE PAST

FREDRICK A. STEWART

"Yes, baby, I am. Tomorrow, could you take me somewhere? I think I know the perfect gift for Mason." I watched Mama Barringer walk away like she won the lottery. I started racking my brain, thinking about what she could get my husband that I hadn't already thought of. Maybe it was something from his childhood that he wanted but never got. I wanted her to tell me so badly.

I watched her from the other room. The smug look on her face was irritating. She seemed so proud of herself. The suspense was killing me. I can't believe she will make me wait until tomorrow to find out.

"Shada!"

"Hu."

"What's wrong with you?"

"Nothing I was um… thinking about… what I would eat tomorrow."

"Alright, look, slow down on the wine, seems like you've had enough."

"I curled my lip and frowned at my husband as he walked off, shaking his head. I hope tomorrow comes quickly.

Dawn's early light arrived as the sun appeared over the horizon. It pressed hard to get above the low-laying clouds that stubbornly refused to depart. The day was in motion. Mason prepared for his workday. Mama Barringer and Baby Moreen were already up eating breakfast. They both are early risers.

The Barringer household was alive and well. I made Mason's lunch and set it by his keys so he wouldn't forget it. Mason came from our bedroom, gathered his things, and kissed everyone goodbye.

As soon as he left the house, I breathed a sigh of relief. "Ok, Mama Barringer, where are we going? I couldn't sleep a wink last night thinking about it."

"Dang! You must want to know bad."

"Yes, I do, please tell me I'm about to burst."

"Wow, you are thirsty. She gets a kick out of using the young kid's language, as she likes to call it. "Ok, ok. I'll tell you when we're on our way."

"Mama Barringer, that's not fair."

"If you'll excuse me, I have to get grandmas baby ready for the day." I think Baby Moreen was siding with her grandma, she flashed her toothless smile as they walked upstairs.

I dropped my head in disbelief. How could she do this to me? I slowly stumped into my room like a spoiled brat. Once everyone was ready to go, we headed to the garage. I tried to act like I no longer cared about where we would get my husband's gift. "Baby Moreen, you see how your mama is acting."

I gave my mother-in-law the side eye while waiting for the garage door to open. "Ooh, child, that man got you spoiled something terrible."

"I need the address to where we're going."

"Alright, Alright, I'll tell you." Mama Barringer gave me the address and name of our location. "Why are we going there?"

"You'll see when we get there."

When we pulled up, I realized why we were there. "Are you serious? he is going to love this." I almost burst into tears. Mama Barringer nodded her head, "I think it's time." We unloaded baby girl and entered the building; I couldn't believe this was happening. An hour or so later, we emerged from the facility, we were both on cloud nine.

We headed home to start prepping for Christmas dinner. We put on some Christmas music, lit the fireplace, and began chopping, cutting, and dicing with a few sips of egg nogg in between. By the time Mason arrived home, we were in full swing. He said he could hear us from outside. We were definitely in the Christmas spirit. He changed out of his uniform and began helping prepare Christmas dinner.

The atmosphere was a feeling of delight and nostalgia. Mason and Mama Barringer shared a remembrance as they took a moment to gaze at Mason Sr. and Andrew's ornaments. Both of them were custom-made with their pictures on them. I couldn't help but feel emotional as I stared at Mama Moreens.

Even with the memories of loved ones, we lost looming, I knew this would be the best holiday ever. As Christmas Eve arrived, the ambiance in the Barringer household reached a new plateau. The atmosphere was saturated with peace and harmony. Gifts, gatherings, or food would not overshadow the sacrifice our savior made for us. We acknowledged him for his love and obedience. Baby Moreen participated as well.

We received the news during her last checkup that the hole in her heart was no longer visible. We wondered whether her angel would deliver the information to her himself. All the gifts were wrapped and ready to be presented to each other and to our guests. The majority of the food was cooked, baked, and prepared.

After exchanging gifts, Mason was going to deep fry a turkey in the morning. The anticipation for Christmas day was hard to contain. Mama Barringer and I whispered about Mason's gift to each other whenever he left the room. We were like two little schoolgirls with a secret eating us inside. Tonight, we will rest our weary bodies in anticipation of the arrival of a new day.

Tomorrow our home will be filled with family, friends, and loved ones, courtesy of our lord and savior, the newborn king. Our human alarm sounded off at seven a.m. The baby monitors from her nursery were strategically placed throughout the house. All hear her calls to attention. Mama Barringer was the first to attend to her needs.

By eight o'clock, we all gathered in the living room. The tradition of praying and giving thanks before any gifts were exchanged or opened was profound. Afterward, we got to it. We must have taken a hundred pictures with baby Moreen and her gifts. The family pictures were the highlight. Mama Barringer changed Moreen's outfits at least three times, our daughter's pleasant personality warms my heart.

Our guests were expected to arrive at one. We planned to begin dinner between two thirty and three, so anyone running late would still make it on time. After all the immediate family gifts were opened, Mason started preparing the turkey. At her grandmother's request, I changed baby Moreen and put on her fourth change of clothes, a beautiful Christmas dress.

The guests started arriving right around one. The laughs and hugs, and pleasantries filled our home quickly. The closer it became to three, the more Mama Barringer and I watched the clock. Everyone that was invited was present by two thirty. We began seating everyone when the doorbell rang. Mason started heading towards the door. Mama Barringer and I both yelled, "I'll get it."

Mason stopped in his tracks as we zoomed by him. We opened the door and immediately started smiling. Mason's present has arrived. Mama Barringer took one side, and I took the other. "Mason, can you come here?" His eyes got as big as saucers when he came around the corner. "Neveah!" He couldn't believe his sister was standing on the threshold of our home.

Mama Barringer let go of Neveah's hand and walked over to Mason. She intertwined her, around his. "Merry Christmas, son." Mason's eyes began to fill with salty tears of joy. "Mama, you invited her?"

"Yes. I figured you would want all your family here for Christmas. I'm sorry for keeping you two apart all these years. I hope you can forgive me."

"Mama, I forgive you, and I love you." The two of them shared an embrace that was long overdue. Mama Barringer motioned for Neveah and me to come and join them. We shed tears like babies. We hugged each other tightly, knowing we didn't have to be apart anymore. Mama Barringer took Neveah's hand. "Come with me, let me introduce you to your family."

I looked into my husband's eyes and began wiping the tears off his face. "You knew about this?"

"Yeah, but it was all your mother's doing."

"I can't believe it; this is the best Christmas present I ever received."

"We were hoping you would say that." My husband and I entered the dining room with the rest of our family. We enjoyed a delicious meal, the company of our loved ones, and the blessing of our Creator. The rest of the evening was wonderful. More gifts were exchanged, and we made Neveah a scrapbook with pictures of dad, Andrew, and Mason. Most of them were taken at Safety.

For a brief moment, I thought about my biological family and what they were doing on this Christmas day. I wondered if they were having a big dinner with family and friends. I hoped they were enjoying themselves.

"Mason."

"What's up, sis?"

"I didn't bring any presents, but I did bring some spirits and that scotch Dad liked."

"That's what's up. Where is it?"

"It's out in the car, I'll go get it."

"Naw, I got you. Let me get the keys. I'll go get it." Mason returned a few minutes later with a box full of cheer. "Sis, you weren't playing, you brought the good stuff."

"I didn't know what to bring, so I grabbed some bottles."

"Yes, here it is. Dad's favorite. How about we set this aside for later?"

"So, how does it feel."

"Unbelievable! I never thought this would happen."

"Did it feel awkward?"

"Yeah, a little bit, but your mom did a great job explaining it to everyone. She doesn't seem as bad as you made her sound."

"That's because you're getting the new and improved version." The evening carried on into the night. The cheers and laughter continued nonstop. Baby Moreen hung in there as long as she could, by nine o'clock, she was worn out and ready for bed. Around nine thirty, everyone started making their to-go plates. Hugs and kisses were handed out as family and friends said their goodbyes.

A decision was made about who would host the next Barringer Christmas dinner. After everyone left, the cleanup began. We sent Mama Barringer to bed, she had given all she had, and was visibly tired, and a little tipsy. Neveah volunteered to stay and help with clean up. We worked in the kitchen, putting food away and washing dishes.

The biggest piece was making room in the fridge for all the leftovers. Mason took care of the living room and dining room. When we all finished, we sat outside on the enclosed porch to have a nip of Scotch. The night was calm for a winter evening. The heat of both fire pits and some warm blankets combated the coldness in the air.

Mason and Neveah enjoyed a toast of their dad's favorite Scotch. I gave it a try, but it was too much for me. I was tagged as the little puppy who needed to stay on the porch, which I was ok with, I was fine with my wine.

"Ok, Neveah, so what were you thinking when Mom and Shada showed up at the bar."

"At first, I thought they were lost. I've never had anyone come into the bar with a baby. When your mom asked if she could speak to the owner, I got a little worried. I told her I was the owner and asked if I could help her. She started to speak, then she saw the picture we hung up at Dad's table. She walked over to it and stared at it for a while.

She sat at his table and slowly ran her hand over his name. I approached the table, "is there something I can help you with?" She asked me to have a seat and explained who she was. She started by apologizing for not allowing Dad to be in my life.

I could tell her apology was sincere. She said she had few regrets, but that was one of her biggest. She begged me to come here today as your surprise Christmas present. I didn't know what to say at first. In my mind, I was thinking, 'there's no way I'm going over there.' Then Shada approached and placed my niece on my lap, "this is your niece, Moreen."

That beautiful Barringer smile captivated my heart instantly. When I looked at Shada, I knew right away who she was. She's as beautiful as you described her. We all sat there for a while, getting acquainted. The bar started getting busy, so I had to return to work. Before they left, your mom asked me to promise I would come, "I promise." She lit up like a light.

After they left, I started thinking about everything your mom said and our discussions. Then something dawned on me. Every year on my birthday, I receive a deposit for a hundred, sometimes two, sometimes three hundred dollars. My mom started an account for me when I was a baby that the money went into. I have been receiving these funds all my life.

Before my mom passed, she told me about the account. My mother has been gone for some time, and I still receive a deposit in that account every year on my birthday."

"I told you dad sent your mom money to help with you."

"No, that money went into a different account on the first and fifteenth of the month and stopped when I turned twenty-one. My birthday is after Dad's. The last deposit I received was after he passed, and it was a nice amount."

"You think Mom has been sending you money all this time?"

"That's the only thing that makes sense. I thank she was giving me something from both of them on my birthday."

"So, Mom has known when your birthday is all this time."

"I believe so."

"Wow, that's amazing, she is something else."

Mason and Neveah continued their discussions long after I went to bed. "Bro, I guess I better be getting home, it's after midnight. Sis, you don't have to go anywhere. Shada already fixed up the guest room, no drunk driving on my watch. You can stay the night unless you want me to wake Mom up and tell her you are trying to drive intoxicated.

"Oh, you one of those tattle tale little brothers, I see." What are you talking about, little brother."

"Um, I'm the oldest!"

"I don't know about all that, I'm big brother!" as he beat on his chest.

"Alright, big brother, please show me to my room. I need to lay it down, this room spinning like a merry-go-round. The night ended because it had to, definitely not because they wanted it to. It would not be the last night that they enjoyed their sibling comradery. The year ended with celebrations of forgiveness, reconciliation, and empathy. We had all become someone new.

Winter retreated, and the new beginning of Spring was eager to get underway. Flowers bloomed in an array of colors and designs. Their scent filled the air as far as the senses could travel. The sun's warmth was as refreshing as a drink from a spring creek frozen throughout the winter. Butterflies and bees fluttered and buzzed around, pollinating and replenishing what lay dormant through the winter months.

The novel of the new season burst at the seams. Everything felt fresh and renewed. But life would not be satisfied with such pleasantries. Its menacing persona has joined forces with past transgressions. Their ominous duo is a reminder that everything is not always what it seems.

CHAPTER 12.

I Don't Know You

•●•

SAFETY FROM THE PAST

FREDRICK A. STEWART

"**M**ason somebody is at the door, can you get it? I'm feeding the baby."

"Alright." I checked the camera. A lady was standing at the entranceway, she looked confused but vaguely familiar. When I opened the door, it startled her, as she turned around to leave. "Hello, may I help you?" The lady stopped in her tracks. When she turned back around, she seemed nervous. Her words stammered over her response.

"Um, hello. I'm looking for someone. My name is, she closed her eyes as to regroup. "Um, does Shada Shields live here?" She didn't look like a detective or was associated with law enforcement, but her question alerted me.

"Well, her name isn't Sheilds anymore, but I'm her husband, Mason Barringer, and you are…

"She's married?"

The slight smile on the lady's face was confusing. "Yes, she is. I'm sorry, who are you?" "My name is…, um, I'm…, Oh lord, please help me. I shouldn't have come here, I'm sorry for bothering you." She turned around to leave.

"Wait, wait, are you ok?" I was concerned she was about to pass out. Her breathing was shallow, and she seemed disoriented.

"No, not really."

"Can I get you something to drink, a glass of water, maybe?"

"Yes, that would be nice."

"Please come in and have a seat, I'll get you some water."

"Thank you!" I returned from the kitchen with the water and handed the glass to her; she was shaking so badly that she used both hands to drink it. After she drank the water, she seemed to calm down a little.

"Are you ok now?"

"Yes, thank you."

"I'm sorry to stare, but you look familiar. Have we met before?"

"No, I don't think so."

"Well, how do you know, Shada?"

"My name is… Patricia, Patricia Shields." My eyes widened like I was trying to get more light. "You mean Patricia Shields, as in, Patricia Shields, Shada's mother!"

"Yes." Before I could gather my bearings, Shada inquired from the top of the stairs, "Mason, who was at the door?" I walked out of the dining room and looked up at my beautiful wife standing at the top of the stairs holding our daughter.

"Honey, can you come down here, please."

"What's wrong? You look flustered?" Shada cautiously walked down the winding stairs. Patricia came out of the dining room into view. The closer Shada went to the bottom of the stairs, the more puzzled she looked. "Is everything alright?" Neither of us uttered a word. "Wait, I remember you." I looked at Shada with surprise, "You know who this is?"

"I don't know her personally, but I met her at the grocery store a while back. She was in the checkout line with several people ahead of me. She didn't have enough for the stuff she was trying to purchase, and the people behind her were getting impatient and started yelling at her. She had the cashier take some of the food off her purchase.

But she wouldn't take off the toy she had. I paid for her items, the food, and the toy. After I paid for our stuff, I walked outside where she was standing and asked why she didn't put the toy back." She said it was a gift for my grandchild." Shada seemed confused, especially when she noticed the same toy in Patricia's hand. I looked at my wife, "Shada, look at her."

"I am looking at her."

"What is your baby's name?" Shada reluctantly answered, "Moreen, why?"

"Can I hold her?"

"What! Mason, what is going on here?"

"Shada, this is your mother."

As soon as my words were spoken, the blinders were removed from Shada's eyes. All the years of living or having objective reality about her mother were forced back into actuality. Patricia extended the toy to Shada, "Can she have this?" Shada had a look of complete disbelief. The anger she fought so hard to bury forced itself from the grave into existence, "I don't know you! Get out of my house!"

Shada's scream startled and scared Baby Moreen so badly, she burst into crying. Shada ran up the stairs with her. I could tell Patricia was trying to hold back her tears as she apologized for coming by. She walked towards the door, before she turned the doorknob, she turned and looked at me.

"You have a beautiful family. Thank you for taking care of my daughter and granddaughter."

"It is my pleasure. Is there anything I can do for you?"

"Yes, there is." Patricia reached inside her purse and pulled out two letters. One letter said, "read first." The second had the number two. "Can you please give these to her?"

"Of course. Can I give you a ride somewhere?"

"No, I've caused enough trouble. It won't be any trouble. Patricia lifted her head; she had the saddest look I've ever seen. "You are a good man; Shada is lucky to have you."

"Thank you." I opened the door for her. Before leaving the house, I turned and stared at the top of the staircase, bewildered at the events. I returned home a couple of hours later. Shada was sitting in the living room. "Where have you been? "I took your moth…" Shada shot me an evil look. I revamped my statement. "I gave Patricia a ride home."

"Where does she live? Never mind, I don't care."

"Shada, I think you …"

"Mason! I don't want to talk about her."

Not wanting to be on the wrong side of her anger, "Ok. I'm headed to bed. Are you coming?"

"No, not right now."

"Ok." I kissed my wife on the forehead and started towards our bedroom. I remembered the two letters Patricia asked me to give her. I took them out of my pocket and extended them towards her. "What is this?"

"Letters Patricia asked me to give to you."

"I don't want them."

"Shada, it's not going to hurt you to read them. They may provide some insight on things." "I said I don't want them!"

"Fine, I'll leave them here on the table if you change your mind."

"Whatever," was Shada's indignant response. "Goodnight." I left my wife alone with her thoughts and emotions. I headed upstairs to our daughter's nursery to kiss my princess goodnight. Looking at her sleeping peacefully always brings me joy.

The more I admired this beautiful gift we have been blessed with, the more I could see the resemblance between her mother and grandmother. I bowed my head and closed my eyes. I prayed to our Father in Heaven to watch over our daughter, protect her, and soften my wife's hardened heart toward her mother. *"In your son's name, I pray, Amen."*

After Mason disappeared upstairs, I jumped to my feet. I paced back and forth with no destination. My fists clenched in a death grip of pain and anger. Unjustly upset at Mason for showing kindness to the woman who all but destroyed my life, my thoughts poured out like boiling lava.

"Who in the hell does she think she is? Showing up here after all these years like everything is supposed to be ok. She thinks she can abandon me and return to my life like nothing happened! Can you hold my baby? Hell no! You can't hold my baby!"

I haven't been this enraged since I met Mason. All sorts of scenarios and misguided thoughts ran through my mind—anger, followed by waves of confusion, disbelief, and then unadulterated rage. My emotions played a ruthless game of cat and mouse with my heart and mind.

"There is nothing she could say that could justify her actions of leaving me. Because of her, my whole life has been in shambles."

The smoldering heat from my anger ignited an emotional wildfire that sought to consume me. The blistering winds of desertion and neglect fan it. The inferno-like intensity attempts to incinerate everything I've overcome and accomplished in the last few years. For my safety, I must seek refuge.

I stood motionless, desperately wanting to scream at the top of my lungs. Too mad to cry, I trembled with anger, infuriated. I was too distraught for rational thoughts. I could hear Crazy calling, "*come to me, my sweet.*"

I did the only thing I knew to do. I closed my eyes and called out to my lord. "Father, please help me. I can't do this without you." My prayer to my father was intense and personal. My plea was to forgive my anger and answer what I didn't understand.

I sought strength and insight while I was in his presence. It seemed like hours before I opened my eyes. I realized I had knelt in the middle of the living room floor. The burning anger had subsided. The confusion was still present, but there was a coolness in the air. I stood to my feet and sat on the couch.

There were no thoughts; my mind was blank. Nothing looked familiar. I sat in silence. Not even the ticking of the clock made a sound. His presence was still upon me. After a few minutes, things seemed to come back to recognition. I arose from the couch when I noticed the two letters Mason had left on the coffee table.

I picked up the letters staring at the writing on the envelopes, the handwriting on the first letter looked familiar. I reluctantly opened the letter marked open first.

"Hello, my love. I hope this letter finds you well and in good health. With a heavy heart I must tell you my time on this earth is coming to an end soon. A part of me wants to push you away so you don't have to witness my decline. But I know you wouldn't leave me anyway, so I pray death will find me soon.

There is nothing more the doctors can do for me but try and make me comfortable until it's all said and done. There are some things I need you to know. I planned on telling you these things when I felt the time was right, but I have run out of time. So, I pray you will not be angry with me. The first thing I want you to know is that I loved you from the first moment I saw you.

When I saw you walking down the street, I could see you were a lost soul wondering with no direction. You were so beautiful; I could tell the world had used that against you. You were walking in the rain, oblivious to the world around you. You carried your pain like a mother transporting her child.

I prayed God would give me a second chance at being a mother. I knew if I received that opportunity, I would love that child with all my heart, he sent me you. To explain what is needed, I have to start from the beginning. About a week after August twenty-first, I was picking up some food for dinner at the grocery store.

A lady approached me. She was very friendly, but it was her smile that caught my attention the most, it was warm and inviting, almost like I knew her. We went back and forth about the ridiculously high prices of everything in the store, you know I could go on forever about that. We finished our shopping together and checked out.

As we walked out, she asked about the beautiful young lady who was usually with me. Automatically, I assumed she was the police or someone with ill intent, so I didn't give her any information. "Why are you asking about her?" I don't know if she recognized I was getting upset or that I had slipped my hand into my purse, but she paused.

"I'm sorry, I'm not trying to start any trouble, I'm looking for someone I lost a long time ago."

"Does this person have a name?"

"Yes, her name is Shada Shields." As soon as she said your name, I knew my worst fear had become a reality. The longer I stared at her, the more you appeared. Her physical features were like I was staring at an older version of you—everything from the long hair, the full lips, and light complexion.

Even then, I tried to deny what my eyes revealed. I couldn't overlook how she was standing; it was the same way you stand, with one leg straight and the other slightly turned to the side. She bites her bottom lip when she gets nervous, how many times have I fussed at you about that?

The slight trimer in her voice reminded me of the first day you and I met. All these things and more made it obvious that you were birthed from this woman's womb. In my soul, I knew the lady that stood before me was your biological mother. We stood in awkward silence for a moment.

"Well, I need to catch this next bus; it was nice talking to you." She held her head down like she had been scolded. In my mind, I wanted her to get on that bus and never return, but my heart overruled my selfishness.

"Wait, can I give you a ride somewhere?"

"No, that's ok."

"Please! We need to talk."

Patricia turned and stared at the bus that had pulled up. She looked back at me. The sadness in her eyes cut deep into my soul. "Ok." We loaded up the groceries and started our journey. There was so much I wanted to know. More than anything, I wanted to know how she could abandon such a beautiful child.

The more I looked into her eyes and listened to the words she spoke, the easier it was to withhold my judgement. Her voice shook as she revealed her past. She turned her face towards the window when she became emotional.

Her words spoke of regret, naiveness, and shame. I could tell she was still hurting. She didn't play the victim; she took accountability for the things she allowed to happen. Your mother didn't have to share any of her life with me, she didn't owe me anything, but I appreciate her doing so. I'm sure you have many questions for her, and you deserve to know the answers too.

That's why I hope and pray you will give her the time to explain. Everything wasn't what it seemed, and you deserve to know the truth. I didn't have her come by the house because you were dealing with losing your babies and were still hurting mentally and emotionally. I wanted you to be in the right headspace to deal with the things she has to tell you, so I gave her our address and told her to write you a letter so she could reach out to you when the time was right.

I hope you understand why I kept this from you until now. A part of me was afraid of losing you. However, I wouldn't want anyone coming between me and my child if there was a chance to fix what was broken. I hope and pray you understand.

Regardless of what happens between you and Patricia, I'll always love you until I take my last breath. With all my love, your Mamma Moreen.

When I finished the first letter, I sat back on the couch, perplexed about what I read. Although I was in a room full of furniture, lamps, mirrors, and décor, it felt like I was sitting in an empty space.

I found myself drowning in a tidal wave of emotions. If there were one thing I knew for sure, it would be Mamma Moreen would have never done anything to hurt me intentionally. I concluded she withheld this information because she genuinely felt it was in my best interest. I looked at the second letter. I was reluctant to read it at first.

But I knew the answers I sought were encased within that envelope. I held the letter upon my chest, waiting for it to speak to my heart. I opened the letter and began.

"Shada, I feel silly having to reintroduce myself, but this is your mother, Patricia. I know you have a million questions, and I'll do my best to answer them. First, I need you to know, I did not abandon you.

I made a tough decision to prioritize your safety, and the only way I knew to do that was to have you removed from the toxic environment I called my life. I can understand you being angry and upset with me. I hope and pray that you will understand why I did what I did after you read this letter. Over the years, I have learned to take accountability for my actions and mistakes.

I was young and foolish. I allowed people I thought loved me to exploit my naivety. What I need to share with you is difficult for me. I have to relieve a past that almost killed me. Over the years, I have learned that it's imperative to close and lock the doors to your past to move forward. I was nineteen when I gave birth to you.

I graduated high school the year before, and like many young girls my age, I thought I had everything figured out. I couldn't wait to leave my parent's house and live on my terms. My parents, your grandparents, were very strict. They did not allow me to date or have boyfriends. I couldn't go to parties with people they didn't know.

They were very particular about the girls I hung around. They had to meet them and their parents; if they didn't get a good vibe from them, I wasn't allowed to be around them. I knew they were doing their best to protect me, but I wanted to be free and make my own decisions and choices.

After having multiple heated arguments about being treated like a child, I moved in with my older sister, your Aunt Zora. She was the free spirit as well as the black sheep of the family. I'm sure she was why my parents were so protective and stern with me.

She put our parents through hell. She was involved in everything from underage drinking and smoking weed at school to sneaking out of the house at night. In her senior year of high school, she and some of her friends skipped school, stole a car, and went joyriding. They all had been drinking and smoking weed.

The driver must have been drunk because he decided to go down a one-way street and run every stop sign and red light he encountered. At a four-way intersection, he pulled out before it was his turn to go. He clipped the rear of a car that was in the intersection. The car he hit spun out and slammed into another car.

No one was seriously hurt, but there was a lot of damage. Shortly after, the police tried to pull them over, but he wouldn't stop. They went on a high-speed chase through the city. They flew past the high school we attended. You could hear the sirens and the flashing lights from the classroom windows.

I remember feeling like I knew my sister was in that car. Eventually, the police ended the chase by hitting their back bumper, causing them to spin out and jump a curb. Luckily, no one was hurt. My sister and the other two kids in the car were placed in juvenile detention for six months. The driver, who was twenty, did some jail time.

I remember looking at my sister during her arraignment and feeling somewhat envious, she was living her life on her terms and didn't care who liked it or not. Your father's name was Carlos, Zora introduced us. Carlos was twenty-three when we started seeing each other. I remember thinking he was the finest human I ever saw walking on this earth.

He was about five foot ten. His jet-black hair had deep natural waves. He got a kick out of asking me if I was getting seasick when I brushed his hair. His skin was the color of honey and light brown sugar. There was not one pimple or blemish on him. He was slender but very well-toned. I met his parents once.

His mother was Indian, and his dad was black. So, when I say he was fine, I mean it. He was smooth and silky, like the cream in my coffee. His physical features were one thing, but his voice aroused me. When he spoke to me most of the time, I didn't know what he was saying. His slow and suave tone captivated me.

It was something about how the base in his voice penetrated my body and bounced off the receptors in my mind. Even after he stopped speaking, his words traveled throughout my body until they found that spot! It didn't take long for me to fall under his spell. I was mesmerized by his looks, style, swag, and words.

I gave him everything I had. My mind, body, and soul belonged to him. In the beginning, he treated me like royalty. Anything I wanted; Carlos provided for me. Money, clothes, jewelry, the world was my oyster. I was living the life. About a year into our relationship, things started to change. He wasn't as attentive as he had been in the past.

He seemed to be going through mood changes every other day, and everything wrong was my fault. I was so enthralled with him, I believed anything he said. The first time he hit me, we were at a party one of his friends was throwing. Everything was alright at first until I noticed Carlos went into the house with the party's host. They had been gone for quite a while.

A couple of the guys that were outside approached me. Mostly they complimented me on how pretty I was, "If you were my girl, you wouldn't be sitting out here alone." That meant nothing to me because my heart, mind, and panties belonged to Carlos. After a while, I went to look for him. I checked all over the house before I heard some laughing in the basement.

The wooden steps to the basement were worn and tattered. The basement was cold, dingy, and dark. It wrapped around the center of the house and led to an area towards the back. That area was eerie and creepier than the front of the basement. The cement foundation was falling apart. There was visible mold on the walls, floors, and ceilings.

I entered the room, where I heard the laughter coming from. There was a strange odor in the air and the stale musky basement air. Carlos and four other people were sitting at a table. One guy had something wrapped around his arm. I called Carlos's name, he quickly turned in surprise. "Hey babe, what you doing down here?"

"I was looking for you."

I noticed the one with the band around his arm was trying to hide the stuff on the table. I couldn't tell what it was, but I saw a spoon and aluminum foil. Carlos kept trying to get me to go back upstairs. I told him I was ready to go. He rose from the table, walked over to me, grabbed my arm, and escorted me out of the room.

When we got around the corner, I could hear the other people in the room laughing. "Carlos, you're hurting my arm." The look he gave me was frightening.

"Didn't I tell you to go back upstairs? That's your problem, you don't listen."

"What are you doing down here?"

"None of your damn business. Now get upstairs!"

"But I..." Before I could get the rest of my words out, Carlos backhanded me in the face and knocked me to the floor.

"Now, see what you made me do!" He came towards where I had landed. I didn't know what to do, I thought he would hit me again. "Baby, I'm sorry, but when I tell you to do something, I need you to do it." I agreed as he picked me up from the floor like nothing happened. He began kissing me and telling me how much he loved me.

"Now, go upstairs. I'll be up there in a minute." I wiped the blood and tears off my face and did as he instructed. When I reached the first step, I could hear the people in the room laughing. After a while, Carlos and the other people came back outside. They all acted like nothing happened.

For the rest of the night, Carlos showered me with affection. He sat me on his lap and caressed me, whispering what he had planned for me when we got home.

Everybody at the party was laughing, drinking, and having a good time, except me. I was confused about what happened. By the time we left the party, Carlos was out of it, he could hardly walk. I helped him in and out of the car and into the house. I struggled to get him to the bedroom. I was getting his shoes and clothes off when he murmured, "that's why I love you, you always take care of me." I stared at the man who had earlier assaulted me.

The only thought that ran through my mind was, 'I didn't know love was supposed to hurt.' The next day I went to see Zora. I figured she would be sympathetic to what I had experienced. I would be wrong about that as well. I told her what happened and how Carlos had been acting lately. Her words were as cold and corroding as the basement walls.

"You need to stop tripping, that's how a man shows their love for you, if he doesn't go upside your head, that's when you need to worry." I was shocked at what she said, but somehow it seemed to make sense, he did say he loved me. I figured Zora knew what she was talking about since she was older and more experienced.

"Anyway, little sis, I have some exciting news."

"What is it"

"Well, you know I've been seeing someone for a few months."

"Yeah, and?"

"Well, my friend didn't show up last month."

"What friend?"

"Girl, you are so stupid, my period! You're going to be an aunt."

"Your pregnant?"

"Yes, I am."

"That's… that's awesome congratulations."

"Thanks, I'm so excited."

"Have you told Mom and Dad?"

"Why do you have to bring them up? You know I don't talk to them."

"You're not going to tell them?"

"I don't know. It's not like they would care anyway."

"You know that's not true. It's their first grandchild, they will be so excited."

"Um, I doubt it. If it was you, I could see them being excited, but not me."

That's not true."

"Girl, please, you know you're their favorite. Anyway, we're having a party this weekend you and Carlos should come through."

"Yeah, of course."

"Well, look, I have to go, I'll see you this weekend."

CHAPTER 13.

Introduced to Evil

•●•

SAFETY FROM THE PAST

FREDRICK A. STEWART

Ileft my sister's house feeling more confused than when I arrived. Everything she said was hard to digest. Even her goodbye hug felt cold and forced. Before Carlos left for the day, I told him about Zora being pregnant and her weekend party. He didn't seem concerned at all. I did my best to lighten the mood. I tried being affectionate and sexy. I wrapped my arms around him, "So when are we going to have a little one?"

Carlos looked at me with a frown on his face. He took my arms from around him and shoved me on the couch, "I guess when you get yourself together." I sat on the couch stunned. I didn't know what else to do to make him happy. Nothing I did seemed to work. I felt like I was about to lose him. I couldn't imagine life without him, he was my entire world.

I called Zora for some advice, but she didn't answer. I didn't have anyone to talk to. I contemplated calling my parents. But I decided against it. I had to show them I was an adult and could handle life without their help. I stayed up late, waiting for Carlos to come home. I couldn't sleep until I fixed what was wrong with our relationship. He staggered in at about one thirty a.m.

I tried to be as sweet as I could. "Hey, babe, can I get you anything?" He stopped and stared at me. "You can get out my face." He had become so mean and nasty towards me. "Babe, please, tell me what I did wrong so that I can fix it." He whirled around and grabbed me by my throat.

He smelled like the musty, molded basement mixed with a familiar scent. "You want to fix it! What's broken? Tell me what's broken?" My breathing had become restricted. "I don't know." That seemed to piss him off more. His yelling increased a few more decimals. "So, how will you fix something if you don't know what's wrong? I felt myself getting lightheaded. "Baby, I was trying to help you." I quickly realized those were the wrong words to say. He tightened the grip on my throat, pulled me towards him, and slammed me back into the wall. The slap that followed, sent me hurdling down the hall. The beating I took that night was one of the worst ones I had endured.

After pounding on me, he took the rest of his frustration out on me sexually. When I came to, the merciful morning had come. The sunrise emitted warm rays down the hallway where I had been left. The sympathetic plea of "*come to, my love*" forced me to open my eyes. Where Carlos finished with me was where he left me.

I struggled to get to my feet. I staggered to the bathroom to survey the damage. I didn't recognize me. I remember thinking, *"I fought with the devil and lost."* I took a shower to wash the stale blood off me, the water brought no relief. It intensified the pain of my wounds. Carlos came out of the bedroom as I walked out of the bathroom.

He cut his eyes at me and continued down the hall. "Fix me some breakfast." He didn't want to look upon the damage he had done. After he ate breakfast, he dressed and left for the day. I took a deep sigh; it was ok to breathe again. I cleaned the blood off the hallway floor and straightened up the house. I didn't want to give him another reason to hurt me.

When he returned home later that evening, he had gauze, rubbing alcohol, and flowers. He attended to my wounds. The vicious cycle of love and hate continued for what seemed like forever. Regardless of how bad the beatings and disrespect became; I couldn't leave him. As evil and abusive as he could be, I couldn't break free from him.

I believed he needed me. If I left him, it would destroy him, and I couldn't live with that. I loved his life more than my own. I would do anything to prove my love for him. During one of the few ceasefires, I was cleaning up our bedroom. I began changing the sheets when I noticed something under the mattress on his side of the bed.

It was a small, flat, leather travel-size shaving case. I pulled it out and sat on the edge of the mattress. Inside the case were a burnt spoon, a rubber band, some dark brown powder wrapped in aluminum foil, and a needle. I was naive to what I was looking at, but I would soon learn a life lesson that could only be repaid through a debt of pain and suffering.

Carlos wasn't in the destructive mode he visited frequently when he came home. He seemed concerned or worried about something. I figured this was the best time to inquire about the case. "Carlos, are you alright?"

"Yeah," He headed straight for the bedroom and closed the door. I heard him rustling around before he came rushing out. "Patricia, where is …" he stopped when he saw me holding what he was looking for. "Carlos, what is this?" He stared at the case like it was his first time seeing it. "It's something to help me relax.

I don't always use it, only when I need to clear my mind." It was apparent he didn't understand what I was asking him. "Carlos, what! Is it?" I think that's when it dawned on him, I didn't know what I was holding. He came and sat down with me. "You don't know what this is?"

"No, that's what I keep asking you. What is it?" The relief that appeared on his face was confusing. "It's something that helps me cope. I have a lot of stuff going on in the streets, and sometimes I need to escape. This gets me in a better mental state of mind. When I don't have it, I do crazy things, like hurt you. I don't like hurting you, I love you.

I keep thinking you'll leave me, and when that crosses my mind, I lose it. I would probably kill myself if you left me." His words ate away at me like a ferocious beast. I became one with the burden he was carrying. His affliction I made my own. "Baby, I'm not going anywhere. I would never leave you. I love you. There's nothing I wouldn't do to make you happy."

I would greatly regret the words I spoke that day. Carlos slowly removed the case from my hands. He opened it and laid everything out in a neat row. He started preparing the substance that was in the foil. When it was ready, he withdrew it into the needle. "Do you love me?" I didn't know it at the time, but the answer I gave him would almost cost me my life.

"Of course, what else must I do to prove it? I love you more than life itself." Carlos tied the band around my arm. "Take this trip with me." He pushed the needle into a vein in my arm and injected the substance, the feeling of euphoria rushed to my brain. My body immediately felt weightless and numb.

I felt like I was watching myself float in the air. I noticed Carlos injecting himself with the substance. He took me on a flight to the devil's door, I opened it and walked in. Believe it or not, the beatings decreased as long as we got high together. When we weren't, the nightmares returned. About three months after my introduction to evil, Carlos came home drunk.

I wasn't his first choice to get high with; others shared that role. He began yelling and cussing at me, I don't remember what for, usually, he didn't need a reason. Through the years, I learned it was best if I didn't respond when he was in that mode. The beatings weren't as severe. This night would be different. My silence was his trigger. He came into the room, "you don't hear me talking to you!"

"Yes, Carlos, I do."

"So, now you're ignoring me!" His eyes squinted till they were almost closed. That was the telling sign of what kind of beating I was in for. Usually, I would assume the position of covering my head and face. This time I covered my stomach. As he was about to strike, I screamed, "Carlos, please, don't! I'm pregnant."

The punch he was about to deliver froze in midair. He stared at me for a moment with a scowl on his face. Eventually, he backed out of the room and left. I found out I was three months pregnant the day before. I don't know how I made it through my pregnancy with you. The beatings I received persisted but differed from the pre-pregnancy ones.

They were more precise and laser-focused on my stomach. Now they included kicks as well as punches. I don't think he wanted me to give birth to you. I am ashamed to say I used the substance in the aluminum foil a few times while I was pregnant. I think it was to combat the pain of the abuse that I thought would stop because I was pregnant.

After you were born, my focus shifted, but it was too late, I became a minion to the substance. There were times when we would have parties that I wasn't strong enough to resist the pressure, urge, and temptation. I also found out; Zora was a heavy user of the substance. When she gave birth to her daughter three months earlier, she was forced to have a c-section due to the damage to her veins, the doctors felt it would be safer for her and the baby.

Sometimes, we would use so much of the substance I couldn't remember one day from the another, my life became one big blur. Things happened under my nose that I was oblivious to. As you got older, I usually asked the lady down the street to watch you until the next day or two, depending on the level of euphoria I reached.

If she weren't available, I would put you in your room with some food and let you watch tv. I did my best to make sure you were not around my downfall. I checked on you often or until I passed out. I never wanted you in that environment. As time progressed, I became more and more addicted to the substance.

I wasn't strong enough to quit using or get out of that abusive relationship. I had become a slave to the demon in the aluminum foil. Days, months, and years rolled by. I had become a functioning addict. The parties grew in size and frequency. We were either at Zora's or our house. One night we were over at Zora's. There were a lot of people there. I knew some of them, but the others I had never seen before. Zora had a bad habit of letting her daughter hang around the adults while we partied. The men that I didn't know gave me a bad vibe.

I found out later they were the ones Carlos and Zora purchased the substance from. This night there were more drugs and alcohol than usual. The men weren't getting high. They stood around in different areas of the house, watching us. After a while, Carlos and Zora disappeared with them. When they came back, the men left, but Carlos and Zora looked nervous and shook.

As the night progressed, we all were pretty messed up. I passed out on the couch. Some were sitting off by themselves, zoned out. The rest were playing spades or shooting craps. I awoke at about two-thirty; everyone, including Carlos and Zora, was gone. I struggled to get to my feet. I staggered around the house, looking for anyone.

Zora's bedroom was down the hall at the back of the house. My body didn't feel right. I almost felt paralyzed. The substance in the aluminum foil never made me feel like that before. My vision was so blurry, I couldn't make out what I was looking at. Every step felt like I had cement boots on. I bumped into walls and crashed into tables.

I somehow made it to Zora's room. I opened the door; I could see two figures in the bed. One was on top of the other. I squinted my eyes, opening and closing them, trying to find my focus. I could see briefly, and then it was blurry again. I recognized both figures. It was Carlos and Zora. The room and everything around it started spinning, I couldn't hold my balance anymore.

I stumbled backward and fell to the floor. When I came to, I was at home in my bed. I tried to sit up. My body ached from head to toe. I had the worst stomach and headache imaginable. I quickly dashed to the bathroom and threw up everything in my stomach. Carlos came to the bathroom door. "Are you alright?" I couldn't say anything.

Between the vomiting and heaves, I struggled to breathe. My heart was beating so fast that I could only sit at the base of the toilet bowl and hold on for dear life. When I finished emptying my system, Carlos came into the bathroom and helped me. He put me back in bed. "Are you hungry, I'll make you something to eat."

I was still gasping for air, struggling to breathe. When I could form a sentence, I asked him why he was in bed with Zora. He looked at me perplexed. "What are you talking about? Zora saw you on the floor and called me back to get you up. You must have hit your head on the floor, you were out when I arrived."

"I saw you two in the bed; she was on top of you." Carlos shook his head. "Babe, I don't know what you're talking about. You must have really been messed up last night. Maybe you were having a bad dream or something. Why don't you get some rest? I'll make you something to eat, you'll feel better once you get something on your stomach."

I didn't have the strength to say anymore. I closed my eyes and went to sleep. I awoke a day and a half later. I could hear Carlos in the living room. I made my way out the bed and down the hallway. He was there with you.

You were both playing and laughing. When you saw me, you jumped up and ran to me. "Mommy, you woke!" I hugged you as long as I could. "Daddy said you were sick and needed some rest. Are you ok now?

"Yes, baby, I'm fine now."

Carlos came over and hugged me. "Baby, you had me scared, I thought I was going to lose you. You said you would never leave me." I flashed a fake smile." I remember looking at you. You were so innocent, oblivious to the madness that was going on around you. We sat in the living room and continued playing the game you and Carlos were playing. We all made dinner together and ate as a family. Carlos stayed around the house for a good week or so.

About two weeks after I was sick, things started returning to how they were. Actually, it got worse. I put you down for a nap and sat outside on the porch. It was a beautiful day. Ida came by to check on you. She was the lady who would watch you when I couldn't. "Hello, Patricia, where is my baby?" Ida was the neighborhood grandmother.

She watched over the kids in the area. If they were hungry, she would feed them. She would open her door to them if they needed somewhere to stay. She would help anyone if they wanted help. "Hello, Ida. She is taking a nap."

"Ok, I haven't seen her in a while, thought I'd check on her. How are you doing? I heard you had gotten pretty sick."

"I'm fine, I'm doing a lot better." Ida was known for saying what was on her mind. "Baby, you have done let that man get you on that stuff." I couldn't say anything, I held my head low and stared at the ground. "I remember the first time I looked at you; you were so beautiful. I hoped and prayed you wouldn't let that man hurt you and get you hooked on that stuff. That's a bad monkey to get on your back, when he gets on there, it's hard to get him off."

"Thank you, but I'm fine." Ida took a step close to me and grabbed my arm. "Those tracks in your arm say different." I snatched my arm back, still unable to make eye contact. She sat down beside me. "Baby, you can beat this demon. Right now, it has a good hold on you, something terrible.

It's not going to let you go unless you fight. I mean, fight with everything you have left in you. You fight to get your life back, you fight to be set free, and fight for that baby girl, because if you don't, she just may be the next one sitting out here wondering how her life got so messed up. And when you can't fight anymore, fall to your knees, and you scream and yell out to God until his heavenly throne shakes from the shudder of your voice.

You can do it. You're not the only one who has been at the mercy of that cold-blooded killer." Ida pulled up her sleeve to reveal the track marks of the liquid demon. I quickly made eye contact with her. "Yes, me too. I was sixteen when I was introduced to it. For twenty years, it took complete control of me. I was its slave, anything it asked of me, I was willing to do. When I was at my lowest point, I tried to kill myself.

I purposely tried to overdose, but God's mercy said, "No." I lay on that floor, shaking and shivering as the demon circulated through my veins. The people that were with me left me there to die. I could hear God's voice telling me, 'It's not over, I have a plan for you." I spent years in and out of hospitals and rehab centers.

I've been clean for over twenty-five years, so I know it can be done. You have to decide when you've had enough and are ready to fight for your life again. "And another thing, that man isn't no good for you. As far as that goes, neither is that low-down sister of yours."

"Please, Ida, I don't mean no disrespect, but that's my sister you are talking about."

"I know who she is, and I know she isn't good, neither of them. But what I want to know is, when will you quit sitting around here with blinders on, acting like you can't see what's happening around you?"

"What's that supposed to mean?"

"It means they have been sleeping together, and that baby she got belong to him."

"Why would you say something like that?"

"Because I speak the truth, and the truth sets you free, and if you don't accept the truth, it's going to be the death of you.

I'm sorry you must hear it that way, but that's the only way to tell it. Ida stared at me with sincere empathy. "You bring my baby by to see me, I don't mind watching her." Her words tore at my heart but were confirmation that what I thought I saw was real. When Carlos came home that night, there was a guy with him.

I recognized him as one of the men that was at the party. Carlos said he needed to talk to me in the bedroom. When we got to the room, he pulled out the substance in the aluminum foil and started preparing it. The whole while, he told me how much he loved me and reminded me that I said I loved him and would do anything for him.

I told him that I didn't want to get high. He kept telling me how badly he needed me. He owed the guy in the front some money, and they would kill him and Zora if he didn't pay him.

"I need you to do this for me, I wouldn't ask you to do this if it wasn't life or death."

"What do you need me to do?"

"I need you to take care of the guy out there."

"What do you mean take care of him?

"You know, hang out with him, and if he wants to do something, make him feel good. If you do this, it'll get him off my back for a while."

"Carlos, have you lost your mind? You want me to sleep with another man."

Baby, I wouldn't ask you to do this if it wasn't important, I don't want to share you with anyone. Could you do it this one time? Look, I got you something to help you. You won't even know he's in here. Baby, I love you so much, you always take care of me."

I allowed Carlos to inject me with the liquid demon. Within seconds the room started spinning, everything became blurry, and I couldn't feel anything. I laid back on the bed and floated away. A minute after Carlos left the room, the door slowly opened. All I could see was a blurred image walking towards me. I closed my eyes, hoping I would never open them again.

I wish that was the first and last time, but it wasn't. He used my love for him as a crutch. My desire to please him was ten times more lethal than the substance. I injected the illusion of his love into my veins. It careened through my body, filling me with the fallacy that the abuse and mistreatment was his showcase of love and affection.

I couldn't say no to him. No matter what he asked of me, I was willing to prove my undying devotion. My desire for him to love me was my real addiction. He used my body in exchange. My mind was useless to him, and my love carried no value. I was traded like goods that had no good in them.

Whenever he had a debt, I became his payment. I had become disposable. He would use me to pay his debts and currency to purchase the demon in the aluminum foil. I grew to hate myself. I didn't care what happened to me. I often wondered, 'why was death taking so long to free me." Many times, I thought to expedite the process.

You were my only joy; I didn't have to be high to relish in your love. The day came when I decided I couldn't take any more abuse. I had lost all respect for myself and the desire to live. I went over to Zora's to tell her I was leaving Carlos. I don't know why I thought that was a good idea, but it was my only thought.

There was a guy there I had never seen before. It always pissed me off Zora allowed her child to be around these men and allowed that baby to sit on their laps. I asked Zorra if I could talk to her in her bedroom. She got upset at first. "Don't you see I have company?"

"Yes, Zora, but it's important." Eventually, she agreed. We headed to her room. I noticed her daughter wasn't coming with us. I looked at Zora. "Aren't you going to get your child? "she can stay with me." Zora agreed, "she is alright." I knew Zora was becoming increasingly addicted to the substance, but I never imagined it would reach that plateau.

We went into the bedroom. I forgot what I would tell her and went off about letting her daughter be in there with that man. She shrugged me off like she didn't want to hear what I had to say. Once I finished ranting, I told her about my plan to abandon Carlos and return home to Mom and Dad.

She didn't like me chastising her about her daughter and was displeased about my departure. After we exchanged a few unpleasant words toward each other, I stormed out of the room. When I returned to the front room, the man's hand was between that baby's legs. I lost it. I yelled and screamed at him, ran into the kitchen, and grabbed a knife. I returned to the living room, but he ran out the door.

Zora cursed at me like I was the one in the wrong. She told me to get out of her house and never come back. By the time I got home, Carlos was already there. I opened the front door, and Carlos grabbed me by my hair and snatched me into the house. He slung me all over that place, repeatedly yelling, "You want to leave me, you want to leave me."

When he was done putting his hands on me, he did what he usually did. When it was over, he walked to the bedroom door and stood in the doorway, "I'll kill us both before I let you leave me." I lay on the floor, too scared to cry but wanting to die. A memory entered my mind. When Zora and I were little, my parents kept us in church.

Every Sunday was devoted to service, and every Wednesday, bible study. Once, Zora asked our parents, "why do we always have to attend church? My father quoted Proverbs 22:6, *Train up a child in the way he should go, and when he is old, he will not depart from it.* Her smart-mouth response of, "I'm not he," got her slapped in the mouth.

As I lay there, a sickening realization came to mind, 'I've tried everything else it couldn't hurt to try God.' I crawled off the floor onto the bed, closed my eyes, and called out in silent prayer. When I opened my eyes, my mind was made up, that would be the last time he would do that to me. I laid in that bed for over an hour thinking, plotting, and scheming.

Then it came to me. I would have to do the unthinkable. I would have to make a sacrifice only a mother could make to protect her child. I knew it was a matter of time before you would become a victim of the abuse I endured, and I would not allow that to happen. The next day I took you with me to see Ms. Ida.

For my plan to work, I knew I would need some help. I waited for the right moment. It didn't take long for the opportunity to present itself. Saturday nights were when the big parties usually took place. Several people, including Zora and Carlos, were at the house.

Enough drugs and alcohol were flowing throughout the house for my plan to work brilliantly. I didn't take you to Ms. Ida that night, I needed you there. I ensured you were safe in your room before I implemented my plan. A couple of hours into the party, the police raided the house. They made everyone get on the floor.

A few people tried to run but were caught immediately. While we were lying on the floor, handcuffed, Carlos looked at me, "Don't tell them anything, keep your mouth shut." I whispered to him, "I have been quite way too long." When the police escorted us out of the house, it looked like everyone in the neighborhood was out there, including Ida.

When I saw her, I nodded my head to say thank you. I asked the female officer who escorted me out if you could stay with Ida, your babysitter. She agreed and gave you to her. That was the last time I saw you. I fought and struggled with my addiction for years. Once I was released from jail, I returned to my slave master.

My body fiend for the warm rush through my veins, I had become dependent on the substance. Sometimes, I would get deathly sick if I couldn't get it into my system. I never used the substance to get high, It was more of an escape or diversion from reality and relief from the pain. I have been clean for ten years.

The drugs have wreaked havoc on my mind, body, and soul. Last year I had a heart attack and was hospitalized for some time. I prayed God would allow me to look upon your beautiful face again before he called me home. It was by God's grace; I ran into Moreen at the grocery store. Before Moreen became terminal, she sent me the first letter to give to you.

When I felt ready, I went to the address Moreen gave me. She no longer lived there; you both were gone. It wasn't till later that I found out Moreen passed away. I extend to you my deepest condolences. That was the first obstacle I faced in finding you. I would not rest until I could look you in your eyes and tell you I'm sorry. I almost gave up hope of ever seeing you again.

I went back to the house where Moreen lived to ask the new owners if you had a forwarding address. They said they didn't have one. As I stepped off the porch, a lady was walking by. She asked, did I live there? I told her no; I was looking for someone who used to. The lady shook her head. "I miss my old friend,"

"You knew Moreen. She laughed a little. "We were thick as thieves." She told me about Moreen's battle with cancer and how she had almost given up until this beautiful girl came into her life and gave her a reason to live again. I asked the lady whether she knew the girl's name. She said the most beautiful name I have ever heard, Shada Shields.

I fought hard to keep my emotions intact. I explained to Ms. Stella who I was and how hard I had been looking for you. She invited me to her house around the corner. The number she had for you was no longer in service. But she knew someone that might be able to help me. Ms. Stella called me last week and told me that one of her granddaughters had a class with you at the college.

She said you used to live in some apartments across town but weren't sure if you still lived there. I checked the apartments. The manager confirmed that you used to live there but couldn't give me your new address. It wasn't until I saw you at the grocery store when you helped me pay for my groceries that I knew I had found you.

I couldn't tell you then, it wasn't the right time or place. I was taking a risk, not saying anything, but I had faith we would meet again. Shada, please understand I was not in a good place back then. I have fought tirelessly to overcome my addictions. I have been in and out of countless rehab facilities, counseling sessions, and mental health hospitals.

In the last five years, I can honestly say I have embraced my sobriety. I did what needed to be done to protect you from the life I was a part of. I didn't love myself back then, I'm just now getting to that point. It may be too little too late, but at least I know how it feels. The one thing I never stopped doing was loving you.

I hope my absence in your life has not caused you any hardship. That was never my plan. I only wanted your life to be filled with happiness, and I felt you had a better shot at that with someone else than you did with me. In conclusion, I should tell you what happened to your father.

When he was released from prison, he involved himself with some guys who didn't want anything but their money. When he couldn't produce it, well, you know, they collected. Your aunt Zora passed away from a drug overdose a few years ago. I don't know what happened to her daughter. She let men do things to that little girl that no child should ever endure.

I pray she is alright. Whether or not this letter ever finds you, I want you to know I loved you then, I love you now, and I'll love you to my dying day. You are my only child, proof that I walked this earth.

With love, From your mother, Patricia Shields.

After reading both letters, I wasn't sure what to think or how I was supposed to feel. What I thought I knew became a mangled mess of emotions and confusion. A part of me wanted to remain angry and hold onto the grudge that had been my crutch for the better part of my life. But was it abandonment? Or sacrifice.

How could I still be angry when her actions may have saved my life? Bewildered, I went upstairs to my daughter's nursery. I gazed at this gift from heaven, thinking, 'could I have made the same decision Patricia made if it meant protecting her from immediate danger and harm.'

While my mind wrestled with my thoughts, I noticed something in my daughter's crib. It was the stuffed animal Patricia brought for her. I picked the toy up. It was a funny-looking little plaything. It was blue with a big belly and big eyes. There were socks stuffed in its fur pockets. I wasn't sure what it was supposed to be, but somehow it made me smile.

"Hello." Mason was standing in the doorway. "I see you put the toy in her crib."

"Yes, I did."

"Do you mind if I ask why?"

"Because it was a gift."

How could this man who's been to war, faced death, and expected to do the unthinkable in combat have such a pure and loving heart? There are times when I don't feel like I deserve him.

I placed the gift back in the crib with our daughter, walked over to my husband, and wrapped my arms around him. I laid my head on his chest and listened for the sound that soothes and comforts me. His heartbeat is my favorite melody, I could listen to it for the rest of my life. We quietly closed the door to the nursery and went to our room.

We lay on our bed. I wasn't ready for my song to end, so I laid my head back on my husband's chest as he held me close.

"I read the letters."

"Really."

"You seem so surprised?"

"For one, I figured your stubbornness wouldn't allow you to read them."

"I'm not that stubborn!" his chuckle was annoying. "That's your story, I'll let you tell it."

"I guess you're starting to wear off on me." I could sense he was smiling, I'll let him have that one. "So, what were the letters about?"

"The first one was from Mamma Moreen. Patricia saw us together on the bus. For whatever reason, she didn't say anything to us, I guess she wasn't ready. Shortly after I lost the twins, Patricia ran into Mama Moreen at the grocery store. They did their shopping together. After they checked out, Patricia asked Mama Moreen about me, and revealed who she was. She explained the circumstances and events that led up to my being taken.

CHAPTER 14.

Who Am I To Hold Grudges

•●•

SAFETY FROM THE PAST

FREDRICK A. STEWART

"So, she didn't abandon you? "Not exactly. That is what the second letter was about. That one was from Patricia. She was on drugs and was in a volatile relationship with my dad. She felt the only way to get out of the situation so she could get some help, and keep me safe, was to sacrifice her freedom. That's how I ended up in foster care.

I don't have many childhood memories; I forgot what Patricia looked like over the years. I guessed I blocked her from my mind to deal with the abandonment. Strangely enough, the night the police came was the one event I can still remember. I've never talked about this to anyone, but I'll never forget that night.

I remember our house being full of people. There was a lot of laughing and loud music. Patricia would check on me in my bedroom every half hour or so. She didn't allow me to enter the front room with their company. It's crazy how I remember that night, but I couldn't remember her face. Anyway, there was one man that I never felt comfortable around.

He would always try and hug me or get me to sit on his lap. Whenever Patricia saw him trying to groom me, she would take me to my room and tell me to stay there.

She would bring me food or something to drink. The last time she came into my room, she looked sad, almost like she was ashamed or something. A few minutes after her last check, she returned to my room, at least, I thought it was her. But it wasn't, it was the man I didn't feel comfortable around.

I'm not sure, but I think his name was Earl. He asked me how I was doing. I told him I was fine and asked where my mom was. He said she was busy taking care of some things. He kept telling me how pretty I was while he moved closer to me. I was lying on my bed but quickly sat up and called for Patricia. That's when something happened.

My room started shaking, followed by a loud noise. I would describe it as a humming or buzzing sound. Then there was this huge burst of light that appeared in the back of Earl. It was so bright I couldn't look directly at it. I used my forearm to shield my eyes, but I could only see a figure in the light.

I couldn't make out a face. The figure absorbed the light like it was glowing from inside of it. It grew so tall; its head was touching the ceiling. I still couldn't make out a face, but its body was huge. Once the light and figure appeared, Earl never said another word, he didn't move. It was like he was frozen.

The figure moved towards me; I don't want to sound crazy, but I believe it passed through Earl and stood between us. A feeling of peace and safety came over me. Its voice was different from any other I've ever heard. *"Do not be afraid,"* was the only word spoken.

The last thing I remember is the figure wrapping something around me. I guess I passed out. When I woke up, my room was empty. The police were there, carrying Patricia and others out in handcuffs. I was always too scared to say anything about that night. I didn't want anyone teasing me or saying I was crazy."

"What do you think it was?"

"I always thought it was…" or it could have been, I don't know what it was."

"It's ok, you can say it."

"I thought it was an angel. But why would an angel come and save me? I didn't know anything about God or Angels. And from what I just read; we weren't the church-going kind of family."

"Just because you didn't know God; doesn't mean he didn't know you. If he gave his only son to die for our sins, why is it so hard to believe he wouldn't send his angels to protect you? His words say that I knew you before you were conceived in the womb. Since he created you, he knows you, and if he knows you, he is there for you."

I hugged my husband as tightly as I could. His words, as usual, were comforting.

"So, what do you plan on doing? Are you going to see her?

"Babe, I don't know. What if she is still on drugs, I don't want anything to do with that. Her letter said she has been clean for ten years, but I don't know."

"There is also the possibility that she has been clean like she said. Shada, it seems like she has gone through a lot to find you. At least give her a chance. Tomorrow is not promised for any of us. If you have the opportunity to reconnect with her, why not?"

"You're right, who am I to hold grudges? My past hasn't been all that squeaky clean either."

"That's my girl."

I lay in the arms of the man of my dreams, having prolific thoughts. I have gone through some painful and horrific things, but they are glimpses of my past. I am starting to realize that the trials I went through prepared me for now. It took me a long time to get here, but by the grace of God, I have arrived. Life isn't all about self. It's about helping others who have experienced trials and need help finding peace.

The next day I awoke with Patricia heavy on my mind. I thought about how mean I had been to her, yelling at her, telling her to leave my house. I wondered if she even wanted to see me now. Mason gave me Patricia's address, by then, I had talked myself out of seeing her.

My emotions were all over the place. My brain and my heart had stopped communicating with each other. I was at a stalemate with my thoughts and actions.

"You alright, Shada?"

"Hello, Mama Barringer, I'm fine."

"Ok, where is grandmas baby?"

"She is taking a nap; I think she's been asking for you."

"Of course, she's been asking for her grandma."

"Are you sure you're alright? You seem preoccupied with your thoughts. Shada! Shada, the house is on fire. The baby took the car to school."

"Hu, I'm sorry, I'm swept up in my thoughts."

"I see, you want to talk about it."

Mama Barringer came and sat down by me. She took my hand. "What's bothering you?" I began telling her my dilemma. My topic enthralled her. She gave me her undivided attention. She never said a word until I was done. "Baby, that woman has been through hell. The last thing she needs is for her only daughter to add to her misery.

Go to your mother, accept her apologies, forgiveness, or whatever she tries to give you. Give her that opportunity to put all that stuff behind her, once and for all." I knew she was right. I needed to hear it from another woman, another mother. "If you want, I'll go with you. I know it won't be easy, but it's necessary."

"I appreciate you, Mama Barringer. But I need to do this on my own."

"Ok, I think I hear my grandbaby waking up."

"Yeah, that's her, let's go get the princess. Wait! Did you say she took the car to school?"

"Child, come on here."

The next day Moreen and I prepared to visit Patricia. As we were walking out, Mama Barringer reminded me. "Don't forget it's girl's night with Neveah at the bar. See if your mom would like to join us." I got a kick out of that. "Will do."

We arrived at her apartment. I took a deep breath, "you can do this." Walking up to her apartment was the first step, the only thing left was to knock on the door. My knocks were quick, no answer. I waited impatiently. Again, I struck the door with force, but still no response. I returned to the car, somewhat disappointed. I buckled Moreen in and headed to the driver's side when a lady came out her door. "Excuse me, are you looking for Patricia?"

"Yes, I am. Do you know where she is?"

"Give me a minute." The lady closed the door, opened it and came out to where I was standing. "You must be Shada." The lady had a big smile on her face. "Yes, I am. How do you know who I am?"

"I know you don't remember me, but I used to watch you when you were little. My name is Ida. I told her you would come. She hasn't stopped talking about you since she returned from seeing you, and that must be that beautiful grandbaby."

"Yes, that's her. Do you know where I can find Patricia?"

"Yes, the ambulance took her to the hospital yesterday, she was having pains in her chest."

"Oh no, do you know what hospital?"

"They usually take her to general, over there on the twenty-sixth street."

"Ok, thank you so much." I rushed around to the driver's side of the car.

"Shada, can you tell her I'll be up there later this evening? and baby, your mother is not a bad person, she has gone through some things."

"I will, and thank you," Ida's words about my mother caused an emotional shift in my thinking. My eyes began to water. I couldn't make sense of what I was feeling.

I don't know the woman in the hospital, but every fiber of my body urged me to hurry and see her. I called Mama Barringer to find out if she would watch Moreen, I didn't want to take her to the hospital.

I dropped the baby off at home and departed quickly. I was at war with myself. 'What if I was too late, and she passed away while I was deliberating my thoughts.' A sickening feeling came over me, tears would no longer stand by. They would commence like rain pouring down, trying to feel an ocean.

I wiped them away as quickly as they came so that they wouldn't distort my vision. My heart raced like a sprinter who needed to make up valuable ground. My nerves were at war with me, they caused my breathing to become short and shallow. I inhaled deeply to try and regain control of my frantic respiration.

Once I arrived at the hospital, I took a moment to get myself under control. I closed my eyes and gripped the steering wheel firmly. I called out to my God, who had forgiven me before, and I needed to forgive me again. My selfishness caused me to forget about all the grace and mercy I have received over the last few years.

It has taken center stage and demands to be the main attraction. I repented for my sins and asked to be free from my lack of empathy. *"In your son's name, I pray, Amen."*

The sliding doors opened as I walked into the hospital. Two people were ahead of me waiting to talk to the front desk attendant. When it was my turn, I approached the front desk. "Hello, I'm here to see Patricia Shields." The attendant checked her computer. "She is in the intensive care unit; family members can only visit her. What's your name?"

"Shada Barringer."

"Ok, you're on her list, her daughter, right?"

"Yes, I am."

"Can I see your license, please?" The attendant checked my license and directed me to the intensive care unit. I prepared myself for whatever I saw. I stopped at the nurse's station and asked for my mother's room number. "What is your relationship to the patient?"

"I'm her daughter." The nurse checked her chart. "Your Shada Barringer?"

"Yes, I am."

"She has been asking for you."

"How is she doing?

"She is stable. She had a mild heart attack a couple of days ago. This is concerning, considering she had a major a year ago."

"Is she having heart attacks because she is still using drugs?'

"No, it's from her previous drug use. Most of her veins have collapsed, which is putting stress on her heart. Most of the damage is irreversible. Her toxicology reports have all been adverse for the last ten years. She is a strong lady. Most people don't stay clean that long after using drugs, as much as she did."

"Can I see her?"

"Of course. She will be in and out of consciousness because of the medicine her doctor has her on, it's mainly to keep her calm and rested to give her heart time to recover." I stood at the side of Patricia's bed; thankful she was still alive. I thought about the stuffed toy she gave baby Moreen. It made me chuckle because I still couldn't figure out what it was, but I was glad I might still get to ask her.

I had a seat and waited. Mason called like he usually does during the afternoon. "Hey, love, what you up to?"

"I'm at the hospital."

"Why, what's wrong?"

"I'm visiting Patricia; she had a mild heart attack a few days ago."

"Baby, I'm sorry to hear that, how is she doing?"

"The nurse said she is stable. I'm waiting for her to wake up, so she knows I was here. I left the baby with your mom. I might leave and come back later, I'm not sure if Mama Barringer has plans today, I should have asked her."

"Babe, stay there as long as you want. I'll call Mom and check on her, and the baby. I'm sure she doesn't mind watching her until I get off."

"Ok, thanks, love, I appreciate you and Mama Barringer. I feel like I need to be here with her."

"No, problem. If you need me give me a call."

"Will do. Love you."

"Love you too."

I got up and approached the bed. I gently picked up her hand and held it, I wanted her to know I was here. After a while, the nurse came in to do her checks. While she was changing her I.V. bag, Patricia awoke. "Hey there lady, how are you feeling?"

"I'm ok. Tired is all." Her voice sounded weak but soft.

"You're going to feel like that for a while. There is someone here to see you."

"Who?" I stood up and stepped over to her bed. When she saw me, her face lit up, her tears started flowing. I guess my tears didn't want to be left out. She slowly lifted her hand. I embraced it with both of mine. "He told me you would come."

"Who said I would come?"

"God did, he said you would come to see me." I broke eye contact with her for a moment. I guess the nurses' tears wanted to join the festivities."

I stayed at the hospital until Ida showed up. Mom must have put her down as her sister, I would later find out they were best friends, thick as thieves even. Ida was the one who called the police that night, as she and Patricia planned. She has been Patricia's support and strength on her journey of sobriety. I didn't know either of them very well, but I was proud of both of them. Patricia was in the hospital for a little over a week, recovering from her heart attack.

I told her that her granddaughter and I would come to pick her up when she got discharged. She was so excited to see her only grandchild. The nurses said that's all she talked about when she started feeling better. It was unbelievable that we had been reunited after all these years. I never thought it would happen.

Not only did I have my mother, but I also gained an aunt as well. I couldn't help but imagine what Christmas would be like this year. Instead of taking Patricia home, she came over to our house to meet the rest of the family. On the way home I remembered to ask her about the stuffed animal she got for baby Moreen.

"I have a question, what is that funny-looking stuffed animal you got for your granddaughter? I have been trying to figure out what it is for the longest." Her laugh brought a smile to my face. If you didn't know her story, and only went off her laugh, you would think she never had a bad day in her life. It reminded me so much of Mama Moreens' laugh.

"It's a Sockmonster!"

"A What?"

A Sockmonster. It's a character in a children's book. The author was my rideshare driver. He picked me up from my doctor's appointment and took me home. Normally I take the bus, but I wasn't filling it this day. We started talking and he told me about a children's book he wrote called, There is a Sockmonster that Lives in My House. He let me look at the book.

I liked it so much that I bought a copy. He even signed it for me. It was funny because his mother's name was Patricia too. When I saw the book and the stuffed toy at the store, I needed to have the toy so I could give it to my grandbaby when I read the book. That's why I was willing to put the food back instead of the toy.

"Why didn't you say anything about being my mother at the store."

"Because the time wasn't right. Believe me, I wanted to, I prayed for years asking God to allow me to see you again. And he did. He was waiting on me to be specific about what I wanted, which was to be in your life as your mother. Baby like Moses wandered through the wilderness for forty years, I wandered through this city for years, hoping to find you."

"I'm glad we were able to reconnect. Where is the book at?"

"It's at my place. Can we stop by and grab it so I can read it to her, please."

"Of course, grandma. I don't know who is going to be worse, you or Mason's Mom."

We took our detour on the route to Patricia's' apartment. We pulled up in front of her building. "You can come in if you like."

"Ok." I went inside, her apartment was cute. She had a collection of figurines and whatnot. Plants and flowers were spread out throughout the apartment. She had some pictures on the wall of her when she was younger. Is this you? She came out of her bedroom with the book.

"Yes, that's me. I took this picture about a month before I found out I was pregnant with you. These are your grandparents, they passed away a couple of years ago. I have a picture book if you want to look at it, I mean if we have time."

"That would be nice, I'll text Mason and let him know we made a stop." She went back to the bedroom and grabbed the book with the pictures in them. We sat on the couch and went through some old photos. "This is your father, Carlos."

"He was very handsome. All the women wanted him, but I was the one that got him. I wish I knew then, what I know now." I could have saved myself years of hardship and pain."

"Patricia, I'm sorry. If it bothers, you to look at these we don't have to."

"Baby, I've gotten over all that. I had to learn to let it go, or it was going to keep pulling me back down. This is your aunt Zora."

"How did you keep from going upside both of their heads for what they were doing."

"At that time, I didn't know how to stand up for myself. I let people walk all over me. It wasn't till I got out of jail that I realized this world will chew you up and spit you out if you let it. I turned the page in the picture book. "This is your aunt Zora and her daughter."

A cold chill raced through my body. I quickly closed the book. "I think we better be leaving; I don't want to keep everyone waiting. I stood up and rushed to the door.

"Is everything alright?"

"Yes, we need to get going, that's all."

"Ok. that's fine." We rode in silence the majority of the way. When we pulled up to the house my anxiety was in full effect. I was shaking and trembling. "Shada are you sure you're alright, you seem like something is bothering you. If you're not ready for this, I understand."

No, it's not that. I'm fine, I felt a little sick for a moment, that's all."

"Alright, we can do this some other time if you like."

"No, we're good." We ventured inside. Everyone was sitting in the living room waiting for us. Hellos, hugs, and introductions were distributed. Mama Barringer was holding Moreen. "I bet you would like to hold your granddaughter." Patricia looked at me, her eyes asked if it was ok. I nodded yes.

"Yes, I would love that very much." Patricia held her granddaughter for the first time. While she was holding the baby, Mason asked if he could see me in the bedroom.

"What's the matter, you came in looking like you saw a ghost."

"I did see a ghost. You remember me telling you about Karmen, right?

"Yeah, the one that was killed in prison?"

"Yes, Patricia was showing me some old pictures. I turned the page and saw Karmen in a picture with my Aunt. She was my half-sister and my cousin."

What do you mean half-sister? I didn't tell you this earlier, but my dad and aunt were messing around behind Patricia's back. My aunt ended up getting pregnant by my dad. Karmen was my aunt's daughter.

"Good lord, are you going to tell her?

"I don't know, I don't want to start our relationship off with that mess. Plus, she is dealing with enough, I don't want this to be the thing that sends her back into the hospital. I'll deal with it later, right now let's just go have dinner." We joined everyone else in the living room.

Patricia was still playing with Moreen. Mama Barringer finished setting up the dining room table. "Patricia, are you ready to eat?"

"Yes, I am. I haven't had real food in over a week, and it smells delicious."

Mason couldn't miss the opportunity to let everyone know that Mama Barringer was the best cook in the state. We all sat down to eat. Neveah called to let us know she wouldn't be able to make it. The bar was very busy due to the basketball team having a home game tonight.

Dinner was delicious as usual. It was nice to have both of our mothers present with us. After dinner, Patricia, Mama Barringer, and Mason went into the living room. "Ladies, I'm about to pour myself a nice drink, would either of you like one? Mama Barringer wanted her usual red wine, from France. "Patricia, would you like anything?"

"No thank you, I don't drink anymore." I think it dawned on him all at once, or maybe it was the look I shot him. "I'm so sorry, I wasn't thinking."

"It's ok sweetheart, go ahead and enjoy your drink, I've gotten past the point where it's a trigger." For the first time, I saw Mason look unsure about his actions. "Plus, I have a book date with my grandbaby." Patricia picked up the Sockmonster book and began reading it to baby Moreen.

They both were enjoying themselves tremendously. Baby Moreen recognized the picture of the Sockmonster. "munter, munter." We all looked surprised but couldn't help but laugh. "Ok, baby girl, I'll get your munter."

"Can I see her room please?"

"Of course, come on." Patricia and I went upstairs to the baby's nursery. "This is so beautiful. Ah, you were a pooh bear baby too. Shada can I ask a favor of you." I don't know why when people have a troubled past, and they ask a question like that, we automatically assume the worst. "Sure, what is it?"

"Could you please, fix your husband, and your mother-in-law their drinks? This is their home, and I don't want them to feel uncomfortable around me. It would take a lot more than the sight or smell of liquor to drag me back down that hell hole."

I nodded yes. There is so much more I need to learn about this lady, I don't want to be judgmental towards her. We retrieved the baby's toy and headed back downstairs. Patricia and baby Moreen continued their story time. I went to the kitchen and prepared both drinks and brought them to their perspective drinkers.

They both had that, "What are you doing," look on their faces.

It's ok." I could see Patricia, taking a quick look up from reading. She flashed a smile and carried on. The night finished with pictures being taken, and Patricia putting Moreen to bed. The pictures we took Patricia looked at repeatedly, during the trip to her apartment.

About halfway there she became emotional. "What's wrong?" She turned her head towards the window, so I couldn't see her tears. I guess I know where I got that from. Her voice quivered when she spoke. "I have missed so much of your life; I don't know how I could ever make up for that."

"You don't have to make up for anything. We are starting a new beginning together, you, me, baby Moreen, and the rest of the family. She wiped away the remaining tears from her face. Nervously, she looked at me. "Do you think you'll ever...ever feel comfortable calling me mom?"

"I'm sure in time, it will feel right. Until then we'll keep working on our relationship." My answer gave her a ray of hope, at least that's what I gathered from the smile on her beautiful face. Once we arrived at her place, I helped her take her things inside her apartment. Our initial attempt at embracing each other was awkward.

Eventually, we both closed our eyes and held each other tightly, like we imagined, and wished for, all those years apart. We both became emotional wrecks in a matter of seconds. We wiped each other's faces free of cries. I told her I would give her a call in the morning. She asked if I could let her know I made it home safely tonight.

"Of course," was my reply. I returned to my car, before I pulled off Patricia was on her way to Ida's door, to show her the pictures of her family. I had to chuckle. I drove home thanking God for bringing my mother back into my life and delivering her from the drug addiction that snatched her away from me. I gave thanks for all the blessings he has given me. *"In your son's name, I pray, Amen."*

CHAPTER 15.

The War Inside Me

•●•

SAFETY FROM THE PAST

FREDRICK A. STEWART

Over the next six months, Patricia and I spent a considerable amount of time with each other. She was present for baby Moreen's first steps, as well as her first birthday. Our relationship flourished like tulips in the dawn of Spring. Eventually, I told her, how Mason and I met. As well as the events that led up to our encounter.

I was reluctant to tell her the full story. So, I left some details out. I didn't know how to tell her about Karmen and me, but, as fate would have it, part of the story showed up knocking at my door.

"Mom, can you get the door, I'm changing the baby."

"Ok, I got it. Hello, can I help you?"

"Yes, Is Shada Barringer home?"

"Who is asking?

"My name is Detective Dean, and this is my partner Detective McAfee."

"Wait here." Mom rushed upstairs; she was breathing heavily trying to catch her breath. "Shada, there are two detectives at the front door asking for you."

"Mom, sit down and relax, you know you're not supposed to get all worked up like that. "Baby, is everything alright?" I took a deep breath and let it out quickly.

"Yeah, can you finish getting Moreen dressed?"

"Of course."

I preceded downstairs and stepped onto the porch. "Good afternoon gentleman, how can I help you."

"Hello, Mrs. Barringer. How are you doing?

"I'm fine, what can I help you with."

"We wanted to stop by and let you know the case has been dropped due to lack of evidence, and you are no longer a person of interest."

"And you couldn't call and tell me that over the phone?"

"Well, yes, we could have, but we wanted to see if you remembered anything since we last talked."

No, I haven't."

"Ok, then um, like I said the investigation has been closed."

"Ok. is that all?"

"Yes, um, do you mind if I ask who that was that answered the door."

"Yes, I do mind, good day gentlemen."

I stepped inside, Mom, was waiting with a worried look on her face. "Everything is ok Mom." Her worried look intensified. "Baby, please, tell me what's going on." There was no way of getting around it. We sat down and I told her everything. When I was done, she looked more concerned than before.

"I was supposed to protect you, I failed you in so many ways." Her agony ripped at her soul. I could tell she felt terrible about all the things I told her. I knew she blamed herself. "Mom look at me. From this day forward. Your past, and my past, no longer matter. The mistakes we made, the things we went through, and the hardships we endured, are all gone.

They have been buried in the sea of forgetfulness. Those things can no longer affect us unless we let them. I do not want you torturing yourself over that stuff anymore. One of the most important things I have learned over the last few years is how to forgive, and that started with forgiving me. We deserve as much forgiveness as anyone else. I took my mother's hand and prayed the prayer that Mason prayed with me at Safety.

The more time I spend on this earth the more I realize life can be unbearable at times. As beautiful as it can be, it hoards a sinister side. It has no quarrels letting us know it does not play fair. Once again it would grin an evil grin. Its thirst for anarchy is unbridled. Its narcissistic portrayal is embellished as it craves to play the victim.

It finds enjoyment in the wreckage of unsuspected turmoil. Its menacing behavior is exhibited out of malice, and the pompous pleasure of knowing that it can. It has searched for me like a child playing hide and seek, I wish not to be part of its diabolical amusement.

"Mom, what are you looking for?"

"Mason I'm trying to find my phone.

"Is it in your purse?"

"No, I've pulled everything out of it, it's not in there."

Mama Barringer, it's right here on the charger, you plugged it up a few minutes ago.

"Oh, lord. I forgot I put it on the charger. "Thank you, baby, I swear it feels like I'm losing my mind sometimes."

"You're fine mom, it's been a rough couple of years for you. I might have to get you on a cruise ship so you can relax. A nice vacation might do you some good."

"That's my baby always looking out for his mother like your father did."

"I told Dad I would take care of you." My mother looked at me with the saddest expression, "I miss him so much."

"I miss him too."

I gave her a big hug hoping it would ease some of the pain. "How about we take you to dinner for your birthday?"

"Oh, I would love that, the old girl still has a pretty good appetite you know."

"I know you do Mom."

"Another trip around the sun. Eighty-three years and counting. Never thought I would make it this far." Shada and I looked at each other puzzled; Mom turned eighty-five today. We planned a surprise birthday party for her at the diner. For many years she has put her blood, sweat, and tears into that place.

We invited some family and friends as well as some of the regulars that were faithful patrons. "Mason, are we going to pick Andrew up along the way?"

As much as I wished I could say yes, the truth would not be denied. "No, Mom, Andrew is gone; he passed away."

"O shoot baby, I'm sorry, I forgot."

The ride to the diner was soundless. A couple of times I would look in the rear-view mirror at my mother sitting in the back seat, staring out the window. At times she looked as if she was seeing everything for the first time. We pulled up to the diner and unloaded everyone from the car.

Mom started walking towards the diner and suddenly stopped. "Are you ok, Mom?" She didn't say anything at first. She stood silent staring at the building. "Guess we better get inside; it's fixing to rain." We continued to the diner, I unlocked the door and let Mom walk in first. Once we were all inside the lights came on and everyone yelled, 'happy birthday.'

I expected to see surprise and excitement on her face, but instead, there was a look of confusion. "Mason, whose birthday is it?"

"It's your birthday, Mom." A moment later she presented the question, I'm eighty-five?"

"Yes, Mom, you are eighty-five." The look on her face disappeared and was replaced with the smile I had expected to see. "I'm eighty-five!" she proudly proclaimed as she walked off to greet her guests. I could feel my wife staring at me, but I refused to look in her direction.

I watched my mom laugh, giggle and enjoy herself for the rest of the evening. She interacted with everyone as if the last seven years of her life never happened. She enjoyed her party so much she got on the dance floor and cut a rug or two; the old lady still got some moves.

I couldn't let the opportunity of a lifetime pass me by. We cleared the dance floor as the DJ put on her favorite song. "May I have this dance?" She took my hand, and we swayed back and forth to the soft melody, creating a memory that would be forever etched in our hearts.

I danced with my first love as I did as a child. Even after the music stopped playing, we relished in the moment. It was her special day and our exceptional moment. Once our dance was over, we sat down for dinner and presents.

"Mason, who has been cooking in my kitchen?"

"Nobody, Mom, we had the food catered."

"Oh, ok then. I didn't want it to get ugly up in here." Eighty-five or not, the little lady still has some fire in her. We finished eating and began opening her presents. She received almost as many as Baby Moreen did on her birthday, and she has so many we might not have to go Christmas shopping for her this year. Mom opened presents until she got tired of opening presents. "Ok, that's enough for now, I'll open the rest later."

"Alright, Mom, but there is one present you need to open now."

"Uh, alright where is it? A good friend of mine, who is an artist, that specializes in painting portraits, created a compilation piece gathered from photos of my mother and father on their wedding day, and their last anniversary. He combined the pictures and made a beautiful portrait that shows how they grew through the years. "Isiah, can you bring it in?"

"Happy birthday Mrs. Barringer, I have known you ever since Mason and I were in kindergarten. It was my pleasure to work on this piece for you, I hope you enjoy it." Isiah uncovered the portrait. Mom's, eyes grew big as saucers. She gazed at the portrait with love and affection.

"We were so young then. Thank you so much, you did a beautiful job." She stood up and hugged Isiah. "You two were always trying to steal food out of my kitchen." Everyone in attendance laughed. It was a wonderful sight to see her so elated. When the party was over, I could tell she was worn out, but filled with joy. She hugged everyone like it was the last time she would see them. On the way home the birthday girl fell asleep in the car.

I woke her up, once we arrived home.

"Mom, we're home."

"Ok, baby, I thought we were headed to the club, I could have danced all night." I laughed at the dancing machine, "not tonight lady it's bedtime."

"Aww." I helped her out of the car and into the house. She said her goodnights and headed up the stairs. "Mom let me help you."

"I'm ok baby I got this." She made it up two stairs before she missed the third step and almost fell back down the stairs. Luckily, I was close enough to rush to her aid and catch her before she did. Tears ran down her face. "Mom did you hurt yourself!"

"No baby I'm not hurt, your dad always helped me up the stairs, I miss him so much." Shada came and took her arm. "Come on Mama Barringer, I'll help you get ready for bed." Helplessly, I watched as the loves of my life slowly maneuvered up the stairs and disappeared into my mother's bedroom. I fixed myself a drink and had a seat on the back patio.

I love being outside in the warmth of the nocturnal summer nights. The coolness of the air relaxes me, allowing me to reflect on the events of the day. After a few minutes, Shada joined me on the patio. I started a fire in the fire pit, the sound of the crackling wood and flickering flame adds to my relaxation.

"Hey, how are you doing?"

"I'm fine," was my standard answer. "I think we should move Mom's room downstairs in your office, and you can set up the basement as your work area.

"Yeah, I was thinking that also, I'll get started on it tomorrow."

"Also, I think we should make a doctor's appointment for her to see a specialist."

"See a specialist for what?"

"She is showing signs of memory loss."

"There is nothing wrong with my mom's memory, she's dealt with a couple of rough years, that's all, she is missing Dad, she might be stressed or grieving but that's about it."

"Mason all I am saying is it wouldn't hurt to have her checked out."

"My mother is fine!" Shada.

"Ok. I'm headed to bed are you coming?"

"No, not right now."

"Alright, well good night, love you." No reply came from my mouth, no acknowledgment of love you returned to her. The next morning my wife came into the basement where I had spent the night.

"You didn't come to bed last night."

"Yes, I know."

"Why not?"

"I couldn't sleep so I started moving the stuff out of my office."

"Is that the only reason?"

"I said I couldn't sleep what else do you want."

"I want my husband to come to bed at night, and not talk to me like I'm nobody."

"If that's how you perceive it, then that's your problem."

"Excuse me!"

"No excuse me, I have to get ready for work."

"You didn't sleep all night, and now you're going to go to work."

"Yes, I am, somebody has to pay the dam bills around here."

"What the hell does that mean? Mason."

"I don't have time for this, I have to get ready for work."

"So, we're not going to resolve this? I looked at her with heated anger. I spoke no more words. I walked away from my wife, the mother of our daughter, the love of my life. The battle wasn't with her. It was my internal conflict that I couldn't control, I guess you always hurt the ones closest to you.

When I came from the basement my mother was sitting at the kitchen table.

"Mason, are you alright?"

"Yes, Mom, I am fine," was my standard answer.

"When I get home, I'm going to move your bedroom into my office, so you won't have to walk up the stairs."

"Ok, but that's not what I'm talking about."

"Mom, I'm late for work I need to get ready." I kissed her on her forehead and hurried upstairs. Escape and evade. The next few days were filled with unnerving silence. My wife and I closed our minds to resolving our issues. We walked by each other as if neither of us was there. We ate our meals in silence and slept with our backs toward each other.

No warm embrace thawed the frozen tension that had us bound. We were as strangers standing in a sun shower being drenched with the reality that love alone is not enough. Another week passes and we still have not found the combination to unlock this torture chamber of intimate distancing.

Every time she walks by me or gets danger close, I can feel the heat of her body as it whispers, *"take me I'm yours."* Her scent harassed me viciously. It follows me everywhere. Her luminous fragrance of ripe pomegranate and lush lotus in full bloom became my antagonist. I longed to embrace her. This was our first disagreement since we were married.

We had no idea of how to escape this anguish, we were gasping for air in a chamber void of oxygen, we were suffocating from silence. Another week of lonely emptiness feels our home. Everything seems out of place. Where the joy of laughter once resided, the cold shimmer of silence has moved in. The enjoyable and intriguing conversation that used to run rampant, has now been evicted due to lack of compensation.

Before I left the house this morning, I almost spoke to the stranger that has become my partner. I almost expressed how much I miss her, how bad I want to hold her, how much I love her, but pride would have none of that, it silenced me like a sniper's rifle. Before I walked out the front door to go to work, I took a glance at the beautiful woman holding our child.

We made eye contact but neither of us uttered a word. Is this what death feels like? Anger pacified me as I slammed the door and retreated to higher ground. About two hours into the workday, I received a call in my office, I rushed to the phone hoping it was my wife,

The voice on the other end of the phone was not the soft voice I wished for. "Hello, is this Sargent Major Barringer? My disappointment was on display.

"Speaking!"

"This is Sargent Simmons of the fifth precinct police department. I'm calling regarding Marie Barringer."

"That's my mother, what's wrong?"

"Nothing is wrong, she is fine." One of my patrol officers picked up your mother."

"What do you mean picked her up?"

"She was wandering around in the Fremont neighborhood. The officer asked her if she was alright, and she told him she didn't know where she was. She seemed confused and disoriented. Can you or someone come and pick her up?"

"Yes, I will be there right away."

"Thank you, sir, we will let her know you are on your way."

I ran out of my office. When I entered my car, I called home. "Hello, Shada I need you to meet me at the fifth precinct, they picked Mom up, she was wandering in the streets lost. When did she leave the house?

"About an hour ago. She said she was going for a walk."

"You didn't check on her?"

"Mason, I fed the baby and laid down with her, I didn't get any sleep last night."

"Can you meet me at the precinct please?"

"Okay, I'm on my way."

I arrived at the precinct; Mom was sitting in one of the interrogation rooms. She looked scared and bewildered. When she saw me, she rushed towards me. "Mason, please take me home! I don't like it here."

"Yes, Mom we are going home right now." I thanked Sargent Simmons for taking care of her and calling me. I put my mother in my car and drove off. I didn't say anything until I saw my mother had calmed down. "Mom, what happened?"

"I don't know, I remember leaving the house but that's all. Mason, I was so scared." I assured my mother everything was alright, but I knew it wasn't, I also knew my wife was right, she needs to see a doctor. We arrived at the house right after Shada and the baby. Once Mom saw them, she lit up like a light.

She hurried to Shada's car and took the baby out the car seat. She walked into the house with her, like she was oblivious to the events that happened. My wife and I met at the front door of our house. I looked into her soft eyes and said the only thing that could or should be said. "I'm sorry!

Shada, I'm sorry that I didn't listen to you about Mom. I'm sorry for taking it out on you, I didn't want to accept I may be losing my mom." Before I could say another thing, my wife put her hands on my face.

"My love, we are in this together. Where you lead, I will follow, all I ask is that you understand I only want what's best for our family, and if I have a concern, you trust me enough to listen and take what I'm saying into consideration."

"Shada I promise I will." I held my wife as close as I possibly could without hurting her. The warmth of her physique sizzled through my whole body. The kiss she gave me weakened my knees. "I am so sorry, I missed you badly." A suggestive grin appeared on her face. "Well, my love, why don't you come to show me how much you missed me."

Her words were as enticing as her beauty. My heart responded, *"If I had only one night to live, I would spend it pleasing you."* We disappeared into our bedroom; we needed time to reconcile.

While we engaged each other Patricia stopped by. "Hello, Marie."

"Hello Patricia, come on in."

"Where is everybody?"

"They back there making us another grandbaby."

"Oh, ok, well, let's not disturb them." After a while, we returned from our room. The two grandmothers were sitting in the living room with their granddaughter. They both gave me that look that elderly women give you when they know what you were doing. "Hello, Patricia."

"Hello, Mason." Shada went over to where the ladies were sitting. I guess when you get to a certain age, you don't bother whispering, you say what you want to say, and my mother has reached that age. "Girl, did you put it on him?" Shada smiled and put her hands on her hips. "Now, you know I did."

"Mason."

"Yes, mom."

"We would like a boy this time, ok baby." Very seldom do you hear of a marine retreating, but this would be one of those times. As I hastily walked out the door, all three of them, with their sneaky smiles shouted out, "bye Mason." Once I entered the safety of my truck I realized, it was four against one in my home, yes, I need a boy next time.

The next day I took a personal day from work so I could talk to my mother about going to the doctor. When her memory fails her, she can't remember much of anything. Other times she is sharp as a tack. Normally my mother is an early bird. Usually, she is up and scampering around the house by zero eight hundred hours. Today there was no sign of her as the clock struck nine. I stood outside her door listening for any indications of movement or sound, there was none.

I have known the fierceness of battle. I have engaged in my adversary's failed attempts at ending my life. I've tread in places where the wrong step could mean certain death, needless to say, I have known fear. But what I'm facing this morning I am not prepared for. I felt helpless, scared, and afraid.

In battle I knew my enemy's intent, now I have no idea of how to prepare for what I may encounter on the other side of this door. I stood paralyzed. I closed my eyes as I stood at my mother's bedroom door. I pleaded and prayed to God to allow me to look upon the face of my mother once again and see life.

I opened my eyes and raised my arm, as I shook with fear, as I prepared for the worst. My fist came down on her door, slowly repeating the motion three times. No answer came from within. A rush of adrenaline caused me to quiver. My heart race increased with every moment of not knowing. I slowly reached down towards the doorknob; my eyes squinted to keep the tears at bay.

With one turn of the knob and push of the door, I would be face to face with the reality of life or death. The door slowly opened. All the breath I was holding in my lungs escaped in one huge exhale. I entered my mother's room in no way prepared for what I might encounter.

She was lying on her side with her back towards me. "Mom, are you ok" No answer returned to me. I slowly walked towards her hoping and praying for some sign of life. I called to her again "Mom." I was almost standing in front of her. I received final confirmation that the privilege of life had not forsaken her.

"Mason I can't remember what he looks like." I collapsed to my knees. Although there was relief in hearing her speak, her words cut through me like a mameluke sword. My prayer to God was a personal thank you. When I opened my eyes, I stared into the face of lost memories. Memories that were part of her life for over fifty years. She looked sad and dejected. I noticed she was holding some papers that looked tattered and aged.

"Mom, what are these papers?" I eased them out of her hands. "Those are poems your dad wrote when he was in Vietnam. After we were married, he shared them with me. He said he never knew fear like he did while he was over there. The nightly bombing, air raids, and firefights were more than enough to make him question if he would make it out alive.

Writing poetry was his escape from the war. It helped him deal with the uncertainty of not knowing if he would make it home or not. I never knew my dad wrote poetry, but as I started reading, I realized there was more to the big man than I ever imagined.

I sat on the floor next to my mother's bed reading the inner thoughts and reflections of the man I idolized. The first poem I read was a short story about his childhood, and how he viewed the world through the eyes of a young black male. The next poem was different. I had the feeling that my father was dealing with internal conflict, that caused him to look at life through different viewpoints.

While I was thoroughly engulfed in my father's writings my mother's soft voice interrupted me. She placed her hand on my shoulder and requested I read it out loud. Taken back by her request, I eagerly read the writings of my father.

The war that rages inside me demands I wave the white flag and surrender all fortitude, self-worth, or decency that I may have had.

It demands I surrender all knowledge of my past, forcing me to forget, I was revered as a king in a far-off desert land.

It holds me as a captive like a refugee in a foreign land, barely giving me the necessities of life, while torturing me into believing, I'm less than a man.

It beats at my soul until I have nothing left, then watches with enjoyment as I breathe my final breath.

Its anger is kindled when I don't give up the ghost and rages into a violent tantrum when I call upon the Lord of Host.

I try and have the love of my savior and cry out "forgive them for they know not what they do" but how could it torture me so savagely and not have a clue of the pain it's putting me through?

The war inside me has decided my fate. It has condemned me to death for crimes against the state.

There will be no jury, I won't get to testify, I won't receive council of law just the judgmental lethal injection of mankind.

A concoction of poisons that will slow my heart rate and incapacitate me into a vegetable-like state.

The poisons that are used can't be found in a chemist's lab but in the insidious toxins of a world that has truly gone mad.

It will use love against me with the hope that I'll believe that no one could love someone as hideous as me.

It will cause the ones who are supposed to love me and stand by my side, to look me in my face and tell a serpent's lie, then stab me in the back with the proverbial dagger of my demise.

Its main ingredient will be hatred because of the color of my skin, tricking me into believing I'm inferior to other men.

I'm sure it will add bigotry to force me to be politically correct, even though its acceptance is like a noose around my neck.

There is more it will add, it doesn't want my death to be quick, it wants to make sure it destroy a whole generation with the trickledown effect.

This war inside me has destroyed many men, who have given up the fight, and caved from within… but I, I will fight this war inside of me, its victory won't be an easy win.

I won't succumb or be brought to an end, by the effect of destructive or disruptive forces that I battle with from within. I will fight the good fight; I will fight the good fight for the totality of man.

CHAPTER 16.

Songs Of Victories

•●•

SAFETY FROM THE PAST

FREDRICK A. STEWART

Silence demanded the room. My mother knew this side of him but struggles to remember it, her memory is failing her. I never knew of my dad's creative mind, but I will treasure it, and hold it dear like a priceless jewel.

We sat listening to what silence had to say, what was heard was the unforgiving sound of time as it ticked by. I turned and looked at my mother, gloom mimicked her face. She tried desperately to force a smile into existence, but she was not successful.

"Mom, I need to make you an appointment to see the doctor." She looked at me confused. "Why? I feel fine."

"I know you do, but we need to have your memory checked."

"Why, did I forget something?"

"Well, yesterday's event has me concerned."

"Yesterday!"

"Yes, you know when you went for a walk and couldn't remember how to get back home, and we had to come to pick you up from the police station."

"Baby I didn't like that place; I don't want to go to jail again."

"Mom, you didn't...The confused look on her face was heartbreaking.

"I'm sorry baby I won't forget again."

"It's ok, Mom, I want to make sure everything is ok."

"Alright baby, we can go to the store. Where is my grandbaby?"

"She is at the daycare today."

"I don't know why you take my baby to that place; she can be right here with me."

I kissed the beautiful lady on her cheek and walked out of the room. She continued fussing about her grandbaby being at daycare until I was out of hearing range. Shada was sitting at the table working on her schoolwork. I walked downstairs quietly trying not to disturb her.

My first thought was to ask her to make Mom's doctor's appointment, but I realized that was my burden to bear, and I would have to take point. I headed into my office when Shada looked up from her studies. "Hey, you." Her soothing voice was a pleasant distraction. "I'm sorry, did I disturb you.?"

"No, I was about to take a break, and check the baby's video monitor."

"I got fussed at about her being there."

"Yeah, I'm sure you did. I told her it was your idea to have her there."

"Wow, you threw me under the bus like that."

"Yep."

"How did your talk with her go?"

"As expected, she doesn't remember much of it, other than being at the precinct. Before I realized it my wife had come across the room and wrapped her arms around me. "It's alright my love, I'll call the doctor's office right after I check on the baby.""

"No, I'll take care of it. You have enough to handle."

"Are you sure, it's no problem?"

"I know, but I need to take care of this." Shada took hold of my hands. "It pains me to see that look." She removed a lone tear that had gone AWOL from the corner of my eye. "I wish life had as much compassion for me as you."

"Where in this together my love." Her words gave me comfort, her gentle kiss eased my pain. I retreated into my office to make calls, set appointments, and finish transforming it into my mother's bedroom. Over the next few months, my mother saw several doctors from her primary care to a neurologist.

The various cognitive, neurological, and memory tests sometimes confused her. But CT- scans didn't sit well with her at all. She did not like being in the tube. When all the testing and procedures were finished, the diagnosis of Alzheimer's dementia was no surprise to us.

The doctors recommend setting up daily routines and schedules. We rearranged our agenda, so they worked in accordance with hers. Meals were planned and prepared so she could eat early enough to coincide with her sleep pattern. Shada would go on walks with her during the day.

We found programs for older people that she could participate in, she still enjoys being around people laughing, talking, and having a good time. She especially likes her girls' nights out. She and Patricia are becoming thick as thieves. My mother's life was changing, and in the midst of it all, ours was forced to transition.

I finished getting her bedroom moved downstairs. We hung her birthday portrait up in the living room so that every day she could be reminded of the love that she and Dad shared and always have a remembrance of what he looked like. The ugly side of life continues to seek ways to destroy us. It has evolved into a vicious and dreadful beast, snarling and seeking to extinguish everything in its path.

Fear is its weapon of choice. But we will not quiver in terror. We will face the beast head-on as a mighty unit. Love and compassion will be our weapons of victory. We will trade blow for blow until the head of the beast lay at our feet. Our songs of victory will ring out throughout the land.

Over the last year, our family has grown substantially. The loss of our beloved has impacted our lives. The birth of a new generation has reenergized us. Loved ones have been reunited with a new understanding of the importance of strength and forgiveness. Matters of the brain and heart have changed our daily routines.

Yet there is one more deed that needs to be fulfilled.

"Good morning, beautiful."

"Good morning, handsome."

"So, you know our anniversary is coming up next month. And I don't know if you remember, but I promised you something in exchange for what I asked you.

"Oh, I remember. I was wondering if you still remembered."

"I do, and I'm ready to make good on my promise."

"Mason Barringer, are you ready to make me your wife again?

"Yes, I am, until death do us part."

"Does that mean I get to pick up my wedding dress?

"You mean to pick out your wedding dress."

"No. I've had this dress ready and waiting since we married, but I think I might need a new ring to accompany my dress."

"Oh, that's what you think. Well, if that's what you want, you definitely deserve it."

"Yaa, I have to call Neveah so we can go shopping. She is going to be my bridesmaid."

"Wait, Neveah is your bridesmaid."

"Baby, I told you this wedding ceremony has been planned since I said I do! at the courthouse. All I have been waiting on is you."

"I see. Well, let's put this thing in motion."

I couldn't wait to call Neveah and tell her the news.

"Hey, sis."

"What's up, sis? How are you doing?"

"I'm good, guess what? Your brother is going to marry me again."

"That's what's up. When is the day?"

"It will be on our original anniversary date." `

"Dad's birthday."

"Yes, are you still down to be my bridesmaid?"

"You know it…"

"What's the matter?

"Can you come by the bar later on, I need to talk to you about something."

"Of course, I'll drop by after I take Moreen to the daycare."

"That's fine, I'll see you then."

"Alright." I wondered what Neveah wanted to talk to me about. I hoped it wasn't anything serious. Mama Barringer was getting ready for the van to pick her up. Today is field trip day with her activity group, she gets so excited on field trip days. After Mama Barringer left, Moreen and I headed out.

On the way to drop the baby off at daycare, I called my mom to check on her, that has been our routine since she was in the hospital.

"Morning, Mom."

Good morning baby, how you doing?"

"I'm good, I have some exciting news."

"What's that?"

"I'm getting married."

"I thought you were already married."

"I am, but we never had the ceremony because of Mason's Dad passing. "So, I get to marry him all over again."

"Baby, I'm so happy for you."

"Thank you, we'll have to go shopping for you and Marie's dress later this week."

"I get to be at the wedding?"

"Of course, you do. Mom, don't start crying."

"I'm sorry, I can't help it."

"Alright, crybaby, I'll talk to you later. Love you."

"Love you too."

'She is so funny.'

"Baby girl, we must get you a dress for Mommy and Daddy's wedding."

"Yaa, da da."

"Uhh, daddy's girl. Alright, little lady, here we are. I took Moreen inside, kissed her and headed to Neveah's. When I arrived at the bar, Neveah was opening for the day.

"Come on in. How are you doing? Excited for the big day."

"I sure am. I never thought I would find a man I would want to marry twice."

"You go, girl, I'm still looking for someone to marry for the first time. Would you like a mimosa?"

"Please and thank you."

Alright, here we go."

Ok, so first, let me say I'm not accusing you of anything. I'm not saying I believe what the person said, that's why I asked you to come here to talk."

"OK."

So, the night I was supposed to come over, but I couldn't because of the game, the bar was packed. These guys came in, and they were cool for the most part. The one guy must have thought he was God's gift to women. He tried to holla at every female that was present, including me.

He was nice-looking, but something about him didn't sit well with me. After he made his rounds, he noticed Dad's plaque and table. He told the guys he was with that he knew Dad, and Mason and him were like brothers. He went on to tell them that you were the person he told them about, who did that thing a few years ago.

One of the guys told him they had to drop the investigation due to a lack of evidence. Then the guy started talking about how you and he hooked up. And you didn't want to stop seeing him, even begging him to give you some when he came to the house after Dad's funeral.

Shada, like I said, I'm not accusing you of anything. I want you to know what's being said before it gets back to Mason. I sat at that table, fuming with anger. I could feel my body shaking like I had a fever. I looked at Neveah. Do you remember me showing you problem child?"

"Yeah, did you bring her with you?"

I snickered a bit, "No, I didn't. The name of the guy you're talking about is Terry Settles. I described him and the other two guys as well. "The two guys Terry was with are detectives. They have been trying to connect me to some murders that happened a few years ago.

When I introduced Terry to the problem child at the house after Mason's senior's funeral, it didn't sit well with his pride when he tried to shoot his shot. I told him that I would make it his last time if he ever disrespected my husband or our home again.

Sis, I told you I have a past, but it wasn't that kind of past, it was, um, a lot more serious." My sister-in-law put her hands together and interlocked her fingers as they rested on her mouth.

She said nothing for a few seconds. "Well, sis, we have much more in common than we knew. You know, Terry gave me his card. I'm sure he wouldn't mind meeting me somewhere.

"Naw, sis, I'll let Mason handle this."

"Ok, if you change your mind, let me know, I haven't put in work in years."

Neveah and I raised our glasses in cheers. We didn't speak any more about the topic, but we gained mutual admiration for each other. When Mason came home, I let him relax and unwind before I gave him the news about Terry. His only quarrel was that he wished I would have told him sooner rather than later.

I agreed I should have. Communication is a huge part of marriage, something we're both still learning. Terry will receive a visit from a pissed-off Marine, but it won't be about buying a car. As time progressed to our anniversary and wedding ceremony, our lives continued to change.

We were experiencing the devastating effects of dementia. Although Mama Barringer was in the first stages of the condition, there were times when we didn't think it was dementia that caused her to do certain things. She has reached the age where she says what's on her mind. Sometimes it can be pretty funny, other times, it's quite embarrassing.

She definitely doesn't bite her tongue when it comes to her grandchild. My mother is still having complications with her heart. She has doctor visits regularly and has been instructed to change her diet and eating habits; I have to stay on her about that.

She vowed that no matter what, she would be present for our wedding, even if she has to wear her hospital gown instead of a dress; I pray she can make it. Often, I think of what her life could have been like if she never met my sperm donor, and then I realize I wouldn't be here. All we can do now is keep lifting her in prayer and assure her she is loved.

Our daughter is walking, talking and getting into everything. It's like having a little tornado that lives in our house. Her laughter and adventurousness are the highlights of everyone's day, she keeps us on our toes, but we wouldn't have it any other way. I have been forced to accept that she is daddy's girl.

Her first words, of course, were da da. She repeated it from the time I picked her up from the daycare until when arrived at home. I am glad the generational curse has been broken, and she will grow up with a father to watch over and protect her. As for Mason and me, we are still learning to love, respect, and cherish one another.

At times we lose our way, but we've vowed not to let our anger or frustration last more than twenty-four hours before we address the issue. So far, it has proven to be an effective tool. Now and then, I start a little something for the pleasure of making up. As good as that man makes my insides feel, I have to ask God if it is a sin.

Today I will give my wife the wedding ceremony she deserves. She has allowed me to take care of my father's passing without asking, "what about me." She has poured her heart, soul, mind and body into being my support system in my times of need. Even today, as we stand on the hollow grounds of Safety, she unselfishly stands by my side as I close the final chapter. Today is more than our wedding ceremony, it is a celebration of lives.

I have been permitted to bury my father, Mason Barringer, and my baby brother, Andrew Barringer's ashes, under two new fruit trees in the Orchard of Safety. Their names, as well as their birth and death dates, have been carved into the trees.

Now they both can rest in the place where angels tread. Today is a celebration of lives that meant the world to me and the lives that are my world. Shada often says I saved her that day at dinner; the truth is, we saved each other.

As we both stand at opposite ends of the bridge that crosses over the stream into the orchard, I couldn't help but reflect on how much life has changed for us. My mother was talking with Neveah and Shada earlier in the day. I overheard her say, "I gave birth to two sons, I lost one, but now I have two daughters."

My precious baby girl, who keeps trying to get into the stream to play with the fishes, will make a great big sister, we are expecting our second child, hopefully a boy. We invited a small number of friends and family to gather with us. I know it did Shada's heart well to have her mother present this time.

Because of Patricia's health issues, she needs a wheelchair to get around, but she wouldn't let that stop her from being at her daughter's wedding. We both started walking towards the center of the bridge, I could see the shimmer in her eyes. Her dress flowed as Neveah carried her bridal train. The closer we came to each other, the more I realized who this woman was.

She is the mother of my children; my life partner till death do us part. No longer does she answer the superficial names of her past. The only name she answers to now is Mrs. Shada Barringer, my beautiful wife. As the minister began to speak, we took each other's hand, "dearly beloved, we have gathered her today." A mild guest of wind maneuvered through the crowd and wrapped around us. It was as if the land was saying, *"bring your hearts to Safety."*

THE END

THE WAR INSIDE ME

The war that rages inside me demands I wave the white flag and surrender all fortitude, self-worth, or decency that I may have had.

It demands I surrender all knowledge of my past, forcing me to forget, I was revered as a king in a far-off desert land.

It holds me as a captive like a refugee in a foreign land, barely giving me the necessities of life, while torturing me into believing, I'm less than a man.

It beats at my soul until I have nothing left, then watches with enjoyment as I breathe my final breath.

Its anger is kindled when I don't give up the ghost and rages into a violent tantrum when I call upon the Lord of Host.

I try and have the love of my savior and cry out "forgive them for they know not what they do", but how could it torture me so savagely and not have a clue of the pain it's putting me through?

The war inside me has decided my fate. It has condemned me to death for crimes against the state.

There will be no jury, I won't get to testify, I won't receive council of law just the judgmental lethal injection of mankind.

A concoction of poisons that will slow my heart rate and incapacitate me into a vegetable-like state.

The poisons that are used can't be found in a chemist's lab but in the insidious toxins of a world that has truly gone mad.

It will use love against me with the hope that I'll believe that no one could love someone as hideous as me.

It will cause the ones who are supposed to love me and stand by my side, to look me in my face and tell a serpent's lie, then stab me in the back with the proverbial dagger of my demise.

Its main ingredient will be hatred because of the color of my skin, tricking me into believing I'm inferior to other men.

I'm sure it will add bigotry to force me to be politically correct, even though its acceptance is like a noose around my neck.

There is more it will add, it doesn't want my death to be quick, it wants to make sure it destroys a whole generation with the trickledown effect.

This war inside me has destroyed many men, who have given up the fight, and caved from within… but I will fight this war inside of me, its victory won't be an easy win.

I won't succumb or be brought to an end, by the effect of destructive or disruptive forces that I battle with from within. I will fight the good fight; I will fight the good fight for the totality of man.

ABOUT YOUR AUTHOR

Fredrick A. Stewart was born and raised in Battle Creek, Michigan, the Cereal City. His favorite memory of growing up in Battle Creek is the wonderful smell of fruity pebbles being cooked on Saturday morning.

He progressed through the Battle Creek school system and graduated from Battle Creek Central, class of 87, Bearcat Go!

He is a proud father of four adult children who reside in Michigan along with his eleven grandchildren.

After living in Battle Creek for an extended time, he moved to Denver CO. where he met his late wife and two stepdaughters.

The birth of his fifth child and youngest daughter was the inspiration that set him on the path to becoming a published author. She provided him with countless hours of material. She is also his motivation when life shows its sinister side.

During the onset of Covid -19 Fredrick momentarily switched from children's books to urban fiction. His first fiction book, Ten Miles to Safety, took third place out of eight hundred entries in that genre at the Bookfest Awards Spring 2023.

The sequel, Safety from the Past is his sophomore project in the Urban fiction genre.

Mr. Stewart appreciates everyone who has supported him on his writing journey, and plans to continue providing entertaining literature while using the power of the creative mind.

www.ingramcontent.com/pod-product-compliance
Lightning Source LLC
Chambersburg PA
CBHW030357030726
47497CB00002B/378